Also by John Turner

The Wicked Kind

Dodging Bullets

~A Novel of Deception~

John Turner

REGULATOR
PRESS

ISBN-10: 0692380426
ISBN-13: 978-0692380420

Published in the United States of America by Regulator Press.

Inquiries: admin@regulatorpress.com

This book is dedicated to my daughter Paige, whose love of reading was the spark that started me on this journey, and to my son Shaun, a chip off the old block if there ever was one.

And finally, to Mike Mullins, a man whose continued friendship has meant the world to me. This one's for you, amigo!

You and I used to shine like a jewel

—Ryan Adams

There's three sides to every story, baby

—Don Henley

Dodging Bullets

Prologue

A Good Day to Ride

The phone rang loud and it rang early, a half-dozen skull-rattling blasts cut short by the machine. The caller hung up as the message greeting beeped, the sharply modulated tone reverberating like a shot before abruptly stopping. Benjie rolled to his left, checked the time on the bedside clock.

What the hell?

Pain radiated from the center of his forehead, and he eased back onto the pillow, eyes closed. Then his cell phone went off, the *Born to Run* ringtone chasing away any lingering hopes for sleep. Damn I love that song, Benjie thought, reaching for the phone and flipping it open.

"What."

"Buenos días, Benjie mi amigo."

"Speak English, asshole."

"Come on now, don't be that way."

Benjie lowered the phone and breathed deep, the pressure behind his eyes building by degrees. After a long moment he raised the phone back to his ear and spoke slowly. "What do you want? And why are you calling so early?"

Kenny let out a small, humorless laugh. "You see, Benjie, that's your problem. Too much sleep. Remember that story I keep telling you, the one about the bird and—"

"Yeah, the worm story. Whatever, dude. I haven't liked worms since I was a kid. Now, what do you want?"

The line went quiet, followed by a slight tapping noise.

"I'm having a little get together tonight, out at my place. Some business associates are coming by to discuss a new thing I'm working on. I want you to meet them. Afterwards, we can get up on our other deal."

Benjie thought about the *other* deal. "It's getting hot," he said, not sure if it was a question, or a statement.

"Maybe," Kenny said. "It's nothing I can't handle though." His words hung stark and resolute, magnified by the silence that followed.

Benjie sighed. "What time?"

"Make it nine. We'll get business out of the way first."

"I'll be there." Benjie started to flip the phone shut. Kenny interrupted.

"One more thing. Be in a good mood tonight. I've arranged for some nice señoritas to join us. Just for you my friend!"

HE ROLLED UP a little after nine and curbed his bike across the street, taking a moment to survey the scene. The sprawling ranch-style house made him smile; Kenny Lopez had done all right for himself. It seemed like only yesterday he was living in that cheap apartment deep in a Santa Ana barrio, and now this. Benjie was truly impressed.

Then again, Benjie wasn't doing too badly either, even if he did like to keep things more low-key. That funky shack down on the peninsula suited him fine. He was close to the Wedge and the Santa Ana River Jetty, satisfying his surfing jones, and the Coast Highway ran nearby, the perfect escape for days when he felt like riding his fat machine up to Malibu or maybe down south to Mexico. It was not a bad setup at all. We'll just leave all that early bird shit to people like Kenny, Benjie thought with a laugh, as he crossed the street and made his way toward the house.

He approached the pair of hand-carved front doors and stopped to listen, the muted sounds of music and laughter filtering through. He thought about the new business thing Kenny mentioned, surely just another of his elaborate schemes designed for only one purpose: to bring in more money than the last. Benjie wondered if it would ever be enough.

Before he could knock, the big doors swung wide open, spilling into the soft porch light two stunningly beautiful women. Dressed like twins in short skirts, high heels, and low-cut tops, they giggled when they ran into Benjie's large frame.

"Ooh look, Kim. It's a biker. A great big one," the redhead said as she looked up into Benjie's eyes.

The blond one replied, mimicking handlebars and a throttle. "I like bikers, lots. Let's go ride on your hog, dude. Vroom, vroom."

Benjie gave a dubious smile and squeezed between the two women, easing into the wide foyer. He briefly considered making a play before throwing off the idea in amusement; he'd been so long without a woman, he wasn't sure he knew how anymore.

Turning the corner, Benjie saw a group of people gathered outside by the pool, the French doors leading to the backyard wide open despite the cold. He spied Kenny off to the side, standing over a large built-in barbecue, focused deep in thought. Kenny took his grilling seriously. Benjie made a beeline, ignoring the mostly unfamiliar faces along the way.

"Dude, you get way too intense when you cook. You need to ease up some, learn to relax. Maybe sleep in once in a while." He reached out and smothered Kenny in a hug. "So, where are these cats you wanted me to meet?" Benjie got right to it; he didn't like to waste time.

"Those guys? Shit, they bailed. Gave me some jive about a big blowup in Vegas and split town quick." Kenny slipped

3

gracefully from the embrace. "We're meeting up again next week."

Benjie's radar blipped. "You working a Vegas angle now?"

"Not exactly," Kenny said, bent over the grill while staring at a prime cut of beef. "These guys have action all over Nevada. You want a beer?" He reached into a small cooler and removed two bottles.

Benjie popped his and took a long pull. He turned and scoped out the yard. "What's the occasion?" he said.

"No occasion. Just some friends over for a good time."

Benjie watched as most of the partygoers migrated into the living room to escape the cold, pulling the French doors shut. "Kind of chilly for a cookout, ain't it?"

"Could be." Kenny grinned. "But you know me. I'm not the type to wait around for the weather."

Yeah, I know you all right, Benjie thought. Always having things *your* way. He killed his beer and threw the bottle into a small tin garbage can, the harsh clanging sound echoing sharply, not unlike the thoughts in his head. "About our deal, you said you wanted to go over something."

"Sure thing, Benjie," Kenny said, his jaw set as he stared down at the empty beer bottle lying in the can. He turned and motioned toward the house, and a young Hispanic man approached. "Tomás, keep an eye on this for me please, while my friend and I go talk."

The kid was the houseboy, Kenny's idea of living large.

Tomás took over the grilling while the two men retreated to an office at the far end of the house, where they took seats on opposite sides of a large mahogany desk. Kenny opened a polished teak humidor and removed a couple of fat Cuban cigars. Benjie waved his off, choosing his Marlboros instead.

"When are you going to get some class?" Kenny said, shaking his head dismissively. "Start enjoying the finer things, like a nice Cohiba or a Montecristo."

"No dice, amigo. I have zero interest in laying down fifty bucks a pop to smoke a rolled-up turd, even if it would make me all classy and *so-phees-tee-cated*."

Benjie comically drew out the word, laughing at his humor. Kenny simply smiled and methodically lit up, working his cigar in a series of measured puffs until the end glowed red like an ember. He shook out the wooden matchstick and dropped it into a jade ashtray large enough to hold a football. Then he spoke to the end of the cigar in that cutting tone of his, the one he'd perfected over a lifetime of such encounters.

"You're one of a kind, you know that, Benjie? You're like fifty cents in a two-dollar world."

An awkward moment ensued as Benjie stared across the desk. Every now and then Kenny came up with some wise-ass comment. That shit got old fast, and tonight Benjie was in no mood. "Where do we stand," he said, making no effort to hide his irritation.

"Well, as I mentioned earlier, it's getting warmer," Kenny said casually, completely ignoring Benjie's discomfort. "There's change in the wind, no doubt about it. But I'm on top of things, and plan on staying that way. We just need to remain vigilant, and keep our focus."

Focus. Right. Kenny and his *focus*.

Benjie studied his friend, genuinely amazed at the way he always maintained control, his mind like some kind of freakish computer, one that's never turned off. It had been like that from the start, and Benjie had come to count on it. Streetwise as he was, he knew it took a guy like Kenny to work it right, muscle and guts getting you only so far.

"You think they'll come back on you?" Benjie said.

Kenny considered the question. "I can't say. It could break either way." He showed no hint of concern, the guy born with a poker face. "There is one little thing that might blow up, if we're not careful. Remember Butch Davey?"

"Frank? I thought he split for Santa Fe last summer."

"He did. And now he's back. I've had him working on some things, small stuff, just to throw him a bone."

"What's the problem?"

"He's been running his mouth, big talk from a little man. He keeps it up, the wrong people start listening."

"And?"

"And I want you to find this guy and contain him, teach him some manners." Kenny leaned back in his chair, stared at the ceiling for a long moment. "We have a lot of eyes on us, Benjie. If we're not careful, we'll have foxes in the henhouse."

Benjie laughed inside, foxes in the henhouse reminding him of that crazy-ass Terry Stone down in Nicaragua. He watched Kenny, who was seemingly lost in thought as he rolled his cigar slowly between his fingers while blowing a precise stream of smoke to the ceiling, the hushed room betraying the faintest hint of the party going on at the other end of the house.

Benjie took in the room.

Dark-paneled walls hung with tasteful artwork; bookcases filled with neat rows; sturdy leather-bound furniture set on a large Persian rug spread over a spotless hardwood floor. An antique Tiffany desk lamp joined with a corner torchière to provide soft lighting, perfectly complementing the mood. Benjie imagined Kenny doing a lot of heavy thinking in this room. Just like Benjie was doing now.

"A man's destiny can only be determined after he has unencumbered himself from the prejudice of his enemies, and the sins of his past."

Kenny's voice broke the tranquil stillness of the room. Benjie stared at him blankly. Dude was always coming up with shit like that. What the hell did it even mean?

"These people, Benjie, they'll look for any way in they can, any weakness, and they'll exploit it. I need you to close that loophole."

"Are you looking for a permanent solution?"

"If it becomes necessary. I'll leave that decision to you."

"There might be some blowback."

"Then we'll just have to make sure we stand clear." Kenny allowed a small pause for the words to sink in. "How soon can you leave?"

"Where is he?"

"Nogales."

Benjie went silent, his mind clouded by some kind of low-grade white noise buzzing in the background. He thought about the news article he'd read recently, the one about Kenny, and wondered how it fit in. And then there was that other thing, the problem that refused to go away, and the solution he'd been avoiding. A word came to mind, *fatalism*, and Benjie fought to push that negativity aside.

"I can leave tomorrow," he said, his voice restrained by the distraction of his thoughts. "Take care of some other business while I'm down there."

"Perfect," Kenny said, clapping his hands and jarring Benjie back on point. "Now that it's settled, let's get back to the party. I don't want Tomás jacking up my food."

As they started for the door, Kenny remembered a call he had to make, said he'd follow along shortly. Benjie continued to the living room, finding it filled with people now, perhaps twice as many as before. He spotted his two lady friends out by the pool, shivering in the cold, the redhead clearly wasted. Figuring chivalry made an excellent icebreaker; Benjie worked his way through the crowd. "Ladies," he smiled on approach.

"Look, Kim, it's the biker," the redhead slurred, rocking back on her heels.

The one named Kim glanced up from lighting a cigarette, her eyes the deepest, clearest blue Benjie had ever seen. Or at least that he could ever remember seeing. "Can I have your jacket? I'm freezing my ass off here." She said it like he owed her, and Benjie responded by looking her over, way longer than casually.

"If I did that, then I'd be freezing *my* ass off. Not to mention your friend here." He nodded at the redhead. Kim took a long drag off her cigarette, blew the smoke into Benjie's face, her eyes fixed on his.

"First off, my friend can go inside if she's uncomfortable. Second, you don't look like the kind of guy who gets cold too easily." She spoke confidently, deliberately, and it turned Benjie on. Before he could come up with a response worthy of the casual repartee, Kenny interrupted them.

"I see you've met my friends," he said, stopping alongside Benjie while motioning to the redhead. "This is Roberta. And this fine young woman is Kim. It's nice to see you two have already started."

Benjie nodded and the girls grinned. Kenny sucked out all the air.

"Kim recently started working for me as an administrative assistant," Kenny said. He reached out to steady Roberta as she swayed like a sailor on leave. After an awkward moment, he suggested drinks.

"Whiskey and water," Benjie said, staring hard at Kim.

"Chivas, neat," she shot back, her eyes softening the edges of her words.

"All right then," Kenny said. "Roberta, why don't you join me?" He turned and led her into the house.

Benjie and Kim shuffled a bit, smiling like two freshmen at a high school dance. Benjie grasped for something clever to say, but his mind went blank. "Administrative assistant?" he finally said. "Sounds important."

Kim's eyes brightened and she ran her fingers through her long hair, her grin mischievous. "Yeah, I suppose so. And here I thought I was just his fuckin' secretary."

She laughed, slight at first, and then she couldn't stop. It was the sexiest damn laugh Benjie had ever heard, of that he was sure. He started in with her, the two of them close together, cracking up foolishly; the air was back and it felt good.

Kenny returned with the cocktails and passed them around. Roberta crowded in, standing along the edge of the pool, taking up space and giggling like an idiot. Kim picked up on the annoyance and she moved closer to her friend, taking her by the arm while suggesting they all move inside the house where it was warmer. Roberta stared at Kim dumbly, took two feeble steps forward, and then she pitched backwards into the pool, dragging Benjie in with her. She shrieked and clung to him like dead weight, pulling them both under.

"Goddamn it, someone get this drunk bitch off me before I drown her ass!" Benjie yelled, his voice garbled by a mouthful of water.

Inside the house, people crowded at the French doors, pointing and laughing at the spectacle unfolding. Kenny and Kim dropped to the edge of the pool as Benjie shoved Roberta to them, and they pulled her out, sobbing and shivering. Benjie swam to the far steps and Kim ran to him, apologizing for her friend. Kenny called for Tomás.

"Take our friend to the guest room and get him a change of clothes while you dry his out."

"What about my goddamn boots?" Benjie said, anger still in his voice. "They're soaked, and I got to ride tomorrow."

"No problem," Kenny said. "Tomás can put them in the oven. Won't take but a few hours to be good as new." He glanced at Kim, then back to Benjie, and he smiled. "Besides, I don't think you'll be needing those boots for a while anyway."

Benjie took a long look into Kim's perfect blue eyes. Kenny's right, he thought. To hell with the boots.

THE CELL PHONE alarm rang at first light. Benjie sat up, feeling disoriented, a dull ache in his chest. He felt someone sleeping next to him. When he looked to his side, he saw Kim. A smile crossed his face.

Wow, I guess I *am* doing all right.

He eased out of the bed and went into the bathroom, where he found his clothes laid out on a small table, his boots on the floor below. He recalled last night and the unexpected dip in the pool, and it made him laugh. Sure, it pissed him off when it happened, but now it all seemed kind of funny. After a long shower he dressed quickly, stopping long enough to admire Kim sleeping in the bed. He considered delaying his trip for a few hours. There was plenty of time to get things done, even if he didn't get down there until later tonight, or tomorrow for that matter. But then Benjie remembered that other business, the thing with Butch, and he decided he'd better get with it.

He sat down and reached for one of his boots, struggling to get his foot in. He shoved hard, forcing it to fit, cursing Kenny and his damned home remedies; clearly the oven had shrunk the leather. Benjie finally got both of them fitted and he took a few tentative steps, wiggling his toes to clear some space. After a few minutes he gave up. In a day or two they'd stretch out fine. It was time to roll.

He made his way through the empty house and out to his bike, firing up the engine to let it idle in the cool morning air. He gazed up at Saddleback, framed in a crystalline blue and cloudless sky. It was a good day to ride.

Benjie wheeled the bike around, a '47 Knucklehead he bought off some crazy Indian in a no-name burg out on Route 66, deep in the badlands of New Mexico. It was his first summer out of the military, after it all fell apart, yet months before the real shitstorm came. He was tramping aimlessly then, trying to find his place in a hopelessly broken world. He tore that bike down and rebuilt it from the ground up, every last nut and bolt passing through his hands, therapy for a battered soul.

He worked the suicide clutch and caressed the jockey shifter, old school, because that's the only way Benjie knew. Looking back at Kenny's house, he mused at the ways of life and the irony of all that had come to pass. And then he put the bike into gear and rumbled down the street.

He never said goodbye to Kim.

She never knew his name.

Part One

The Setup

One

I woke to the sound of wind in the trees, a curious wheezing that nearly fooled me. From somewhere deep in my brain I confused it for a dream, before my consciousness made out the faint whistle of leaves against the random gusts, and the telltale scratching of that big oak outside my window stirred me to the edge of waking.

Rolling over, I checked the time on the bedside clock. It was early. Far too early for a Saturday morning. I sank back into the pillow, my brain faltering through sleepiness as my mind gained speed. Ten minutes later I surrendered, and stumbled out to greet the day.

Outside my kitchen window an array of lights shimmered in the distance, blazing a path that stretched from Irvine to Newport Beach, and clear out to Palos Verdes. The wind had brought sharpness to an already incredible view, like a slight film wiped from a lens, exposing detail not normally seen.

Sporadic gusts assaulted the trees, making them billow and dance, ghostlike in the dim outside lighting. I stood there lost in the moment, feeling insignificant against the vastness of all those lights, all those people, all those different lives being played out on the same grand stage as my own. My attention was drawn to one particular light, far off to the west, yet impossible to see. Every now and then I played a silly game, one where I pretended to see that light—see *her* inside the house, see our kids playing out front, see the minivan I still made payments on. Sure, it was all right there in front of me, close enough to touch.

But like a wisp of smoke in the breeze the picture would scatter, my temporary amusement giving way to a cold reality: despite the physical separation of a mere twenty-five miles, in truth we lived a continent apart.

Turning from the window I worked my way to the couch, weaving a path through the Pokémon cards, Hot Wheels, and WWE action figures strewn about the floor—the remnants of my son's last visit; silent reminders of a child's innocence. I preferred keeping the evidence of his time here exactly as he left it, drawing a bittersweet comfort from the chaos. At least until the clutter started bugging the crap out of me and I forced myself to put it all away.

I dropped onto the sofa and contemplated my next move.

The morning sky gradually turned light, the wind surging in huge bursts of kinetic energy, followed by peculiar stillness. Without warning, the calm between gusts exploded into the piercing howls of coyotes, echoed down from the foothills; ominous sounds conjuring visions of ravenous nocturnal creatures intent on devouring anyone unlucky enough to cross their path. They stood as a stark reminder: no matter how far we extend our sprawling suburban utopia into the far reaches of the county, ultimately we remain the intruders. Down there in the flatlands—in the sea of all those lights—man may have tamed nature. But up here in the shadow of Santiago and Modjeska peaks, we live like renters, foolishly telling ourselves that no matter what the cost, we will never be evicted.

I recalled summer days and my high school cross-country team training for the upcoming season in these very foothills. It seemed more than a lifetime ago, those dreams of state championships that never came to pass. We worked our asses off running the firebreaks and ravines choked with dust, bronzing our rail-thin teenage bodies in the sun, and we shared a camaraderie that remains with me to this day, a connection to each other and to the pursuit of victory, the common bond of sporting teams since the dawn of time.

How could I have known all those years ago that one day I'd find myself living in this place, reflecting on such memories as filtered through the prism of all that has passed?

Yeah, that was a long time ago. If I ever had a plan, it sure in the hell didn't work out.

Settling back into the familiar comfort of the worn sofa cushions, I breathed deep, attempting to quell the gathering storm in my head. The nightlight from my daughter's room joined with the emerging dawn to bathe me in soft shadows, and through this uncertain light I took in my world: the wall clock ticking away time; my neighbor stirring in the unit above me; the wind funneling through the chimney in a spooky, hollow drone.

I considered my various possessions, the sum total of a life that no longer thrilled me; the television and computer and mismatched furniture fought over and scavenged from the fire sale of my former life. Somehow all that stuff didn't seem so important now.

My guitars hung solemnly on the wall, further reminders of a time perceived as simpler, if not altogether happier. Knockoffs of far more expensive models, in a way those instruments reflected the story of my life, one of grand visions and elusive dreams that didn't quite make it, a sure fix on a reality that always fell just a little short. It reads the story of chronic underachievement, of a life rationalized and settled for. A harsh assessment perhaps, but true nonetheless.

I stood and moved across to the bookshelf, scanning the rows while silently reading titles. It was all about books lately. Before that it was old movies, as I got sidetracked on an epic film noir kick. Seeking out such classics as *Detour* and *Out of the Past*, I spent many late nights with tough-guy actors like Robert Mitchum, Sterling Hayden, and Richard Widmark;

sinking way deep into the dark and brooding protagonist thing, digging the nihilistic vibe of those B-movie classics. Predictably, my interest waned, and over time those old movies disappeared into a box in the closet. At least I'll know where to find them when I get back on *that* kick again.

So now it was a book thing; and quite an erratic collection for sure, with authors ranging from James Lee Burke to Ernest Hemingway to James Ellroy, with a little Cornell Woolrich and Jim Thompson thrown in for good measure. I had straight fiction, nonfiction, and loads of pulp fiction, and I usually kept two or three books going at a time. I used to read just one book at a time, but as I got older my attention span grew shorter, or something like that.

My eye caught a Raymond Chandler collection and I pulled it down, savoring the feel of the paper, the weight of the pages on my fingers. Books are my treasure, each one so similar in form yet completely unique in how they play with my imagination.

I reached for my reading glasses and turned up the light, exploring the table of contents. The wind howled outside my patio door, blasting its way from the canyons to the sea. I stopped on *Red Wind*. What was it Chandler said about the Santa Anas? When they blow, *anything* can happen.

Two

L ater that morning the telephone rang. A common enough occurrence I suppose, but in keeping with the uncertain nature of my life in those days, *this* call was a portent of trouble ahead. I listened as the answering machine picked up.

"J.T., it's Vince. Where you been, bro? So listen up, we're playin' tonight at Weeds, and I want you there. Don't punk out. Call me."

The call ended and I stood there staring at the flashing message light, thinking. Why didn't I answer? My behavior as of late had turned disturbingly anti-social, my life becoming more hermit-like by the day, and talking on the phone was not high up on my list of groovy things to do. Somehow it all felt wrong.

The voice on the line belonged to my friend, Vince Taylor. I suppose you'd call him my best friend, if forty-five-year-old guys *have* best friends. Born and raised in Lake Charles, Louisiana, Vince had an easy Southern way about him, always friendly and instantly likable. He and I went back about fifteen years.

Vince fronted a cover band called the Loose Screws, and he played bass and sang lead. They'd been together for a few years and were fairly popular on the circuit of dive bars and biker roadhouses they gigged around the county. Sure, some of the joints they played were decidedly low-rent, with a borderline criminal clientele, but music's a tough racket and you take what you can get.

The rest of the lineup consisted of Eddie Dowd on guitar, Nick Stewart on drums, and Robbie Smith on keys. They were all decent guys—for musicians, that is—although Nick could be a real asshole and Eddie was definitely a strange cat. I'd go see them play on occasion, although it wasn't necessarily for the music. God knows I could survive the rest of my life never hearing *Brown Eyed Girl* or *Slow Ride* again, especially by a roadhouse cover band. I'd go because doing nothing all the time gets old. Really old.

You see, ever since my divorce I'd found myself with too much time on my hands. It was time I never asked for, time I didn't need, and I had no clue what to do with it. Worse, I was caught between two disparate lifestyles: single-dad mode on Wednesdays and alternating weekends, and swinging single-guy style in between.

Swinging. *Right*. Swinging by the neck was more like it.

A lot of guys I knew—the married ones mostly—tried to convince me that I had it made; look at all that tail you can chase and you don't have to answer to anyone about it. To them, I was rolling in clover. What they all seemed to overlook was the simple fact that my life had turned to shit overnight and there was no pleasure to be found in the aftermath.

The truth?

I still loved Lucinda, and it killed me to see my kids only part-time. But apparently *I'm* the fool for believing in such hopelessly outdated concepts as love and family.

I tried recalling the last time I went out but couldn't think back that far, a sure sign it was high time for me to drag my sorry ass out into the world and see how the other half lives. Weeds was a dump but the Screws always made it fun, attracting what you might call an "eclectic" crowd. Besides, I hadn't seen Vince for a while, providing as good an excuse as any.

So that was the plan. I'd hang out for a set or two, drink a few cocktails, and then split before the whole scene got too depressing. What the hell, that qualified as a life, right? I looked at the clock and sighed. Now that my social calendar was set, only one thing remained; find a way to kill the rest of the day.

Three

Weeds roadhouse was a funky shack. Funky and old, as in 1920s old. Over the years it had existed, in one form or another, as a restaurant, a bar, and a whorehouse. At times, it was all three at once. Tucked way back in a rural, meandering canyon, the joint seemed to attract every lowlife burned-out hippie type in a fifty-mile radius. Oh, it was surrounded by weeds, too. I'm not sure if that's how it got its name, but if the shoe fits.

I passed Nick Stewart on my way in—he was working a cute brunette who looked fifteen and bored—and over at the side of the stage I saw Eddie Dowd tweaking the soundboard. I walked up and said hello. Eddie nodded and took a deep drag off his cigarette.

Eddie wasn't a talker, and whatever he said he tended to keep short, doling out his words sparingly as if there were some inherent value in the speaking. He also had an odd habit of drawing down on his cigarette as he stared at you through squinty eyes, and exhaling real slow, the smoke curling around his face like a veil. Like I said, he was a weird dude.

I asked about Vince. Eddie jerked a thumb over his shoulder, indicating out back. I resisted the urge to make small talk, figuring this guy didn't give a shit anyway, and I made my way down a short hallway at the end of the bar and exited through a rear door. It put me out next to a couple of rank-smelling port-a-potties and an overflowing trash dumpster; welcome to the world of showbiz, kids.

I saw Vince sitting in his truck at the far end of the dirt parking lot. There was someone with him. Weaving a crooked line through the haphazardly parked beaters, bikes, and dust-covered pickups—the usual collection of vehicles you'd expect to find behind a joint like Weeds—I came up to the truck and rapped on the window. Vince fumbled with the door before opening it, and I was immediately blasted by a cloud of potent smelling ganja, forcing me back a step.

"Jackson, my man, what is up?"

"The usual, Vince. Who's your friend?"

"Kenny Lopez," the stranger said, extending his arm across the seat. "You can call me Loco."

The guy gave me a look, and right away he bugged me. Do you know how that is? You meet someone and instantly your radar goes up. That's how I felt as I reached across Vince to shake hands with the interloper.

"Jackson Thomas," I said, keeping my tone neutral. "You can call me J.T."

"Well now, seein' as we're all acquainted, how 'bout a toke, Jackson?" Vince grinned, flashing me the small pipe concealed in his palm.

I waved off the dope. "When are you guys starting?"

"Fifteen minutes or so. Right after I get tuned up."

Vince took a heavy toke and handed the pipe to Kenny. I shut the truck door and walked away, shaking my head; Loco Lopez looked like a real piece of work. Dude had the full biker thing going on; leathers and chain-drive wallet, bandana do-rag, skull rings and bracelets. And attitude, lots of attitude.

Back inside the bar I ordered a beer. The joint was crowded, a roomful of hard cases, drifters, and bottom-feeders. I snagged a stool near the jukebox and settled in for a ringside seat to the parade of life, biker-bar style.

As soon as I sat down, a fat drunk chick with too much skin showing pretended to bump into me, acted all surprised and apologetic about it, and then launched into her life story. Like I give a shit? She had zero social awareness as she stumbled and slurred like a fool, and I tried to discourage her by avoiding eye contact, but she wasn't hip to my cues. I laughed inside at the absurdity of the moment, and my place in it.

Back in my younger days I used to love places like Weeds, the out of the way, *rustic* establishments. The funkier the bar, the quirkier the crowd, the more I dug it. Not anymore. Today, that scene just makes me feel old. But then again, back in those days I'd see a guy my age in a bar and think, What's that old bastard doing here? Today, I *am* that old bastard.

Funny how things turn out, or don't, depending on your point of view.

So Fat Chick's standing there yammering on about her new boyfriend and how he lost his job because he's such a loser, and all he does is sit around all day smoking dope and sucking her dry, and the whole time she's batting her eyes in a desperate come-on that was far more pathetic than enticing. I listened patiently, all the while searching for a way out. Despite my contempt, I couldn't bring myself to be mean about it. After all, fat chicks are people too.

My salvation arrived when Vince and Kenny strolled into the bar. I smiled and told my new best friend that I had to go now. She looked at me like I'd just banged her sister, spit out a contemptuous *whatever*, and staggered off to play foosball. Kenny motioned me over then.

He sat at a table with a group of bikers, all of them outfitted with *O.C. Satans* vests.

Terrific, badass Orange County bikers. Who knew there was such a thing?

Feeling wary, I stepped up to the table. Kenny introduced his gang just as Vince and the rest of the Loose Screws ripped into a ragged version of *Slow Ride*. I cursed under my breath; this was shaping up to be one shitty night. I made myself a promise then. Two sets, and then I bail out for a date with Raymond Chandler.

Four

I woke early on Sunday, feeling out of sorts; dull headache and aching stomach, a condition likely caused by the drinks I'd had at Weeds. The smoking didn't help.

I'm a closet smoker, have been for years. You put a cocktail in my hand and the other instinctively reaches for a cigarette. Fortunately the habit never took. Until recently that is; when I stepped out of that closet in a big way.

Ever since the bottom fell out I'd found myself smoking way more than drinking, nearly a pack a day. It seemed to take the edge off. At least that's what I told myself. It also gave me something to do with my hands when I felt like choking someone. Anyway, alcohol was too much of a downer and the smokes were cheaper, but who needs excuses? As John Lennon famously said, whatever gets you through the night is all right.

I swallowed some aspirin and fixed my coffee, and sat down at the kitchen table to recount my night out.

Weeds was a scene, with Kenny Lopez and his crew as the featured attraction. Apparently it's their main hangout, and before my night was over, the joint was crawling with O.C. Satans. They'd been out on a run earlier in the day, up through Malibu to the Rock Store. From there they blasted across the wastelands of the San Fernando Valley, rumbling up the mountain highway to Newcomb's Ranch, deep in the Angeles National Forest. By the time they'd all met up at Weeds they were half in the bag and showing the full effects of the road.

I got all this from a short, stocky dude with a lazy eye and no front teeth, and a huge drooping mustache that would make Sam Elliot proud. He called himself Rude Dog and he smelled like it. Funny how those guys all have nicknames.

So Rude Dog became my second best friend of the night, regaling me with every detail of the day's run. He lost interest in me when he noticed Fat Chick over at the foosball table. Rude's good eye brightened and he whistled in admiration. I told him that I knew her and that she dug bikers, but before I could say more, he'd wandered off to make his play.

Kenny came along after that and he introduced me to the rest of the Satans. There was Snake and Boxhead and Scoots, etc., etc. You get the picture—goddamn nicknames. And they all looked the same too, like widgets popped out of a factory.

But there was one thing that struck me as odd. While a lot of the dudes in Kenny's crew seemed genuinely hardcore—what you would expect for outlaw bikers—Kenny and a few of the others stood out. Sure, they dressed the part right, and they even exhibited something akin to swagger, but still, something was off.

I already mentioned that Kenny Lopez bugged me from the moment I met him. Just why I couldn't say. Not until later at least, when I learned more about the guy. But that night I picked up an uncertain vibe and it made me cautious. While I couldn't quite put my finger on it, I knew it was there.

You get a lot of fakers here in Orange County, weekend warriors living in the nine-to-five world during the week, pulling down beaucoup bucks in white-collar jobs. They dump a big chunk of that change on tricked-out machines, and come the weekend they don their biker gear and hit the road, making the circuit of funky roadhouses and saloons out on the fringes of the county. If you were to drive by one of those places you'd see rows of gleaming street machines, the chrome meticulously polished. A lot of those guys dump thousands of dollars on their bikes. It's the new status symbol in Southern California. Without a doubt the bikes are impressive, but something about the scene feels way too contrived. If you ever encounter a true biker, a *one-percenter*, he tends to stick out like a sore thumb, making the fakers look kind of lame.

So was Kenny Lopez a faker? Could be. Which was fine by me, as it certainly was not my ambition in life to hang out with crazy-ass bikers.

When I'd finally had all I could take I did a quick fade, slipping out of Weeds unnoticed. I got home near midnight, where I made it to the end of *Red Wind* before drifting off to a fitful sleep and dreams of four-flushers and beautiful dames, and Philip Marlowe throwing fake pearls into the ocean.

And there you have it, my big night out, living large in the O.C.

Welcome to your life, Jackson Thomas.

Shit, how in the hell did it get like this?

More on that later. For now, let me just say that time was the killer. Too much time and no way to fill it. Or more specifically, too much time combined with a complete lack of enthusiasm about it. Quite simply, I didn't *feel* like doing anything.

When my kids were around it was easier, and being *Dad* helped keep the wolves at bay. But take them out of the picture and things got blurry real fast. I never realized just how much my identity was tied up in my role as a father, and a husband.

I was having a hell of a time finding my footing, learning how to live on my own while trying to get a handle on normal. Everything felt weird to me. Everywhere I went felt wrong, like I should be someplace else. And each new day felt like an obligation, not an opportunity. Half the time I was crawling out of my skin and the other half I was too hurt and angry to think straight. I was a prisoner of time and my memories wouldn't let me be, and I couldn't hide from myself or what I felt. Believe me; I tried.

Was I a mess? Yeah, you could say that.

It seems I'd turned into one of those emotional cripples I used to jibe Lucinda about whenever she'd drag me kicking and screaming into marriage counseling. Unfortunately, it was *that* kind of thinking that got me here.

My cell phone rang, mercifully cutting off my thoughts. The number was blocked so I let it roll over to voicemail. I refilled my coffee mug and checked the message; it was from Vince.

"Jackson, where'd you run off to last night? I wanted to talk to you. It's somethin' important. Call me."

His tone seemed oddly insistent, so I replayed the message and listened more carefully. It was there in the way he said "something important"*,* an urgency I rarely heard from Vince. He epitomized the term laid-back cool, and it was genuinely difficult to get a rise out of the guy.

I called him back and got his voicemail. Terrific, phone tag. I left a message about his message, and as I flipped the phone shut I figured it'd be about a week before I heard back, and when I did, the important thing would be forgotten. That's just how it went with Vince; his attention span was shorter than mine.

With inspiration in short supply, I moved over to the couch for some reading. I was on a roll after finishing *Red Wind* and eager to dive into some more Chandler. I thumbed through the pages and stopped on *Trouble Is My Business*, just because I liked the title. But my eyes fell heavy after a few pages, and I set the book aside and stretched out for a short nap.

Plugging into a low-key playlist on my iPod, I settled in for a sweet ride. The last thing I remembered was Chris Isaak singing about making love with somebody exactly like you, and you can't do a thing to stop me.

Tell me about it, brother.

AFTER MY NAP I did some chores and ran a few errands. I tried reaching Vince several times with no luck. While I generally paid no mind to the rambling messages he left on a semi-regular basis, that odd tone of voice really had a hold on me. What the heck was my good friend up to now?

Soon the afternoon waned, the sun a bright orange ball over the horizon, casting long shadows clear to the far end of my neighbor's patio. The breeze stiffened, making its move on the beleaguered trees; it was the third straight day of Santa Ana winds, with no end in sight. I tried Vince one last time. On the fifth ring he answered.

"Jackson, what's up?" He sounded out of breath.

"You tell me. You called earlier?"

"Yeah right. Hey, I'm runnin' late for a gig. I'm loadin' my rig right now—" a heavy object dropped in my ear. "Shit, sorry about that, damn amp's a bitch. Tell you what, come out to Smitty's tonight and we'll talk."

I took a deep breath, impatient with the conversation. "Bad idea," I said firmly. "I've got court tomorrow, the custody hearing, and I've got to have my head together." I felt an immediate tightness in the pit of my stomach. The mere mention of the words *court* and *custody* did that to me.

"Just come out for a little while. Kenny will be there. Remember, he's that dude you met last night. Anyway, he's got a business proposition for us, Jackson, and I think you're gonna dig it."

Vince's words caught me off guard. Business involving Loco Lopez? I flashed through a mental slide show from Weeds, Kenny and his gang, and his affected biker look and poseur cohorts. What the hell was *this* about? My brain froze and I lowered the phone, Vince breathing heavily on the line. Inexplicably, something clicked way down in my subconscious, and I raised the receiver, drawing out my words with an agitated sigh.

"This better be good, Vince."

I hung up quickly, cutting off his reply, and I stared at the phone in my hand, perplexed at what had just transpired.

Human nature is a confusing thing, a conundrum of sorts. How else do you explain all of the crazy things we do? I've often wondered what motivated me to say yes to Vince that day. Because had I known the true magnitude of that seemingly innocuous phone call, I would have screamed *No way!*

But I didn't know, and my crystal ball had long since been broken. The truth is, I'd hit a dead end, and everything that was important to me was scattered to hell and gone. In short, it had all become one big drag. So with my prospects slim and getting slimmer, I figured I really had nothing left to lose. I've never been more wrong in my entire life.

Five

S mitty's Saloon resembled an abandoned barn, resigned to a lonely existence at the far end of an unmarked access road in Carbon Canyon. The building hadn't seen fresh paint in decades, its weathered wood siding running at slightly crazy angles before turning from horizontal to vertical, giving it a lazy patchwork quality. The partially lit neon sign over the front door appeared to read *titty's*, an anomaly I found oddly appropriate.

Backed up against a steep embankment, the saloon featured two ancient oaks framing a dimly lit front entrance, with a couple of ramshackle attachments spread out like wings on either side of the main structure, their sloped roof lines blending seamlessly into the manzanita-pocked hillside. The place exuded a certain nostalgic charm, tucked way back in this remote canyon, far away from more respectable joints.

Shithole chic. Nice.

I arrived earlier than expected and parked my car at the dark end of the lot, taking time to reconsider things. I felt a little out of it, weirdly disconnected, like I was a thousand miles from nowhere. Anxiety burned at the edge of my consciousness, vague and unspecified, as I contemplated Lucinda and the kids and court tomorrow. A palpable sense of foreboding dogged me, heightening my unease.

And now, as if all that other stuff wasn't enough, I had this mysterious business meeting with Vince and some shifty character named Kenny Lopez. Clearly I needed my head examined.

I exited my car to the sound of the Loose Screws tearing through *Stranglehold,* the part where Eddie takes an extended solo, and from out in the parking lot it sounded deadly. Entering through a side door, I stood at the far end of the bar and scoped out the half-filled room, the crowd a carbon copy from Weeds. Visions of Fat Chick and her loser boyfriend came to mind; hopefully she rode off into the sunset with Rude Dog, sparing me a continuation of her saga.

On stage, Vince powered through the song, thumping his five-string bass and singing like a man possessed. Sweat rolled off him, soaking his shirt. He'd put on weight in the last few months, his six-two frame bulging noticeably through the middle. I pictured a younger version, from back when we first met. Pushing thirty and a year away from settling down, he still carried that hungry musician look, lean and tight, his thin face offset by a ridiculous mullet of cascading curls that may have been cool back home in Louisiana, but was strictly retro jive out here in California. He was nearly bald now, and his face had filled out considerably, but he was still the same crazy character I took to like a brother from the moment we first shook hands.

The band finished the song and Vince announced a short break. We made eye contact and he pointed to the exit door, prompting me to snake my way through the cluster of wobbly tables and chairs, occupied by the usual assortment of lowlifes, barflies, and shady operators.

"Let's grab a smoke," Vince said over his shoulder, moving toward the door.

I followed him outside and across the front of the bar, into a corralled patio area set under a canopy of shade trees, the smell of eucalyptus and oak thick, intensified by the night chill. Vince jump-started a cigarette for me, steam rising from his shoulders, and I zipped my jacket to ward off the breeze.

"How's it going tonight?" I said. Vince looked at me loosely as he passed the cigarette.

"Who knows? These gigs are really startin' to burn me out. Nick's playin' like shit and Eddie's bein' a dick, and I'm sure as hell sick of singin' these damn songs. Other'n that, everythin's groovy. How 'bout you?"

Vince had a loping quality to his voice, and he dragged his vowels a bit, with a tendency to round off his words. He never quite managed to lose the swampy gumbo dialect he brought out West with him. It was a very relaxed way of speaking, and it put you right at ease.

I took a hit off the smoke and waited for the nicotine to do its thing, exhaling my response. "I'm a little pissed off, about court tomorrow." I was feeling doubtful about my intentions, overcome by negative energy. I took another hit, and one more, just to let the moment pass. "I'm really hoping things break my way for a change," I added bitterly.

"Yeah, no shit, man. So what's up with that bitch judge anyway, why's she squeezin' my bro's nuts so hard?"

"Who the hell knows? I can't figure it out. My lawyer had me convinced that California divorce court had changed. Gotten with the modern times and lost its insane bias against men, maybe even show some willingness to give us poor dads an even break. But no, I got to get Judge Roy Bean's devil spawn. I'm telling you, Vince, that broad's out to get me."

I practically spit my words. Sensing a loss of control creeping in, I shifted gears and asked where Kenny was. The answer blew in from behind me.

"I'm right here, Jackson."

I turned abruptly at the words, staring straight into the face of Mr. O.C. Satan himself, decked out in the exact same garb he had on last night. The dude still bugged me.

"So what's happening, gents?" Kenny said easily, like a man with all night to kill and not a care in the world about it.

"You tell me. Vince says you have some kind of important business to discuss."

My tone edged toward hostility. Kenny responded with an odd little smile, and penetrating eyes that seemed to look right through me. Time stretched out uncomfortably before Vince finally spoke up. "I'll go grab us some beers," he said, turning for the bar.

Kenny leaned casually against the patio railing and pulled a fat cigar from an inside pocket of his leather jacket. He slowly peeled the wrapper and carefully clipped the end, easing it between his lips, taking his time with the flame. I don't care much for cigars; to me, it's just about the same thing as sucking on a lit piece of shit.

"So how do you know Vince?" I said, more to move things along than any real desire for conversation.

"From Weeds, and a few other places his band plays," came the vague reply, Kenny's eyes focused on the end of his cigar as if it was the most interesting thing he'd seen all day.

So you don't *really* know him, I thought.

Kenny didn't care to elaborate. He simply continued his study of the complexities of a burning stogie, while I tried to get a read on him.

He was a little shorter than I was, maybe a hair under five-ten, and built stocky. I guessed his age at late forties, maybe fifty, easy years by the look of it. Either that or he took really good care of himself. He had strong features offset by intelligent eyes, and perfect teeth, and when he smiled he became instantly captivating. I imagined Kenny Lopez was good with the ladies. A sense of sophistication and educated manner belied his biker appearance and I flashed back to last night at Weeds, and the feeling I'd had that it was all a big put-on.

Vince returned with the beers and passed them around. Then he lit a cigarette and tossed me the pack. The wind had picked up a bit, gently swaying the trees, and I turned out of it to light up. The patio was deserted, cloaked in a strange sort of quiet, the jukebox inside the bar barely audible against the breeze. Spooky.

Kenny remained silent, puffing his cigar evenly and blowing the smoke in a very precise manner. He gave off a clear aura of control, although his demeanor was one of detachment. The dude was a walking contradiction. When he finally spoke, it was with a sharp tone behind a stone face, all business.

"Here's the deal, Jackson. A friend of mine named Benjie Cole has something that belongs to me. In Mexico."

I waited for the "and" but didn't get it. Kenny's eyes remained focused on mine, a hardness there I hadn't noticed before. I couldn't tell if he was trying to be cryptic, or if it just came naturally. Vince provided the rest.

"Benjie took Kenny's boots by mistake, when he split town last week. He's—"

"Boots?" I said sharply. "This is about some boots?"

"Well, yeah," Vince said. "But that ain't the important part. Kenny wants us to go down to Mexico and find Benjie, and bring the boots back. And he's going to pay us to do it, Jackson."

"He is, is he?" I said, my tone heavy with sarcasm.

"Yeah. Thirty grand." Vince smiled, a self-assured expression lighting his face.

I did a whiplash double take, from Vince to Kenny and back, my mouth hung open. I'm pretty certain I looked foolish, because I sure in the hell felt that way. My mind sputtered, and about all I could think was, screw these guys and their damn games.

"I'm out of here," I said, barely holding back my contempt. "You two clowns are nuts, you know that? I have no time for this bullshit. My life's going down the tubes and I'm being fucked ten ways from Sunday, and now I hear this shit? Jesus, thirty grand? For boots? What'd you do, Vince, drink the goddamn bong water? Take a ride on the crazy train?"

My reaction was way over the top but I didn't care. I spun around to leave. Kenny's words stopped me short.

"Maybe I should explain," he said, his tone placating, if not just a little condescending. "The boots belonged to James Dean.

People say he was wearing them the day he died. I bought them at an auction last year, paid a hundred grand."

Kenny paused a moment and puffed on his cigar. The look on my face surely prompted his next words, along with a chuckle that held no humor.

"Now, before you get all twisted up trying to figure out how someone like me can afford to pay that kind of money for a pair of boots, suffice to say, I'm not what you think I am."

He flashed Vince a knowing grin.

"I'm really a financial advisor, an extremely successful one. Some people even call me a guru of sorts. Regardless, I've got money to burn. One time, I paid ninety thousand dollars for a motorcycle that belonged to Steve McQueen. It was a pile of shit, but hey, McQueen rode it. And last summer? I bought Eric Clapton's '58 Strat at a charity auction for that drug rehab joint of his down in the Caribbean, paid close to eighty grand for that little piece of memorabilia, and I don't even play guitar. I'm a collector, Jackson. It's what I *do*, man."

Kenny gave me a look that said I should be impressed. I wasn't. Seriously, did he think I'd drop down at his awesomeness and genuflect like some two-bit acolyte? But it made sense now, that feeling I'd had at Weeds. So this dude really was a faker, a wannabe, and it pretty much told me all I needed to know about Kenny Lopez.

I was used to Vince dragging me into all kinds of wacky stuff, but this one took the cake. I mean come on, a freaking scavenger hunt for James Dean's boots? In Mexico? This one was deep off the charts. Before I could come up with a snappy retort appropriate for the absurdity of the moment, Kenny continued his pitch.

"So you see, we're not entirely nuts here. This is a perfectly reasonable and legitimate business opportunity. One, I might add, that doesn't come along every day. We can help each other, Jackson, you and me. And Vince."

He smiled a little too confidently for my tastes, winking at Vince like it was in the bag, while I stood there dumbly, my mind hitting on too many questions at once. Then the obvious jumped out.

"Why don't you just call Benjie," I said, "explain the whole mix-up."

"He's tried reachin' him," Vince said. "But I guess the dude's in the wind."

"And we're supposed to be able to find him? That makes no sense, Vince. And what about you?" I said to Kenny. "Why don't you go down there and take care of this? I mean, this dude *is* your friend, right? That's got to be a whole lot cheaper than hiring us to stumble around Mexico looking for a guy we've never even seen."

"Actually, I met him once, at one of our gigs. And Kenny gave me this picture, to help us out." Vince handed me a worn photo of Kenny standing with a group of bikers. "That's Benjie, there on the right."

I stared at the photo, glanced at Kenny. "He looks like you," I said.

"I get that a lot. People think we're brothers."

I handed the photo back to Vince. "So score one for you, dude. You've got yourself a picture and you know what this guy looks like. Big deal. It's still a lame idea. Honestly, I expect better from you."

Vince's face flushed, signaling I should ease up. But what did he expect? He knew I was wound tight, and he throws this kind of shit at me.

"I would go down there myself," Kenny said, walking to the far end of the patio. He stood there for a long moment relighting his cigar, as he stared out at the dark end of the road leading to Carbon Canyon. "But I can't. Not now anyway. I've got a major deal closing and there's no way I can just split."

"Yeah? Well how's this for a plan. You wait until after your big deal closes, then you'll have even more money, and you can afford to take a whole damn year off to find your boots. Shit, bro, you can make a lifetime vacation out of it."

Kenny turned to me, but didn't make eye contact.

"You're a funny guy, J.T. But remember, this offer was for Vince. He talked me into letting you tag along, and tossing a few extra bucks your way for the trouble. As I recall, he said something about you needing the money."

A smirk crossed Kenny's face as he studied the end of his cigar. I didn't like the way that last part sounded, and I threw Vince a hard stare. He looked away and I breathed in deep, alternately confused and angry, and more than a little ashamed at the truth of my circumstances.

"Okay, so I'll stop being a dick. But you have to admit, this thing sounds wrong. I mean come on, look at it from my shoes."

"I suppose you're right," Kenny said. "If I was you I'd probably say the same thing. But this is a legit deal. I want my boots back, Jackson. In two weeks there's a celebrity bike rally out in Malibu. A lot of big shots will be there, and through connections I've been invited. Money will do that for you, open doors you never thought possible. Anyway, I figure what better way to impress my new friends and fully blow their minds than to show up wearing James Dean's boots."

Kenny laughed out loud, while inside me a war raged. He'd laid the whole thing out real nice, and the truth is, if I didn't have such a hard-on for the guy I might have been more willing to listen. As it was, I simply felt manipulated, and there was already far too much of that going on in my life.

I decided to hedge my bets. After all, I *did* need the money.

"No problem," Kenny said, when I told him I had to think it over. "I understand."

He smiled, and I knew right then that this guy didn't understand a damn thing about me. We stood there staring at each other, one of those weirdly obtuse moments that weigh heavily on you later, as you attempt to sort out what *really* happened. Kenny's phone rang and he took the call, his voice dropping low as he turned away from us. At precisely the same moment, a huge gust of wind shook the trees violently; as if God's own hand had come down to grab my attention. Vince said something, his voice startling me.

"So what do you think, Jackson? You in?"

"I'm not sure," I muttered, distracted as I stared up into the trees. I looked at Vince. "I've got a foot in the door, let's leave it at that. I still need to think it through. When are you leaving?"

"Late tomorrow. Kenny thinks it'll only take a few days to track Benjie down. He gave me the name of a hotel he stays at, and a few other places to look."

"Sounds thin."

"Not really. It's easy money, Jackson. We'll be home in a few days. A week tops."

"A week?"

"Tops."

"Hey guys, it's time for me to go," Kenny said, after finishing his call. "Some late night business requires my attention."

He stood there smugly for a long minute.

Then he said, "You'll give me a call tomorrow, Vince? Let me know what our friend here decides?" He turned and walked away, trailing his smelly cigar smoke, the breeze blowing it back into my face. A few minutes later I heard the rumble of a bike and watched as Kenny scooted across the gravel lot and took off down the canyon road, leaving a cloud of dust and exhaust behind dimming taillights.

"You really think we can pull this off, Vince?" I said. "Find this Benjie character?"

"I know we can," he said eagerly. "And no matter what, it'll be a good time. It's Mexico, Jackson, just think of the possibilities."

Vince's face lit up, his eyes playful. And then Eddie's voice shot out from the distance, harsh and intrusive, announcing the next set. Vince shrugged, checked his watch.

"Time to entertain the masses. You stickin' around?"

"No way, I need to get home and rest up for tomorrow. I sure hope that goddamn judge is in a good mood."

"I hear that. So anyway, good luck with everythin'. And make sure you call me afterwards." Vince walked away, stopping long enough to glance back over his shoulder. "And remember, Jackson, we leave tomorrow night, right after I drop the girls off at grandma's house."

He said it like I'd already decided.

I TOOK THE long way home. I needed time to think, and driving works best for me. I caught the Corona Expressway out to the 91 east. From there I cruised the 15 south, cut across the Santa Ana Mountains via Ortega Highway, and dropped down to the 5 freeway for the homestretch. It took a hell of a long time to get home, and when I did I'm not certain my mind was any clearer.

None of it made any sense.

Sure, Kenny sounded convincing enough, and Vince could sell ice to Eskimos, I'd known that from the first day I met him. But still it bugged me, some undefined thing I felt way down deep.

On the surface the whole scheme seemed completely irrational, absurdly laughable. Yet I could see a thin framework of plausibility, enough to hang my hat on and justify going along with it. Or maybe that's just the way I choose to remember it.

The more I thought about it the more I saw another angle unfolding, an enticing one at that. It was the lure of throwing caution to the wind, of turning my back on all the bullshit swirling around me and just bailing out. Maybe it was time for me to do something completely stupid and irresponsible. Hell, I'd played it straight for so long, look where it got me.

There was a lot to consider or there was nothing to consider, and I knew that to overthink it was to kill it; it would never stand up to scrutiny. Basically it came down to an act of blind faith, and *not* looking before you leap.

Despite knowing all that, I couldn't get past the nagging feeling that Kenny Lopez wasn't trustworthy. Clearly he was a manipulator, the self-serving type who would make sure he came out on top regardless of the consequences. But so what, aren't most successful businessmen conniving assholes? Getting nowhere with that analysis, I decided not to dwell too much on the guy, figuring if I did this thing I'd let Vince act as go-between, keep my contact with Loco Lopez to a minimum; no offense Kenny, it's just business, bro.

I got home near midnight. The wind had barely eased; the trees and shrubs bowed in jerky waves, the lights in the distance sparkled like a million dazzling diamonds. I listened for coyotes but heard only the wind, and a lone hoot owl keeping watch over the night.

Just then a thought grabbed hold of me and wouldn't let go, bringing with it a shudder of fear so complete it nearly made me gasp out loud. It told me this thing was big, far bigger than anything I could ever imagine.

I shook off the warning, firm in the belief that before I made my final decision, more would be revealed. Exhausted, I let myself into the house and dropped onto the sofa, and sat alone in the dark, listening to the wind.

Six

Monday morning brought a change in the weather, the pale dawn cloudy and gray, fat with the promise of rain. I stood at my kitchen window and stared into the distance, trying to picture Lucinda as she prepared for our day in court. The coffeemaker gurgled and spit next to me as it filled the pot, and I listened to it without hearing, my mind numbed by fitful sleep. Already I felt the tightening in the pit of my stomach, the dreadful anticipation that comes from staring straight down the barrel of life's uncertainty.

I filled my mug and took it over to the couch to contemplate my legal situation. Vince wasn't kidding when he said the judge had me by the balls. Twice previously she'd ruled against me, and I had a bad feeling that today would be strike three. I had good reason to be wary.

Lou and I had recently gone to court-ordered counseling, on account of us disagreeing over custody. The therapist was supposed to get a feel for the dynamics involved and report back to the judge with a custody recommendation. But I blew it that day and lost my cool, and the more I tried to dig out of it the worse I looked. The therapist said I was controlling, and Lucinda piled on, seeking validation for age-old grievances. When I'd finally had all I could take I told them both to go fuck themselves and stormed out. You can imagine how that went over. Later, I tried mending fences by sending the therapist an email explaining myself. She responded with an offer of her services to help me work through my "anger issues". Thanks, but no thanks.

Today's agenda was permanent custody of the kids, saving the resolution of the money issues for a later date. Why they don't consolidate things is beyond me. I suspect the lawyers plan it that way, stringing you along and spreading it out one little bit at a time, all the while racking up a huge fee. It's like death by a thousand cuts and it sucks. Unfortunately, once you realize you're screwed, you're in too deep to do anything about it. You've spent too much to turn back, you're too busted to move forward, and the whole time your shyster attorney is in your ear whispering: *hang in there; things will break your way.*

What he really means is: *hang in there; daddy needs a new Corvette.*

Did I mention the whole thing has made me cynical as hell? It's enough to make you put a bullet in your head. Twice.

The telephone rang and I ignored it, refilling my mug as the answering machine did its thing.

"I know you're there, J.T. Come out and answer the phone, man. Ya know, you got to stop bein' so anti-social and—"

"It's called self-preservation, you fool."

Vince laughed. "There you are, Jackson, popping out of your hidey-hole."

I lowered the phone, instantly regretting picking it up, and counted to ten before responding. My voice was low and slow, weighed down by the uncertainty of it all.

"I suppose you're calling to say you're on your way."

"I already told you, we're not leavin' until later tonight." He laughed again, real casual about it.

"And what about *my* decision?"

"Oh, you'll decide right, Jackson."

I let that one go. A few seconds passed before I thought of something left unsaid from last night. "Speaking of leaving, where the hell is it you're going anyway? You said Mexico, but where exactly?"

"I can't remember the name of the place just now, but I got it written down. It's somewhere down by the border."

"Shit, that's the best you've got?"

"Easy there, amigo, have a little faith. This thing is goin' to be a piece of cake, you'll see."

"Then why do I feel so unsure about it?"

"Because that's how you *are*, Jackson."

"Yeah? Well if you're so confident about this deal, why don't you just go by yourself? Or better yet, drag one of those skanky barflies from Weeds down there, show her the time of her life."

"Damn, buddy, why you got to be that way?"

He sounded hurt, and right away I regretted my lousy attitude. "You're right," I said, "that was out of line. I don't mean to come off so heavy with you. It's just nerves I guess, about the hearing today."

"No worries, I understand where you're comin' from with this. And I hope you catch a break today, because God knows you deserve it."

"Amen to that, brother."

The line went quiet and my brain disconnected from the call. When Vince spoke again he caught me off guard.

"There's one other thing I want you to consider, Jackson, before makin' your decision."

"What?"

"I want you to take the full thirty."

He said it matter-of-factly, without hesitation, and at first I wasn't sure what he meant. Then it hit me; he was talking about the money, Kenny's absurd bounty.

"You sure about that?" I said.

"I'm damn sure. I don't care about the money, I just want to get away for a while. I had a mind to split town anyway, and then

Kenny hit me up with this offer. Once he started talkin' about the money, I thought of you right away. I figured it's gotta help with y'all's legal bullshit and whatnot."

Vince stopped talking and he breathed hard on the line. I sensed there was more, so I waited him out. He cleared his throat with one of those smoker's hacks, and continued speaking awkwardly, his voice a hoarse whisper.

"The truth is, Jackson, I figured it would do me some good to hang out with you for a while. You know, like we used to, back before the goddamn world fell apart."

I was moved by Vince's words, and his state of mind. To be honest, I'd never figured money as a motivator for him anyway, well aware that since his wife passed away nearly two years ago he was flush with insurance settlement cash. I also knew that since Leslie's death, Vince had been acting increasingly irrational, his behavior sliding into pure recklessness. If not for his two daughters, I believe he was willing to drive that bus right off a cliff. It was painful to see.

"Just consider it, okay?"

"Sure thing, Vince. I'll call you later today."

"Cool. And one more thing."

"What's that?"

"We're leaving tonight at eleven. Viva Mexico, partner!"

Seven

Vince's phone call and his unexpected generosity brought me no closer to a decision; if anything, it complicated things more. The idea of thirty grand in my coffers was hard to resist, but the road to get there was still messed up, and I remained hopelessly conflicted over the whole crazy scheme.

At nine o'clock I showered, shaved, and put on a nice shirt, and I took the canyon road to the city of Orange. The drive was long and my thoughts were a jumbled mess. Arriving with time to kill, I parked my car on the top level of the garage and took the stairs down. I bought a weak cup of coffee and a soft pack of Winstons from a pushcart vendor in the courtyard near the front of the courthouse. He was out of Marlboros.

I took the coffee and the smokes to a remote corner, far away from any people, and proceeded to pace up and down the walkway, fifteen steps each way, my mind spun into a knot as I feebly tried to make sense of it all.

The early morning clouds had broken up some, and the air had that in-between feeling, like maybe it would rain or maybe it wouldn't. I burned through two cigarettes in ten minutes and started on a third before throwing it aside in disgust. Then I glanced at my watch and sighed; ready or not, it was time to go.

My heart thumped a choppy beat and my nerves taunted me, and I had the distinct sensation of standing outside myself, watching it unfold. I took a last gulp of the lousy coffee and tossed the remains, and headed up to face the music.

The elevator dumped me into a crowded reception area full of men wearing one of two expressions: completely pissed off, or sucker-punched to the gut. I knew both looks well.

Several attorneys took up space in the lobby; bullshitting and backslapping like frat boys, surely getting primed for a day of legal shenanigans. My lawyer appeared, seemingly out of thin air, like some shitty-ass apparition. He joined the other attorneys, shaking hands and flashing a corrupt politician's grin. His name was Craig Stevens and he was a prick. It wouldn't bother me so much, him being a prick, if only he was kicking some ass on my behalf. Unfortunately, the dude was an empty suit, with an intolerable attitude to boot.

Lou's attorney arrived then, and the fun really started. Susan Baker was a real piece of work; an unsmiling chronic hard-ass who I'm convinced was born mean. She started up with the other attorneys, Craig included, and I thought right about now would be a bitchin' time for some crazed Muslim jihadist to come two stepping in here wearing a pair of shoe bombs.

Kaboom! See ya legal eagles.

But seriously, the whole deal felt like one giant conspiracy, solely designed to beat you down and rob you of your dignity.

I watched the attorneys for a few minutes. When I got sick of doing that, I took a deep breath, hitched up the proverbial trousers, and moved toward them.

"Jackson, how are you?" Craig smiled, offering a weak handshake.

"Better, once this debacle is over with," I said, barely hiding my contempt.

Craig suggested we talk privately. I was thinking maybe we ought to do it right here, in front of Susan, save Craig the trouble of filling her in later. The Bailiff approached and whispered in Craig's ear. Craig nodded and whispered something back, and he motioned for me to follow him into the courtroom. Susan waited outside for Lou, who seemed to be running late, as usual. *That* pissed me off. If you're going to screw someone over, at least be on time for it.

I took a seat at the far side of the gallery and Craig walked up to the bench with the Bailiff. Five minutes later Lucinda entered the courtroom. I caught a glimpse of her out of the corner of my eye, but I refused to turn my head. Instead, I tweaked my neck trying to position myself where I could see her but not appear obvious I was looking. She sat at the opposite side of the gallery, and much to my dismay, I wondered what she was thinking. Let the mind games begin.

Susan joined Craig at the bench and the judge appeared from chambers, and the three of them conferred briefly, their backs turned and voices low. I fidgeted in my seat, unease creeping in like a bad omen, my intuition telling me this thing was going sideways fast. Then, as if spurred by my fears, the legal triumvirate turned and disappeared into chambers, the side door clacking shut loudly in a bitter denouement. Instantly my heart sank and I slumped down into my seat, driven under by the crushing weight of disappointment.

The fix was in.

Once again I was aced out, just like the times before, when Lou and I sat in this very same courtroom while the attorneys and the judge hid from view, secretly negotiating our fate. This time was supposed to be different. Craig promised me I'd have an opportunity to give some testimony, tell my side of the story, even it up a little. What a load of horseshit that turned out to be. I tried hard to convince myself that everything was okay, that things would work out fairly. But there was a lot at stake, and the process didn't seem very fair at all. It wasn't right, not by a long shot.

Slowly my thoughts began to drift in the silence of that dead place, that soul-sucking house of pain. I got the feeling that nothing good ever happened there, and even if it did, there was never anyone around to see it.

I thought about how just a year earlier my life seemed fine, better than fine, really. I had a good job and a nice house and two wonderful kids, and a wife I loved without condition. Sure, maybe I pissed and moaned about too many small things, and maybe I didn't always validate Lucinda in the manner she desired, and Lord knows complaining about all the sex you're *not* getting is never cool, but still, in the big book of marital transgressions, you'd think that stuff would rate small potatoes.

But like the tip of an iceberg hides the true threat, all those small potatoes were simply the warm-up act for a much bigger production. When it all blew up, it happened hard and it happened fast, reaching its climax on D-Day, June the 6th. While Operation Overlord may have been the first step in the liberation of Europe, the only thing *this* D-Day was going to liberate was me from my marriage.

That was the day Lucinda told me she wanted out. And there was no room for negotiation, no maybes; she was done and she meant it. She told me before work that day, early in the morning. Man, you got to love the timing of that; here you go, honey, have a nice day—and choke on *this* while you're at it.

For a brief period I fooled myself into thinking it would all blow over, just like previous rough patches we'd gone through. But this time it didn't, and my life went from zero to sixty on the shit scale in about ten seconds flat. By the Fourth of July I was out of the house. A month later Lucinda was bringing her new boyfriend around the kids. When Labor Day arrived, I was acquainted with Craig and it was all downhill from there.

The passage of time did bring some clarity though, and I began to see things in a different light, eventually admitting to myself that maybe our marriage had a few holes in it, and that leaky boat wasn't likely to stay afloat without some major repairs. And that's where I really fell down—in my constant belittling of Lucinda's efforts to make those repairs; in my lame denials that there was even a problem; in my mistaken belief that *wanting* a good life, and actually working at it, was the same thing.

In truth, Lucinda and I were operating on two different emotional planes, and when it mattered most I let her down. She said that she loved me, had for a long time, but the years of trying to mesh our gears had finally worn her down. In the end, I guess what they say is true—love dies. Ours certainly did.

I tried my best to accept the simple truth that Lucinda and I just didn't belong together. It's been hard though, probably the hardest thing I've ever faced, and all it took was one look into my kids' eyes to break my heart all over again. They were her and she was them, Lou's spirit alive in the light of their eyes, and in every joyful laugh. God help those who get divorced when they have kids.

The attorneys reappeared, jerking me back to the dismal business at hand. They chatted away like two old friends on a Sunday stroll. Craig motioned me over while Lou and Susan headed for the door. "Let's talk," he said, his tone ominous.

I followed him across the hallway and into one of the small huddle rooms reserved for attorneys and clients to meet in private. You never hear anything good in those rooms.

Eight

"It's like this," Craig said flatly.

He paused long enough to pull some papers from his briefcase, shuffling them loudly.

"The judge bought into their argument regarding the kids being better off with Lucinda. She's awarded majority custody to her starting today, Jackson."

I stiffened, sucking air, not sure I heard him right. Craig gave me a goofy look, some kind of phony sympathy play, and the truth came down on me all at once. I felt my face heat up as the room closed in, and I craved a cigarette. More than anything, I wanted to run from that room, from Craig, from the whole damn nightmare.

"That's total bullshit and you know it." I nearly shouted, my anger overriding any chance for rational thinking. "This isn't acceptable, Craig. I don't give a shit what you say about it. You have to do something, you have to fix this thing."

My voice boomed in the confines of that little room. Craig shifted in his chair, unwilling to look at me. "My hands are tied here, okay?" he said, his tone weak, ineffectual. "I've made my best arguments and they aren't working. Sometimes these things go this way. Also, you did yourself no favors with the counseling. Judges don't like angry fathers, Jackson."

"Really, Craig?" I shot back. "Well here's a news flash. People don't like attorneys. Especially ones who suck at their job."

There was a slight twinge at the corner of his eye as he ignored me and continued screwing around with those papers. Everything about the guy made me want to scream. We sat like that for a long minute, and finally I spoke my piece.

"You know, Craig, when all this started you promised me everything would be fair and equitable. You said I'd get to have my kids a reasonable amount of time, keep some money in my pocket. Do you remember that, saying those things? Well *that's* what I hired you to do. You said you'd take care of me. What the hell happened, man?"

He waited a long time before answering, his face a mask of indifference as he shuffled his stack of papers. I felt like choking him. Christ, I needed a smoke.

"I want to help you, Jackson," he finally said, flashing a disingenuous smile. "I'm *trying* to help you. But sometimes things don't pan out the way we'd like them to. Now, I will continue to fight for you. I'll go to the mat for you. But it's going to be a long haul and—"

"Yeah right, dude," I said. "You're real stand-up."

He eyed me with a look bordering on contempt, took a deep breath and continued.

"*And*...we're talking about a full-blown custody fight. That's expensive. Fifteen thousand dollars minimum, on top of what you already owe me." He slid a stack of papers across the table, the ones he'd been messing with. I looked down and saw my damn bill.

Can you believe it, the balls on that guy?

Craig Stevens taught me a valuable lesson that day. Never underestimate a person's ability to be a complete asshole.

He snapped his briefcase shut and went on running his mouth, just taking care of business, despite the fact my life was unraveling before his eyes. "You haven't made a payment in two months. I know things are tight, but I can't do my part if you don't do yours." He folded his hands across his briefcase, a self-satisfied look smeared across his face, as if he expected me to whip out my checkbook on the spot.

I glared at him and he looked away. I should've popped him right there. But then again, he'd probably sue me. After a minute spent staring at the side of his head I stood up.

"I'll get back to you."

I turned and walked out, leaving the papers on the table.

STUMBLING TO THE elevators, I gasped for breath. All at once my indignation gave way to pure desperation. None of it was right, and today was the cruelest joke of all. The elevator doors slid open, revealing a full house, and I turned for the stairs instead.

Exiting at the lobby, I pushed through the glass doors and stepped into a sunlit atrium, immediately seeking refuge in a shadowed corner while fumbling for my smokes. It took three tries to light one. Drawing in deeply, I held it longer than usual, before letting out a long stream of white smoke, followed by every last ounce of my heart and soul. Poof. Gone. Right there into the ether.

I smoked my cigarette, the nicotine rush a salve for my shattered nerves, and stared unfocused at where I stood. What now? A couple of kids chased each other around a large fountain, squealing with laughter, just like my kids. I looked away, the sound knifing through my heart.

Then I saw Lucinda, sitting on a bench next to the fountain. She seemed to be waiting for someone. Against all sense of reason, I approached her, determined to stand tall. I had no idea what I would say, only that I had to say it. Stopping a few feet short, I forced a grim smile.

"Lou."

"Jack."

She looked away, timidly it seemed. It occurred to me that she was the only one who ever called me Jack. I always liked that. Nervous seconds ticked by as I tried speaking with my eyes, but they felt empty, and she wasn't looking anyway.

"Listen, Lou, can't you be reasonable here? I mean come on, you know this is tearing me up inside. What did I ever do to deserve this?"

She refused to look at me. I wanted so badly to reach out to her, to hold her in my arms, as if somehow that would make all the hurt go away. She began speaking, slowly at first, her words tinged by a trace of sadness. Or maybe that's just the way I heard them.

"I have something to tell you, Jack."

An anxious pause followed and my heart raced, a sense of doom washing over me. This couldn't possibly be good.

"I'm considering moving," she said. "To San Francisco." She stopped and sighed, like maybe this wasn't so easy for her. Then she took a deep breath and continued. "I've got a job lined up, and a place to live, and a school picked out for the kids."

A car pulled to the curb, startling Lou. The driver was familiar to me; it was her damn boyfriend. He kept the motor running and stared, mad-dogging me lamely. What a jerk. Maybe I should go over there and pop *him*.

Lucinda stood up, still avoiding my eyes, and when she spoke her voice was a whispered tone, one that dredged up far too many memories.

"I'm leaving early tomorrow to go up there and finalize some things." She took a step toward the car. "I'm taking the kids, Jack. We'll be gone for a week. You can see them when I get back."

She turned and walked away, leaving behind a perfumed scent I could never forget, if I had ten lifetimes to do it.

I stood completely still, in mute testament to what happens when life turns to shit and there's not a damn thing you can do about it. I listened to the kids playing by the fountain, wishing I could die. I was perfectly frozen in that singular moment, every detail burning itself into my consciousness. Fifty years from now, when my mind is gone and I'm nothing but a withering shell, I'm certain I will remember that day.

Without conscious thought I reached for my cell phone and dialed a number. I didn't hear it ring, or even the voice answering on the other end. I only heard my own voice, hollow and cold.

"Vince, it's me. I'm in."

Part Two

The Takedown

Nine

I leaned against my car and lit a cigarette, gripped by an odd sense of time unfolding, as if thin layers were gradually being peeled away, revealing dark truths and secret meanings. My intuition pinged, honing my senses to a sharp edge. I'd been feeling it all day, ever since Lucinda tore my heart out with her revelation of a whole new life planned for herself and our kids, four hundred miles from my own. The phrase *rock bottom* came to mind, and I wondered if this was how it felt.

Vince wasn't home when I got there, his house dark, and my repeated calls to his cell phone went unanswered. This was not a good sign. I was hanging by a thin line to this deal, and Vince's absence was enough to break it.

I smoked my cigarette and pondered the gibbous moon set in a cloudless sky, its thin, silvery light casting strange shadows. In a few days it would turn full, bringing with it all the mystery and lunacy ascribed by mankind from the dawn of civilization. I'd read in a book once that Native Americans had a name for the full moon, a different one for each month. As I recalled, January was known as the Wolf Moon.

The breeze kicked up, shooting a blast of chill air straight to my bones. It set the trees to dancing spastically, a full minute of frenzied activity followed by stone silence. Instantly, the calm was shattered by howls echoing down from the canyons. My mind wandered to the thought of some poor soul lost out there in the dark, alone under the Wolf Moon, held captive by wild animals, and his own fate.

Now I'm certainly not the superstitious type, and I'm generally immune to fears of the dark, but I must admit to you that I felt uneasy. Perhaps it was the expectation of what was to come, and the uncertainty of an admittedly foolish endeavor. There was a time I lived for such moments, relishing the anticipation of something new, the excitement of the unknown. I was born with an adventurous spirit, the kind that drives down unfamiliar side streets just to see where they lead. Sadly, as I grew older that spirit faded. Lucinda would say she missed the carefree Jackson, the guy who was willing to bet it all on red, and walk away happy if it came up black. Somewhere along the way I'd lost that person, and in his place lived an impostor, someone who looked like me and talked like me, but wasn't me. Maybe the next few days would bring all that back.

A vehicle approached from up the street, illuminating me in its headlamps. It was Vince arriving late for his own party. He parked his truck behind my car and got out with a nod. I returned the gesture with a glare.

"It's about time," I said. "I was just about to bail on your sorry ass."

"C'mon now, Jackson," Vince said easily, flashing one of his patented shit-eating grins. "You'd never do me like that. I can always count on you."

I shrugged in defeat. That's me all right, good old Jackson Thomas, Mr. Reliable. I made a mental note to work on that as Vince tossed me his keys. "We'll take the Jeep. You move my truck around," he said.

Climbing into the cab, I immediately noticed a cocktail in the cup holder and Vince's hand-carved pipe in the change pocket, the lingering aroma of sparked bud fresh in the air. Terrific, just how baked was he?

I drove to the end of the street and turned around, passing Eddie Dowd's car on my way back. What in the hell was *he* doing here? Waiting for Vince to back his Jeep out of the driveway, I glanced up at the rearview mirror and saw Eddie get out of his car. I tapped my fingers on the steering wheel, acutely aware of a growing discomfort. When Vince was clear, I pulled the truck into the driveway and got out, walked over to where he'd parked the Jeep and handed him his keys, determined to confront the situation head-on.

"What's up with your guitar player over there?" I nodded down the street.

"He's comin' with us," Vince said, real casual about it. He turned and walked away.

I watched them exchange small talk as Eddie pulled a couple of duffle bags out of his trunk, and when they started toward me I tried putting a finger on what it was about Eddie Dowd that bothered me so much.

He was an unassuming guy, the type who blends in, yet one whose presence is always felt—albeit in a negative way. Kind of short, chubby but not fat, he had a face that was wholly unremarkable, save for the hopelessly outdated Fu Manchu mustache he'd been sporting for as long as I'd known him. Eddie's most unique feature was his eyes, heavy-lidded and vacant, especially when he was doing that funky cigarette routine of his. I could never figure out why Vince kept the guy around, outside of Eddie's ability to shred on the guitar.

The two of them met me at the driveway. Eddie wore a decidedly indifferent expression as he bummed a smoke from Vince, barely acknowledging my presence. Vince offered me the pack, not noticing the one I had burning, and the three of us smoked in an awkward silence. After a long minute I made my move.

"I need to take a leak," I said, the errant flick of my cigarette butt coming dangerously close to Eddie. Vince nodded to the house.

"It's unlocked."

***

WALKING TO THE house, I thought I heard them talking about me. I stepped across the threshold and shut the door harder than intended, the sound like a shot. I was on shaky ground and this thing with Eddie only made it worse. After finishing in the bathroom I heard noises in the kitchen, and I walked over there, found Vince mixing a cocktail in a large plastic cup.

"One for the road?" he said with a sheepish grin.

"Naw, it's too late for that. Shit will put me to sleep."

"Late here is early someplace else." Vince's eyes were full of mischief. "Come on, Jackson, it'll start things off right."

A few seconds of consideration—and the vivid image of Craig Stevens's smarmy face when he slid my bill across the table—changed my mind.

"What the hell, make it a jack and water."

"Right on!"

Vince started mixing, pouring way more whiskey than water. I looked around the room. "Where's Eddie?" I said.

"He had a call to make."

I waited for Vince to elaborate on the situation, but he wouldn't oblige, so I pushed the issue. "Why's he here?" I said, putting an edge to my voice. Vince looked up, his face stiff, one eyebrow slightly cocked in an accusatory manner. He held that look long enough for me to feel uncomfortable about it, and then he burst out laughing, handing me the drink.

"Get this, man. Eddie's chick? She kicked him out last night after the gig, said she's done with his sorry ass. Dude's a total sad sack about it too, cryin' all through band practice today like a stuck pig, goin' on about how unfair it is and how he ain't got no place to stay, all that kinda shit. He liked to kill me with all his bellyachin'. Then right out of the blue he asked if he could come with us, got goddamned relentless about it. I finally said yes just to shut his ass up."

"Really? Well thanks for clearing that with me. *Partner*."

My words were sharp. Vince just smiled and tipped his drink. "Ease up there, Jackson, it's all good." He lit a cigarette and inhaled deeply. "The strange part is I don't remember tellin' him about Mexico. Maybe I said somethin' earlier and just forgot about it. Anyway, no worries about Eddie. He can be a cool dude when he wants to." Vince blew out some smoke and hit his cocktail, winking at me over the rim of the cup.

"Well let's hope he wants to, because if not, we're in for a shitty time. He's weird, Vince. You're just too stubborn to admit it." I raised my drink back at him and took a swig, recoiling at the burn. Vince gave me one of his looks, the one that said I worried too much.

He was right about that. I did worry too much. But someone in this outfit had to be thinking straight, and it sure wasn't going to be Vince Taylor. We stood there silently drinking our cocktails. A thought came to me. "What about the money?" I said.

"What about it?"

"Are we talking a split here?"

"Hell no. I already told you, the money's yours, Jackson. Besides, Eddie ain't hip to the whole Benjie deal. He thinks we're goin' down there for a little vacay, so we're cool."

"You sure about that? Giving it all to me? Thirty grand's a lot of money, Vince."

"Of course I'm sure. Look, Jackson, you're the best friend I've got. The only true friend I ever had. I want you to have the money. I don't need it. You do. It's just that simple." He paused, let out a little laugh under his breath. "Think of it this way, buddy. You've just become my new favorite charity."

The minute the words came out Vince knew he'd stepped in it, and his face flushed red.

"Aw, man, I'm sorry about that. I didn't mean to say y'all was some kind of charity case or nothin'. I only meant to say the money would be better, uh, well, that you might be able to...hell, J.T., you know what I'm tryin' to say here, don't you?"

I stared back, attempting to hide my discomfort. "Sure, I know what you mean." I chose my words carefully, painfully aware that I *felt* like a charity case. I threw down a third of my drink in one long pull and held out my cup. "Top this off, will ya?"

"Now that's what I'm talkin' about!" Vince took the cup and started on the refill. "Speakin' of money, take a look in that drawer over there."

I slid it open and stared at a thick bundle of cash bound by a heavy rubber band.

"Down payment," Vince said.

I picked it up slowly and bobbed it in my hand, feeling its heft. "There must be thousands here," I said.

"More like ten. Kenny wanted to give me half but he was a little short, so we agreed on a third. The rest comes on delivery. You good with that?"

I nodded, still staring at the money. "Wow, he really trusts us, doesn't he?"

"Hell yeah he does. And why not? Just look at us, we're a couple of goddamn Boy Scouts."

Vince laughed and chugged his drink.

"Check this out," he said, reaching for a leather satchel on the counter, pulling out a sheaf of bills and tossing them to me. "Travelin' money. That's three grand and change there, courtesy of your good buddy, Loco Lopez. So you see, brutha, everythin' is cool. Very cool. Or as they say down south, *muy bueno, brah*."

Vince laughed out loud, that yuck-yuck guffaw he used whenever he was feeling it. I was compelled to join him, my mind sufficiently blown. It would seem that despite my skepticism, this deal was really going down.

"Let's hit it," Vince said, as he stuffed the money back into his bag and collected his phone and keys. I pointed to the brick of cash in the drawer.

"What should I do with that?"

"Leave it here. It might get kinda dicey, you and me in Mexico with that much bread. Who knows the trouble we'd get ourselves into?"

He smiled warmly and moved for the door. I followed a step behind, feeling just a little better about things, even though the

Eddie issue was still a bother. A few feet short of the front door Vince turned to face me.

"Hey, listen, Jackson, before I forget. I wanted to say thanks for comin' with me."

"No need for thanks. You're the one helping me, remember?"

"No, that ain't true. Look, I realize you don't normally go in for this sort of thing, and I also know you've been in a helluva fix lately. But you bein' here is, I dunno, prophetic. Anyway, you're my bro, and I'm just damn glad you're here."

Vince hugged me, a full-on embrace with genuine emotional weight behind it. We'd only done it like that one other time, on the day his wife died.

A lot of things went through my mind then, about Vince and our friendship, and the cards we'd been dealt in life. At that moment, I was damn glad I'd decided to join him. Crazy scheme or not, he was my friend, and if you can't be there for a friend, well then what good are you?

OUTSIDE, I NOTICED Eddie pacing in the street while talking on his cell phone. When he saw me, he turned away abruptly, lowering his voice. Something about it felt odd; he wasn't talking very loud to begin with.

"Ready?" Vince said.

"Yeah, sure. What's up with your boy over there?" I pointed at Eddie. "He seems extra sketchy tonight."

"Damn, Jackson, stop fixatin' on that ol' boy. I told you, he's cool. Now let's roll."

Eddie finished his call and joined us at the Jeep, looking tense and distracted. I eyed him warily, an awkward few seconds where I struggled with something to say. I had to find some kind of connection with this guy or else the next few days would be unbearable. I blurted out the first thing that came to mind.

"I'm sorry to hear about you and your girl, Eddie. It may not seem like it now, but things will get better."

He looked at me like I was diseased, and slid into the back seat without a word. Vince just shrugged and rolled his eyes. I let it drop, thinking maybe later I'd try for that connection with Eddie. Or not.

After securing our gear Vince said he'd forgotten something, and he darted back inside his house. It was a tense moment sitting there in the car, just Eddie and me, and I got pissed off all over again at Vince for bringing the guy along. It didn't seem to me like our little threesome was going to work out very well at all.

Vince returned and opened the back of the Jeep, shoved something inside. When he climbed into the driver's seat I gave him a look. "Benjie's boots," he said. "I nearly forgot 'em. Now wouldn't that be a kick in the ass? We get all the way down there and have to leave the dude barefoot?"

Vince laughed about it, a real joker, while I surreptitiously glanced back at Eddie to see if he was listening in on something he wasn't supposed to know about in the first place. Vince started the Jeep and eased out into the street. We had one more stop to make before we hit the highway, and I only mention it now because that's when I found the gun.

Ten

Vince had no idea where we were going. More to the point, he knew where, he just didn't know *how*. The conversation went something like this:

"Where we headed anyway?"

"Some place called the Ranchero Hotel. In Nogales."

"Do you know how to get to Nogales?"

"I know it's near the border."

"What the hell, Vince, the border is like two thousand miles long. Were you just going to point the car south and hope for the best?"

"Hell no, Jackson, that's your job. Y'all read so damn many books, I figured you knew."

And there you have it. Vince wasn't real big on details.

So we hit the service station for gas and sent Eddie inside for a map, while Vince set the pump and waited with me inside the car. He fiddled with the radio and pointed to the glove box. "Take a look in there. See if I have any maps."

I glanced at Eddie through the storefront, and gave Vince the fisheye. He shrugged and went on fiddling with the radio. I rummaged through the glove box, felt something metallic at the

65

bottom, my pulse quickening. I pulled the pistol out and held it up by the trigger guard. Vince gave me a sideways glance.

"I'd be careful if I was you. That's loaded."

"What's it doing here?"

"Protection."

"From what?"

"Bad guys."

"Bad guys?" I said.

"Yeah, outlaws. Bandits. *Pistoleros*."

I raised an eyebrow. "Pistoleros?"

"Mexican dudes with pistols." Vince laughed out loud, and when he stopped, his expression turned grim. "But seriously, you can never tell when a gun might come in handy."

"Come in handy? Damn it, Vince, you know what happens to gringo fools who step out of line down there. Are you out of your mind?"

"Easy, Jackson, it'll be fine, don't you worry the least little bit about that ol' pistol there. I been handlin' them things since I was a kid."

"That's not the point."

"Yeah? So what's the point?" He faked a dumb look, just to piss me off.

I gave up and stuffed the gun back inside the glove box, figured later I'd toss the damn thing out the window before the Mexican cops got onto us. The gas pump shut off and Vince stepped out to take care of it. Eddie returned and the three of us huddled at the front of the Jeep and studied our route on the map spread out on the hood. It turns out Nogales is south of Tucson, maybe an eight or nine hour drive straight out Interstate 10. Easy.

But as I would soon learn, nothing about that trip would be easy; before it was over, it would give new meaning to the term *shit happens*.

JUST OUTSIDE Chiriaco Summit, Vince nearly drove us off the road.

I was asleep at the time, in the middle of a recurring dream I'd been having ever since my life fell apart. In the dream, I'm driving a car up a steep hill, my destination unknown. It's very dark out and the closer I get to the top of the hill the steeper it becomes, to the point my car is nearly vertical and threatening to pitch backwards. Despite my fear I push on, determined to make it over. A few feet from the top of the hill I begin to fall, and then I wake up, suspended as it were, between victory and defeat.

I'm sure a psychologist would have a field day exploring the emotional truths hidden in a dream like that. I could care less. For me the dream held but one interest: to make it over that damn hill and see what was on the other side, or to crash and burn below and be done with it. It was the not knowing that got to me. They say if you die in your dreams you die in real life. I've often wondered if that was true, and if so, what it says about such a dream.

That night in the desert there was a new twist to my dream, a sudden vibration shooting through my body as I was about to fall backwards. When I opened my eyes, I saw the Jeep fishtailing across the highway, the frame shaking violently from those grooves they cut into the edge of the asphalt to wake your ass up when you fall asleep. I braced myself and looked at Vince as he struggled to control the vehicle, rumbling across rocks, weeds, and roadside debris, finally skidding to a stop in a cloud of dust alongside a drainage swale. My heart beat wildly and I heard Eddie breathing heavily in the back seat. Vince looked at me through sleepy eyes.

"Well holy shit, that's never happened to me before," he said.

"I think I'll drive now," I said.

Eddie nodded in agreement, and the three of us got out checking for damage, under a night sky awash in so many stars it would take more than a lifetime to count them all. Thin moonlight bathed the desert landscape in a bluish, almost ethereal light. The highway lay empty; resulting in a calm so distinct it numbed your senses, like standing in a soundproof room. It's odd how dead quiet in such a vast space will do that.

I wandered down the side of the road, away from Vince and Eddie. Standing there in the stillness I thought about the song *Peaceful Easy Feeling*, the part about sleeping with you in the desert tonight, with a billion stars all around. I used to fantasize about doing that with Lucinda. Suddenly I missed her more than ever.

I reached into my pocket, feeling for my key ring, easing my index finger through the gold wedding band hanging between the keys. I'd only recently stopped wearing it, when despite my best intentions and most hopeful wishes I was finally forced to admit that I was no longer a married man. So for the first time in nearly ten years, I grudgingly removed the symbol of the only real commitment I had ever made, and watched as time slowly erased the small circle of white flesh on my finger. I'd kept the ring close by ever since, seeking unspoken comfort in its touch.

My reverie was broken by Eddie's harsh voice shouting out that it was time to leave. I squeezed the gold band, muttering a prayer of apology to my beloved Lucinda as I walked back to the car, savoring the feeling of that singular moment in time.

We took off down the highway, under the blanket of all those stars. Like a man adrift, I was overwhelmed by a sudden feeling of uncertainty, as if I truly had nowhere to go and no place to be.

Moments later we exited at Chiriaco, drove past the General Patton museum and it's collection of tanks and war memorabilia, and eased into a Chevron station for fuel and java. On the way back out of the minimart after loading up on supplies, I noticed Eddie wasn't with us. We settled into the car and I sipped my coffee, nearly gagging—it tasted like they brewed it yesterday, through an old gym sock. Did I mention how much I hate crappy coffee?

I soldiered on, determined to get the caffeine jolt I'd need for the long drive ahead. Vince lay stretched out in the back seat, eyes closed. After a few minutes I spotted Eddie approaching from across the street, emerging from the shadows like a ghost.

"That's weird," I said.

"What's weird?" Vince said.

"How the heck did Eddie get all the way over there by that diner? He went inside the store with us, didn't he?"

Vince sat up, puzzled. "I thought he did. He was standin' next to me. He must've walked right back out. I'm tellin' you, that guy's a fuckin' enigma."

"That joint's closed. Why the hell would Eddie be over there anyway?"

"Who knows, maybe he went over there to look at one of them tanks or somethin'. Or maybe he just wanted some alone time, to cry over his chick and all. Whatever, the dude's a trip. How 'bout we just kick his freaky ass out somewhere along the highway?" Vince chuckled and eased back onto the seat. "You okay to drive?"

I nodded a distracted affirmative. Eddie jumped into the front seat and casually searched through the bag of snacks we'd bought, never acknowledging his random wandering. After a moment's hesitation I turned over the engine and rolled out onto the street.

BACK ON THE road, it didn't take long for Vince and Eddie to crash, abandoning me to the droning monotony of the Interstate. Luckily, my gym-sock coffee packed just enough juice to keep me going, and combined with my near constant head tripping there was no way I was nodding off.

After an hour I blasted through Blythe and kept on trucking, crossed the California state line a few minutes later and weaved my way through the cluster of jagged hills beyond the Colorado River. Bored to tears, I reached for the radio dial, but dodgy reception made for nothing but static. I clicked the radio off and retreated back into my head. The muted sounds of the vehicle in motion relaxed me, allowing my mind to drift. A random memory floated by and I grabbed it.

I saw my daughter beaming with pride as I picked her up early from preschool for an afternoon of miniature golf. Sara strutted through the playground that day, gleefully bragging to her friends about our plans, saying it like she was lucky and they weren't. We went to our favorite course, a place I used to go to as a kid. Once inside, Sara dropped her club and took off running across the grass-covered mounds separating the greens, through a wonderful adventure-land of miniature houses, castles, and windmills set about cascading rivers of water and maze-like walkways, each turn revealing a new secret. I lost myself in the watching, before playfully scolding her for not golfing.

Many years have gone by since that blissful afternoon, with much turbulent water passing beneath the bridges of our lives, yet I could see it all like it was yesterday. I glanced into the rearview mirror and caught myself smiling. Damn, those were good days. How could I have ever known they wouldn't last?

Rolling through Quartzsite, I eased fully into it, feeling like I could drive all the way to New York. I tried the radio again, dialing through the AM band. I dig listening to AM radio at night; driving lonely roads with no particular destination, grooving to the vibe of another time and place, one of big American cars and tube radios that glow in the dark, of rock & roll and youth, of a time when people said what they meant and meant what they said. It's an old sound and I like it.

I picked up a clear signal and the familiar musical intro to *Riders on the Storm,* a most righteous road song. I plugged into the mesmerizing groove, the spooky vibe perfect for a night ride through the desert. In the distance there came the first indication of daylight breaking on the horizon, the faint glow of the sun's fingertips reaching up from the far side of the earth, bringing with it the dawn of a new day. Life is made up of moments, each one a step in the journey, stringing together like a chain through our memories. This was a good one.

I was fully absorbed by the music and the rhythm of the road when something up ahead caught my eye. It was the remains of a wreck on the highway, the skeleton of a burned-out motorhome, twisted and black, and the outline of an SUV tangled up in front clearly visible as I passed. A shiver went through me as I thought of some poor souls perishing right there on a forgotten patch of Arizona asphalt.

The kids came to me then, and Lucinda, and I thought of how far we'd let ourselves drift from the things that were most important. I found it sadly ironic that on the very day they were traveling north to San Francisco, seemingly to start a new life, I was heading south on a fool's errand.

Then my thoughts turned to Kenny Lopez and some cat named Benjie Cole, how the lives of those two strangers had intersected with my own, leading me to a place I likely didn't belong. A powerful sense of foreboding washed over me, and with it came the overwhelming feeling that I was making the biggest mistake of my life.

Eleven

We made Nogales, Arizona, just before ten o'clock on Tuesday morning. Nogales, Mexico, loomed in the distance, pushed up hard against the border fence. The ugly barrier of rusted steel and sinister razor wire sliced through the two cities like an unhealed wound, separating us from them.

The terrain was typical Southwestern desert scrub and hill country, the Mexican side overrun with crummy shacks and poorly built structures, and a density of population both staggering and claustrophobic. The two cities may share a name, but that's where the similarities end.

The heat of the day began its ascent, the morning sun bright in an eastern sky lightly painted over with thin clouds. My anxiety level spiked at the sight of our destination; rather than pleasant anticipation of a new adventure, I found myself hoping for a quick in-and-out operation.

We stopped for gas and supplies at a service station minimart located along the terminus of Interstate 19, just a few hundred yards from the border crossing. Across the street was one of those tourist joints that sell maps, cheap souvenirs, and Mexican car insurance. I suggested to Vince that we buy some of that insurance, but he balked, said it was nothing but a scam and besides, his Cherokee was a pile anyway so who gave a shit if it got jacked in Mexico.

While Vince and I debated the merits of cheap Mexican car insurance, Eddie drifted off to the rear of the minimart, disappearing from view. I paid it no mind at first, but after a few minutes I got to thinking about his wandering ways back at Chiriaco and curiosity got the better of me; it was time for a little snooping.

Vince went inside to pay for the gas and I walked around to the opposite side of the building, hoping to sneak a peek at Eddie. I sidled up to the corner and stood there for a moment, listening. The traffic on the boulevard drowned out any potential for eavesdropping, so I carefully peered around the corner, but saw nothing. Where the hell was he?

I ventured out onto the sidewalk, looked up and down the street. Then I walked across the street to the tourist joint, thinking maybe Eddie had gone in there to buy a map or some smokes, or maybe a sombrero so he'd fit in with the locals. I scoped out the shallow retail space, packed with tee shirts and cheesy curios, and at the rear of the shop, a counter where the insurance transactions took place. Still no Eddie. Damn, that guy was a slippery son of a bitch.

I'd just started walking back across the street when two separate things happened nearly simultaneously, the significance of which would not dawn on me until much later.

A loud rumbling erupted to my right, and I turned in time to see a couple of motorcycles shoot out from an alley about a hundred feet away, while at the same moment I saw Eddie running across the street on a diagonal track, headed toward the gas station. While I could never say for certain, it looked to me like Eddie had come out of the same alley as those two bikes.

I stood there on the sidewalk, alternately watching both Eddie and the bikers, who had stopped now in the middle of the street to talk. Eddie didn't see me, and in a few seconds he'd made it across the street to the gas station. When I turned my attention back to the bikers, I saw them stare and point at me, and I froze in recognition.

I knew one of those guys.

The big, scruffy-looking dude, the one in front doing the pointing, he looked just like one of the O.C. Satans I'd met at Weeds. It was one of those moments where you wonder if what you're seeing is really what is happening. I pictured the scene from Weeds, clearly remembered the big guy being all chummy with Kenny. The other guy looked unfamiliar to me, but the big guy, him I knew.

All at once I felt exposed, like I was standing under a spotlight, and I stepped behind a large tree at the edge of the sidewalk. I stayed in that position and watched as the two bikers finished their roadside chat, gunning their engines loudly as they took off down the street.

The whole episode lasted maybe three minutes tops, and as my adrenaline receded, I began to doubt every bit of it. I replayed the scene in my mind while crossing the street to the gas station, distracted by the images. A horn blared and I jumped, nearly swiped off my feet by a passing truck.

I was rattled and confused by events, and as I watched Eddie talking to Vince over by the Jeep, I knew I'd better keep an eye on that guy. I wasn't sure what to make of the bikers, but Eddie was another story. There was something in his shifty and wandering behavior that didn't feel right, and if he was up to no good, I sure didn't want to be the last to know about it. I'd already had enough of that kind of business with Lucinda, and I wasn't about to let myself get fooled again.

Twelve

The border crossing went without a hitch, although Vince's gun never left my mind, and some nervous minutes ticked by before we were waved through by a dull-eyed border agent who barely gave us a glance. All at once we found ourselves thrust into a parallel universe, one of confusion and chaos, and a sense of desperation so real it hung thick in the air, like the ugly layer of smog that threatened to swallow the entire city.

We wended our way through town, down crooked streets jammed with old cars spewing exhaust, past throngs of pedestrians overflowing the sidewalks and countless hawkers loudly peddling their wares, their carts and storefront stands crammed with all manner of seemingly worthless junk. The densely packed buildings ranged from relatively modern construction to primitive tarpaper and adobe, the shops, restaurants, and various other businesses colliding in a crazy spectacle of sight and sound, the sum total of city planning gone awry.

It felt unfamiliar and strange.

It felt *Third World*.

The awareness hit me, just how difficult this was going to be, finding a stranger in a foreign land. Back home it sounded easy enough, but now that we were actually here, it was another story. This was work for bounty hunters or private detectives, not a couple of middle-aged white-bread O.C. homeboys and their myopic sidekick. We were completely out of our element and it showed. After twenty minutes of aimless driving I'd had enough.

"Do you have any idea what you're doing, or are you just running laps?" I said. Vince grinned, a man perfectly at ease with the world.

"Easy does it there, buddy, I got this handled."

He whipped a hard left off the boulevard, nearly throwing me out the window, and accelerated up a narrow street, his eyes scanning intently from side to side as if he knew what the hell he was looking for. After a minute he jerked sideways to the curb and stopped in front of a three-story tumbledown building. A faded sign at street level read *Mercado Sonora.* A group of degenerate-looking characters hovered nearby, shooting the shit like layabouts the world over. Vince kept the motor running as he leaned across me and shouted at them through my open window.

"Hey, amigos. Qué pasa, bros?"

One of the guys turned and stared at us. He looked like he might be the leader of this gang of fine citizens. "What you want, gringo?" he said with a thick accent, the words coming out slow. His sidekicks turned and gazed vacantly in our direction. Vince plowed ahead, unfazed.

"How do we get to the Ranchero Hotel?"

"Are you sure you *pendejos* do not want the Plaza Nogales, or perhaps the Fiesta Inn? The Ranchero is not, how you say, a tourist joint."

As the leader spoke, I noticed a skinny kid wearing a dirty sombrero walk casually to the rear of the Jeep. I turned to see what he was up to, catching a nervous look on Eddie's face.

"Naw, man, we gotta meet up with a friend of ours," Vince said. "At the Ranchero, not them other places you mentioned." He reached behind his seat and pulled a couple of beers from a cooler. "Hey, you guys want some brews? It's kinda hot out here."

"Drinking when you are driving is *muy peligroso.*" A squeaky voice drifted through the driver's side window. Vince and I turned at the same time; saw the skinny dude with the ratty sombrero practically hanging inside the car. He flashed a wide grin and silver-capped teeth, his odor foul.

"Please, do not concern yourself with Ernesto," the leader said pleasantly. "He is *loco y feo.*" He let out a deep-throated laugh, and Ernesto slunk away as the others giggled.

"I will tell you *gabachos* how to find the Ranchero," the leader continued. "But first you will give me all of your *cervezas*, and fifty of your American dollars. And because I am such a good person, I will not call to my cousin, who is the *jefe* of the *policía* here in Nogales, and I will not say to him that three gringo *contrabandistas* are staying at the Ranchero, and they are driving a black Jeep, just like this one."

The dude gave us a fat, stupid smile, showing *his* rotten teeth proudly. Vince looked at Eddie and me and he shrugged. "At least they speak English," he said under his breath. The Mexicans stood there laughing. Terrific, in town less than half an hour and already we were getting the shakedown.

Vince fished some bills from his wallet, handed the cash and the beers over to our welcoming committee. They started guzzling right away, and true to his word, the leader came through with the directions.

"It is very simple, *cabrón*, to find the Ranchero. First, you must take this street to the little one over there." He pointed the direction, while his friends nodded in agreement. The leader shot them a look and the nodding stopped. "At the little street over there, you will turn to the right, and you will drive two blocks to the street is called Camino Del Sol. Turn to the left and go very far, perhaps five miles, to the Apache Bar. Is *muy bueno*, the Apache, maybe you will visit?"

He paused for our response, receiving silence in return. His friends gave us a frown, and the leader sighed.

"You no like? Okay, is no skin off my nose. So when you *maricóns* find the Apache Bar, you must turn to the right, and you will see a very small street with no name. Take this small street with no name to the left, and this is the place you will find the Ranchero Hotel."

The leader stepped back proudly, taking a long pull from his beer, flashing that killer smile of his; he was truly the master of his universe. His friends gathered around him, grinning their approval.

"Thanks, amigo!" Vince shouted, gunning the engine and lurching away from the curb, the Mexican dudes laughing and pointing at us as we drove off.

"That's a shitty deal," Eddie said, once we were clear.

"No shit. And what the hell's a pendejo, anyway?" Vince said.

"Yeah, and those other things he called us," Eddie said. "Dude's a damn beaner smart-ass is what he is."

"Maybe it's time we get ourselves a Mex dictionary, learn some local lingo," Vince said, laughing out loud. "That sounds like a good job for you, Jackson, on account of all that readin' you do."

I stared at my friend, as I do my son when he displeases me. "Next time, I'm asking for directions."

Vince gave me that good old boy guffaw, and he reached under his seat and pulled out a tarnished hip flask. "Come on, Jackson, I thought those fellas were all right." He tipped the flask in a quick hit, offered it to me. "Whiskey?" I waved it off. Eddie spoke from the back seat.

"Hit me, Vince."

"Sure thing, guitar man."

That Vince and Eddie, they're a helluva pair.

Thirteen

A short time later we found the Apache Bar.

It took up a street corner at the end of a dusty avenue lined with old brick buildings and sleepy neighborhood side streets. We were near the outskirts of town, the pace considerably less chaotic than at the border.

Two-stories tall and wood-framed, the Apache sported a wood-plank sidewalk with hitching posts out front, and a spindle-railed balcony running the length of the second floor. The joint wore its weathered and wasted look proudly, conjuring images of 1880s America and rough-and-tumble western towns like Dodge City and Tombstone. I pictured Wyatt Earp sitting up on that balcony, legs propped on the railing, on the lookout for gun-hands and waylayers.

A block past the Apache we came upon the street with no name, and we turned left as directed. The street narrowed to a single lane, the asphalt badly potholed, and Vince drove it slowly for maybe a quarter mile, to where it opened into a dirt cul-de-sac. A massive oak tree grew in the middle of the turnaround, ringed by a raised concrete planter, the tree's shade extending across the street. We parked in front of a brick and adobe structure that took up the end of the cul-de-sac, hugging its gentle curve.

The Ranchero Hotel.

We stepped out of the car and into the mid-morning heat. I sauntered over to the shade of the oak tree to cool off in the breeze. The street seemed oddly quiet, with little evidence that anyone lived in the nearby houses. Maybe all the people were off at work, or taking a siesta or something.

The Ranchero didn't look like much of a hotel, the general disrepair of the place giving off an appearance of vacancy. A shallow portico comprised of arched openings made up the ground level, the plaster chipped and peeling, revealing patches of red bricks blasted by the effects of sun, wind, and time. A rough-sawn wood balcony topped the portico; the balcony crowded with ferns in large clay pots on wrought iron stands, numerous hanging plants turned brown from neglect, rusted wind chimes of various sizes and shapes, and an ornate birdcage swinging empty in the lazy breeze. There were no windows and only two doors on the balcony, both of them blocked by the potted ferns, and if it wasn't for the faded lettering across the roof parapet, I'd have never known we'd reached our destination.

Vince motioned me over. Eddie took off toward an alleyway bordering the hotel—again with the wandering.

"Let's check in," Vince said, lighting a cigarette and tossing me the pack.

"We're staying?" I watched Eddie. "Where's he going?"

Vince took a deep drag. "Never mind that guy. Why shouldn't we stay here? This place looks all right."

"How about we try finding Benjie first, get the boot thing out of the way? This is the place he's supposed to be at, isn't it?"

"Could be. I'm not sure. It's on the list anyway, if that's what you mean."

I felt tension rise inside me. "I thought you said we'd find the dude here."

"Well yeah, but this is just the startin' point. Benjie could be any number of places. But don't worry. Kenny gave me everythin' we need. I got it all written down on the list."

"The list?"

"Yeah, a piece of paper with words written on it." Vince gave me a straight look, before winking playfully. "Shit, Jackson, what're you frettin' for? We'll find this dude. What's the big deal anyway, it ain't like we're spendin' our own money here."

I started to spell out exactly what the big deal was, but quickly gave up. Vince might have had a point about the money, but the vibe of the Ranchero wasn't setting right with me. Besides, it seemed prudent that we should at least make an effort at locating Benjie before we got locked into anything specific. Vince wouldn't budge though, and before I could convince him otherwise, Eddie had returned.

"We staying here?"

"Sure, Eddie, you cool with that?"

"Yeah, why not." He turned to me. "Let's take a walk, Jackson. They got a pretty nice setup back there. A pool too."

Take a look at Eddie now, all friendly and whatnot. I glanced over at Vince; he gave me a little nod. "Go on, Jackson," he said, "scope it out. I'll take care of things here."

Eddie offered me a smoke and Vince handed me his lighter. If I didn't know better, I'd say those two were working me. I waved off the cigarette.

"Let's go."

Fourteen

I followed Eddie down the alley and into a shaded courtyard located directly behind the main building. From back here I could see hotel rooms up on the second floor, although none of them appeared to be occupied. The swimming pool was large and rectangular and it extended to the far end of the courtyard, the water clean and deep blue in color. It seemed like a lot more care was taken with the upkeep of that pool than the hotel itself.

Surrounding the pool was a garden of tall palms and smaller shrubs, with fruit trees evenly spaced throughout, and gravel walkways branching off in random directions. From somewhere nearby I heard the sound of water trickling from a fountain and birds singing in the trees. On either side of the courtyard, beyond the garden, a row of single-story bungalows stretched into the distance, dropping in elevation with the contour of the land, giving the impression we were on a hill.

We walked to the far end of the pool and leaned against a wood fence, and from this vantage point I could see that we were indeed situated on a plateau of sorts, with a commanding view of Nogales spread out before us, the border fence visible in the distance.

The bungalows followed the alley to the bottom of the slope, maybe a hundred yards, turned left for half that distance, before running back uphill to meet the main building, forming a fortress-like perimeter. The area downslope grew thick with vegetation, stubby palms, and patches of grass dotted with wildflowers, with narrow dirt footpaths leading to the rooms below. It seemed to me the Ranchero would make a nice little smuggler hideout. I closed my eyes, pictured the outlaw Pancho Villa holed up here with his *Villistas*, basking in the tropical splendor after a hard day of revolutionary mayhem, on the run from Pershing and his army. Sounds like a movie.

Scanning the bungalows, I wondered which one Benjie was in, or if he was even here. I felt frustration over Vince's lack of planning and general indifference to things. Someone had to take charge, and I had the sinking feeling it would fall on me.

As I thought about these things, Eddie stood a few feet away, casually smoking a cigarette. I thought about him running from that alley at the same time those bikers came into view, and I considered the significance of that, whether or not I should say something to Vince about it. And speaking of those two bikers, why didn't Kenny just ask a couple of guys from his crew to come down here and get the boots? Seems to me that would've made a hell of a lot more sense than sending strangers to do the job. Probably would've been cheaper too. Maybe even free.

And since I was doing such a good job thinking about things, there was something else that didn't add up. Back at Smitty's, Vince said Benjie couldn't be reached. But that made no sense, not if Kenny knew where Benjie was staying. You mean to tell me he couldn't leave the dude a message, or send him an email, or even a telegram? Do they even have telegrams anymore? Something was screwy with the whole deal.

It occurred to me that my final decision to join Vince was based strictly on a knee-jerk reaction to what had happened in court and the news of Lucinda's San Francisco plans. Upon reflection, that seemed like a pretty reckless thing to do. Perhaps I should have asked a few more questions, gotten a better feel for Kenny Lopez before I threw in with him on what was admittedly an absurd endeavor. Instead, I'd let greed and my desire to get even with Lou trump some obvious flaws.

"You ever been here before?" Eddie said vaguely, startling me back to the moment. "Mexico I mean. You ever come down here?"

"Tijuana a couple of times, once down to Ensenada," I said, the distraction of my earlier thoughts making it hard to engage Eddie. "And you?"

"Naw, man, Mexico never interested me."

But it sure seems to interest you now, I thought sarcastically, or else you'd have never wormed your way into this deal.

"This place isn't too bad," Eddie said, his voice coarse. "The town's kind of a dump though."

I nodded in agreement, glancing sideways as Eddie did that thing with the cigarette and the smoke and the weird eyes. I was impatient with the conversation, not really digging the scene.

"It'll do," I said. "We might as well park it here for the night while we scope things out." I stood up straight, ready to make my move back to the car to see what the hell Vince was doing. Eddie's next words blindsided me.

"You mean while we figure out where Benjie is?"

I tried to hide my surprise, but Eddie saw right through it. He laughed, and offered me a cigarette. "Yeah, I know all about that. You thought I didn't?"

I took the cigarette and bought some time lighting it, my mind racing. *He knew all along?* But Vince said—well, never mind what Vince said—how in the heck did Eddie find out? I decided to play it dumb.

"I never gave it much thought," I said.

Eddie laughed. "Shit, you guys weren't exactly being secretive about it. Like when Vince mentioned leaving Benjie barefoot." He laughed again; it was starting to annoy me. "Anyway, I already knew. Kenny told me."

"You know Kenny?" I said, way too quickly.

"Yeah, sure. From Weeds. We play there all the time, and Kenny's biker gang just about lives there. He mentioned this little favor Vince was going to do for him. Why do you seem so surprised by this?"

I didn't know what to say, my mind too jumbled to react. This threw things into a whole new light, and at that moment I wanted to talk to Vince alone, gets a few things straight about who knew what and when. I thought about the money. Did Eddie know about that too? When I finally spoke I tried keeping my tone neutral, make Eddie work for it.

"Do I look surprised?" I said. "I guess we all have our reasons for being here. I knew about the thing with the boots, but that's not my deal. Why would we keep it a secret from you anyway?"

"I don't know, Jackson, that's why I asked. Who knows why people do the things they do?"

Ain't that the truth, Mr. Wanderer.

I was ready to be done with this line of questioning; Eddie helped me out on that one. "I'm going for some beer," he said. "You want one?"

"Sure. I'll wait here for you. I think I'll just lie down on one of those lounge chairs over there by the pool, rest my eyes a little. Man, I'm beat."

"I hear that. It's been a long day. And night."

Eddie gave a weird little laugh, kind of a *tee-hee-hee* thing, and he turned and took one of the winding gravel paths through the garden, leaving me standing there with far too many questions and not nearly enough answers.

I walked over to the lounge chair and lay down. The sun felt good on my face, the breeze through the trees pleasantly cool. I eased into the contours of the thick cushion over the wood slats. In the distance I heard a wind chime, probably one of the rusted ones up on that balcony filled with all that clutter.

My watch said it was nearly noon, and I wondered if we were in a different time zone down here. I thought about Lucinda and the kids and what they were doing up in San Francisco. I was overcome by sadness. At that exact moment, lying there by the pool at the Ranchero Hotel, I felt about as lost and alone as I ever had in my entire life.

What I didn't think about was Vince and the possibility that he'd misled me, or maybe even lied to me. I would square *that* later. I closed my eyes and tried to blank it all out, stop the endless thinking. I hoped Eddie wouldn't return, not for a while at least, so I could get some rest and reset my brain. Twenty minutes was all I needed, and then I'd be ready to deal with whatever needed dealing. At least that was the plan.

Fifteen

My twenty-minute nap turned into a four-hour deep sleep. I woke to the sun hanging low on the horizon, shimmering like fire through the trees, the day's heat giving way to the coolness of evening. My body ached and my head was groggy, and the stiff wooden lounge chair that had felt so comfortable just a few hours earlier now had me feeling my age. I stood carefully and shook out my limbs. I'd crashed hard and it felt good, but now it was time to get moving.

I reached for my cell phone to call Vince, but it wasn't in my pocket. A search of the immediate area turned up nothing. I recounted my steps since our arrival, trying to place where I could have lost it, but my brain wasn't working right and I couldn't think straight. Finally I gave up and turned my attention to finding Vince; I'd deal with the phone later. Dialing in my bearings, I headed for the front of the hotel. When I got there I saw the Jeep was gone, and a quick surge of panic ripped through me.

A strong gust of wind kicked up and blew through the huge oak out in the middle of the cul-de-sac, shaking its massive limbs. Momentarily distracted, I pondered the age of that tree— a hundred years perhaps? I was struck by a sobering thought:

through all my years of living, that big oak has been right here doing its thing, and probably will be long after I'm gone.

The wind chimes up on the balcony sounded sharply in the breeze and the birdcage slammed hard against a wood post, making me jump, my heart tensed and thumping wildly. Ominous vibes revealed themselves, pulling my nerves tight. I had to settle down, and finding Vince and Eddie was a good place to start.

I turned and pushed through the heavy front door of the Ranchero, stepping into a sparsely furnished lobby that had surely seen better days. The desk clerk sat to one side, behind a wide counter. "Excuse me?" I said. "Can you help me with something?"

The guy lifted his head slightly, looked at me irritably over the rim of his glasses.

"Do you speak English?" I said.

"Yes, I speak your language. What do you need?" The clerk's eyes were indifferent. I forged ahead despite his unfriendliness.

"Did a couple of guys come in here earlier today, looking for a room?"

I smiled, tried to make my face appear open and pleasant, but I was sure my anxiety showed through. The clerk took off his glasses and studied me, his eyes probing now.

"Si, your friends were here. They take a room for the week." He waved his hand dismissively and returned to his reading.

I felt heat rise up my neck. A whole week? What the hell was Vince thinking? But that's just the point, he *wasn't* thinking. I put the brakes on my anger, and smiled at the clerk. "Can I have a key to the room?" I asked politely.

He looked me over again, more carefully this time, an uncomfortable moment passing. "It's okay," I said, trying to sway his decision. "I came down here with them and we got separated."

After another minute of silence, he smiled oddly; I'm not sure it was meant to be friendly.

"I will give you the key," he said slowly, as if talking to a child. He turned and reached for a wood pegboard filled with keys. "Your friends are in room number twenty-seven. The last one on the left."

He turned to face me and extended the key, pulling it away quickly. "When you find *estúpido* Benjie, you tell him he owes me *mucho dinero*."

He smiled again, in that same disagreeable way, and handed me the key. As I took it, his clammy palm brushed against my hand, a sinister feeling gripping me.

"Sure thing. I'll let Benjie know."

The clerk resumed his reading, ignoring my response. I turned away from him in a state of confusion. So Benjie *was* here, and now he was on the move. I wondered if Vince knew. Hell, for all I knew, Vince and Eddie were with Benjie right now, knocking back beers and sharing a big laugh over Kenny and his damn boots.

I took two steps toward the door, before being seized by the immediate sense of the desk clerk's eyes upon me. I turned quickly, only to find him engrossed in his reading.

I MADE MY way down the dirt alley along the opposite side of the hotel from where Eddie and I had been earlier. Room twenty-seven was the corner bungalow at the bottom of the hill. When I got there I found a note stuck to the door. It was from Vince. He and Eddie were at the Apache Bar.

Nice going, guys.

I crumpled the note and threw it aside in disgust. When I opened the door to our room I saw our gear piled in the middle of the floor. The place looked clean, with a couple of twin beds and a nightstand against one wall, and a small couch and coffee table under the window facing the alley. A goofy curtain hung over the window, patterned in 1950s style cartoon cowboys and Indians blasting away at each other. The furniture looked to be fifties vintage as well. How old was this place anyway? Maybe Pancho *did* spend time here after all.

The bungalow featured a kitchenette, complete with a vintage Frigidaire, in keeping with the retro motif. To the right of the kitchenette, an archway led to another bedroom and a single bathroom. There was no television or telephone in either room.

After my quick tour around our digs, it was time to find my cell phone. The car was the likely spot. But where the heck was the car? I didn't see it on my way down the alley. Considering the Apache Bar was within walking distance, it wasn't likely that Vince and Eddie had driven there. I stepped outside to investigate.

The sun had slipped behind the hills and darkness had settled in. Two dim bulbs burned on either side of the window with that funky curtain, casting halos of yellow light. The alley turned to the right, behind our bungalow, extending to the other side of the hotel property. I followed it to the end of our unit and found the Jeep parked on a gravel driveway. A thorough search turned up no cell phone. I squeezed through an opening in the hedge in front of the Jeep and onto a concrete walkway leading to our room. Back inside, I spread our gear across the floor, but found no phone.

By now I was pretty fed up, so I decided to shelve the phone search until later. It was time for me to get cleaned up and go locate my knucklehead traveling companions, teach those two some road etiquette. I checked the fridge and found it stocked with beer. Nice to see my pals had their priorities in order. I pulled a bottle and twisted the cap, took a swig. Something caught my eye, over on the counter. It was my cell phone.

Or at least I thought it was. But when I flipped it open I saw no background picture of my kids. I immediately figured it for Eddie's phone, since I knew Vince carried a different model. Eddie must have taken mine by mistake.

So there I was with Eddie's cell phone in my hand, and I got a little curious. I casually scrolled through the list of recent calls. Virtually all of them, both sent and received, were the same number. It was an Orange County area code, no name listed, just the letter *K*. Three of the calls had come in since we'd arrived in Nogales.

Next I checked text messages. There were five of them, all from the same unnamed phone number. Four of the messages were fairly innocuous. The fifth one read: *when you get there, update me with details*. That one sounded odd.

My mind flashed on Kenny; were the messages from him? But why would Kenny contact Eddie? I took a long pull off the beer, rolled that thought around my head. The beer tasted great and really hit the spot. I drank half the bottle down as I thought about those messages. I wanted a cigarette but I didn't have a pack with me. I had the strong sense of events being put into motion, like I was standing inside a big machine with lots of moving parts.

What did it mean?

What did any of it mean?

Lucinda and the kids in San Francisco. Custody fights and asshole lawyers. Kenny Lopez, Benjie Cole, and O.C. Satans turning up in strange places. Weird, wandering Eddie Dowd. Vince Taylor slowly going off the rails. Me?

I laughed out loud, even though none of it was funny. The beer went down and I got another. I started the shower; let it get good and hot. I stood there lost in the moment, thinking, always thinking. *All things in time, and a time for all things.* That's what I told myself, and that's what I so desperately wanted to believe.

Sixteen

I followed the sound of a jukebox from up the street, a high lonesome sound leading straight to the Apache Bar. Pushing through the saloon-style doors, I entered to the final strains of *I'm So Lonesome I Could Cry*; an odd choice for a Mexican bar, yet ironically appropriate for the moment.

The Apache was a big place, and it looked a lot like Weeds, although decidedly more low-rent. To my left was a high bandstand fronted by a warped-plank dance floor, to my right a sea of loosely scattered tables and chairs, and directly in front of me an ugly yet functional bar. A wide mirror covered the back bar, its low shelves haphazardly lined with bottles, a jagged crack running diagonally from the bottom up to the far corner, cutting the mirror in half. The bartender stood off to one side, casually leaning back while cleaning his fingernails with a switchblade knife.

A handful of drinkers sat on barstools; locals, I figured. I caught the reflection of one of them in the mirror, his face distorted weirdly from the crack and bottles of booze. He seemed to be checking me out from under the brim of his straw hat, although he played it off casually. To my right, I heard muffled words in Spanish. I turned and saw two guys hunched low over their table, one of them whispering in the other's ear, the listener staring at me with pitiless eyes.

All at once a heavy vibe fell, and I had the strong sense of being in the wrong place at the wrong time. I decided that I didn't like the Apache Bar very much, and figured the less time spent inside that place the better. Boy was I right about that.

But the really fun stuff wouldn't come until later. For now, there were other surprises to be had.

I turned back to the voyeur sitting at the bar; his head was dipped now and he seemed to have lost interest in whatever it was he'd found so fascinating about me in the first place. That's when I noticed the collection of motorcycle jackets and vests nailed to the wall above the mirror, each one bearing an elaborate insignia, a veritable who's who of outlaw biker gangs. And right there in the middle of that murderers' row I saw a name I'd only recently come to know. The O.C. Satans.

Yep, there it was, tucked between the Hells Angels and the Mongols. What is it they say about being judged by the company you keep? This thing was quickly evolving into some kind of bizarre, six degrees of separation, with Kenny Lopez at its nexus. And the hits just kept on coming.

The hinky vibe notched a few clicks, and all I wanted was to find Vince and Eddie and get the hell out of Dodge. But a quick glance around the room revealed no sign of those two. There was another section of the Apache to check out, beyond the bar and around the corner, but before going over there I had to hit the head.

The restroom was located next to the bandstand, just past a jukebox and cigarette machine. The juke was filled with country and early rock & roll records, with a smattering of Mexican music thrown in to keep things authentic, and I stole a quick glance back at the bar and tried to pick out the Hank fan. Then I stopped at the cigarette machine for a pack but was short by a quarter—the story of my life—and when I finally entered the dank restroom, I found it empty, save for one familiar face standing at the urinals.

"Man, I tell you," I said loudly, my voice echoing off the heavily tiled walls. "It's a tough day in the neighborhood when your best pal abandons your sorry ass in a foreign country."

Vince smirked over his shoulder.

"True dat, jolly mon. But damn, bro, y'all looked so peaceful lyin' there, all sleepy and whatnot. I just couldn't bring myself to disturb you."

"Now that's what I like about you, Vince. You're genuinely altruistic. Always putting the other guy first." I stepped up to the stall next to him and took care of business. "So what's the deal with the room, you planning some kind of early retirement down here?"

"Hell no, amigo. A short visit is one thing, but livin' here is a whole other deal. The room's cheap anyway, so I figured we might as well take it, 'cause who knows how long it'll be before we locate Benjie. Besides, like I said before, it ain't our money we're spendin'."

Vince grinned stupidly, knowing it was damn near impossible to be pissed at him when he did that.

"Speaking of Benjie," I said, "the desk clerk back at the hotel claims he's owed money by our mystery boot bandit, and he'd like us to pass the word. *When we find him.*"

I fixed Vince with a steady glare. His eyes darted away as he fiddled with his zipper.

"Yeah, well now that you mention it, it sorta looks like Benjie flew the coop."

"So what now, genius, Plan B? Do you even have a Plan B? Or is that on the list too?"

"As a matter of fact, I got that base covered. Follow me, there's a guy I want you to meet." He started out of the restroom.

"Vince, hold up a minute, there's something else we have to settle."

He stopped and turned. "What's up?"

"Earlier today, when Eddie and I went to check out the pool at the hotel, he told me he knew about Benjie, and the boots."

"Yeah, so?"

"What do you mean, 'yeah, so'? You told me Eddie had no idea why we came down here. And now I find out he does. In fact, he heard it from Kenny Lopez. What the hell's up with that shit?"

"Easy, Jackson, it's no big thing, okay? I heard all about it from Eddie today. I had no idea he knew, honestly. I'm not even sure when he found out. He and I didn't get into all that. Sure, Eddie knows Kenny, because we play out at Weeds. But so do the other guys in the band, so what? And besides, I didn't think those two ever talked. I guess I was wrong about that. It don't matter anyway, it ain't like this changes anything."

"And the money?"

"What about it?"

"Does he know about that too?"

"It didn't come up when we talked, so I'd have to say no, he has no idea."

"Well *that's* reassuring."

Vince stared at me. "Look, Eddie's a broke son of a bitch, okay? I know that for a fact. So if that dude had any clue there was thirty grand involved here, he'd be houndin' the shit outta me for his share. Got it? So quit your worryin' and let's go meet this guy I told you about."

I tried holding his stare, but it was useless. I was out of line and we both knew it. The idea that Vince would mislead me, or even outright lie to me, was laughable on its face. The tension slipped away and I let out a long breath, along with a good laugh.

"Dammit, man, I'm sorry. I guess I'm just too uptight these days. The way Eddie hit me with this came out of left field, and it threw me, that's all. Anyway, cut me some slack here, will you?"

Vince waved off my words.

"No sweat, J.T., we're good. I know it's been tough for you lately. For both of us, really. So let's just forget all that shit for a few days, have ourselves some fun down here. Cool?"

"You got it."

Vince turned to leave the restroom. I thought of those calls and texts on Eddie's phone.

"Hey, Vince, hold up a minute. There's one more thing."

He stopped and glanced back at me, annoyance crossing his face. "What *now*, Jackson?"

"Do you know his girlfriend's name? Eddie's, I mean."

"I don't know. I think it might be Amy, or Andrea, some shit like that. All I know is she dumped his freaky ass. Now get off it and let's go meet this guy. He knows where Benjie is."

Seventeen

Vince led me out of the restroom, under the rich baritone of Johnny Cash singing his classic tale of forbidden love, and a burning ring of fire. Whoever it was feeding the juke, they sure had good taste in music.

We turned left at the end of the bar and entered a dining area filled with tables and chairs and booths lining the perimeter. At the far end of the room I spotted Eddie sitting in a dimly lit corner. There was a guy sitting across from him, his back turned. As I approached the booth, Eddie tossed me a cell phone. "I think this is yours," he said.

I caught the phone and flipped it open, but found no messages. I was hoping for something from Lucinda or the kids. "Thanks," I said to Eddie, disappointment bearing down on me. "I thought I'd lost it."

"You didn't see mine anywhere, did you?" Eddie flashed me an odd look.

"No," I said too quickly. "I'm sure it's in the room though, or maybe the car." A jolt of nerves made me look away, along with thoughts of those text messages, and maybe a little guilt over my snooping.

"Jackson, this is the guy I was tellin' you about." Vince motioned across the table. "Barry, this is Jackson Thomas, he's the third wheel on this little operation of ours."

The stranger extended his hand. "Barry Fitzgerald," he said. "Good to meet you, Jackson."

"Same here," I said, returning the gesture with a firm handshake. "You can call me J.T. That's what my friends do. At least the ones who don't leave me passed out by swimming pools." I shot Eddie a stiff glance, half-smiling to smooth out the edge. He shrugged, unconcerned.

"Vince sidetracked me."

"No worries," I said. "I know how Vince operates. He has a way of making you forget what you came for." I put on my best version of the shit-eating grin, turning to Vince. "Third wheel, eh?"

"C'mon, bro, you're always number one with me." He smiled, arms outstretched in a forgiving gesture. "So anyway, enough of that. Barry knows all about Benjie, has an idea where we can find him too. Go on, man, tell him."

Vince sat down in the booth next to Barry, while I took a seat alongside Eddie. Barry glanced up from his cocktail. He wore a faded Hawaiian shirt, *Fitzgerald Aviation & Sky Tours* stitched over the pocket, along with the embroidered logo of a vintage prop-driven plane. His tanned face was thin, with a full mustache set over a lazy smile and sandy curls peeking out from under a Jimmy Buffet *Air Margaritaville* cap; he kind of resembled Buffett.

"Sure, bud, I know Benjie. He and I go back a long time." Barry's voice was rich and warm, vaguely Southern. "You guys just missed him." He nodded casually and knocked back his drink, his blue eyes projecting an easy countenance.

A waitress approached our table. She was young and pretty, with a tight little figure showing under her snug jeans and white tee shirt. We ordered a round of drinks and a plate of tacos, and a kid came by with chips and salsa, and a container of tortillas.

"How is it you know Benjie?" I said.

Barry regarded me for a long moment before answering. "We run in the same circles," he said. "Have for a long time. He's a righteous dude."

"Barry was tellin' us that Benjie headed south," Vince said. "To a place called Hermosillo. He's down here lookin' for a guy."

I stared at Vince, struck by the irony; seems we were all looking for someone. My eyes settled on the logo on Barry's shirt, and I gave it a nod. "You the owner, or the pilot?"

"Both. Right now I have two planes, a twin-engine Beech and another I'm rebuilding. I used to have four, but I've scaled back. This little honey right here—" Barry tapped the logo on his shirt. "She was my number one. Midnight Blue. A great bird. She served me well for many years." He paused a moment, reflectively studying the bottom of his glass. "I lost her off the coast of Belize back in ninety-seven."

Barry let out a small chuckle, like good things recalled.

"Oh well. Easy come, easy go, right? Nowadays I run a shuttle service here in Nogales, with the occasional import/export action thrown into the mix." He drained his cocktail, motioning to the waitress for another. "Moving airfreight of course," he added with a wink.

Airfreight? Import/export? Sounded dodgy to me.

"So what's the scoop with this joint?" I said. "The biker jackets nailed up on the wall over there. I thought those guys were pretty territorial. How is it you get all those dudes mixing in the same place?"

"You noticed that, did you?" Barry smiled knowingly. "The Apache is a unique establishment. Think of it as a clearinghouse for the fringe element, in a manner of speaking. The owner's some mysterious Cuban cat who's rumored to be hooked up with Castro. You ask me, that's strictly bullshit. Regardless, he runs an open shop down here, and he takes all comers. But make no mistake about it. He keeps a tight lid on this place. If the scooter tramps get out of line, he's got the local heat on 'em like the proverbial stink on shit."

"Barry was tellin' us he's ex-military," Vince said. "And that he's tied in with a group of—what'd you call them? Expatriated Americans?"

"Sure, slim, there's a bunch of us scattered around these parts, most with the same story. We did our time serving Uncle Sammy, learned a thing or two about dealing with subversive elements, and then parlayed that experience into more fruitful opportunities. Servicing the local needs, if you will."

Barry Fitzgerald grinned wide, mirth in his eyes; he clearly enjoyed playing the role of barroom raconteur.

"The thing of it is, life in the straight world gets boring as hell once you've tasted some action. Down here is about as close to the Old West as you'll ever get. It's the last frontier, man. Desperadoes, shady operators, opportunistic entrepreneurs, they're all right here. If that's your thing, well then this is the place to be."

Barry leaned back in the booth, smiling loosely as if gauging my reaction. He had an appealing way about him, one that drew you right in and put you at ease. He was definitely well versed in the art of being specifically non-specific.

I turned and considered the room, laughing inside at the scene. It would seem I'd fallen through a trapdoor and landed smack in the middle of Rick's Café, in a twisted Mexican version of *Casablanca*, mystery and intrigue lurking about. The more Barry talked the more I filled in the blanks, and it became clear to me that we were operating on the fringes here. Just how far I could never have guessed. Had I been able to, I would have surely run for the hills. The ones back home.

Eighteen

B arry gave us some more information about Benjie Cole, and a picture emerged of the man we were pursuing. Up to that point he was simply an abstraction, the impetus, if you will, for my being in Mexico. Now, for the first time, I began to see him as a real person.

Barry knew Benjie from their time in the military, and in the years since, they'd stayed in loose touch. It seems Benjie made frequent visits to Mexico, although for what purpose Barry wouldn't say. According to Barry, Benjie Cole was a solid dude, and the right guy to have at your back when things went south. I got the impression there wasn't much that Barry Fitzgerald would not do for his friend.

On his last trip down Benjie had seemed distracted; bugged was how Barry put it. They'd made plans to do some fishing together at Bahia Kino, out on the Sea of Cortez, but Benjie pulled up stakes and left town without warning. The way it went down left Barry feeling uneasy. Hearing about it brought to mind the desk clerk back at the Ranchero, and his claim that Benjie owed him money. That struck me as odd, since the guy Barry described didn't sound like the type who'd skip out on a hotel bill, especially a cheap one. Something drew Benjie away from

Nogales though, so suddenly that he literally dropped everything.

Barry never once asked us why we were looking for Benjie, and he seemed to take it at face value that we had legitimate dealings with him, and that we meant him no harm. Of course, we didn't exactly look like a trio of hoods with nefarious intentions either.

After a while Barry started to fade, and he leaned back into the corner of the booth with his eyes closed. The Apache Bar had turned crowded, filled now with raucous patrons, the action heating up. The jukebox continued pumping out mostly gringo music, and the next song up was Townes Van Zandt, *Pancho and Lefty*. Barry sat up suddenly, his face beaming.

"Now there's a song. *Pancho met his match you know, on the deserts down in Mexico.*" Barry sang along, strumming his air guitar while harmonizing to the next part of the song, something about dying words that nobody heard. I was struck by a funny thought; you don't suppose Pancho was down here searching for some guy's boots, do you?

"Ya gotta love ol' Townes. Crazy as a cross-eyed mule, but damn, what a songwriter." Barry laughed out loud.

"Speaking of music, what gives?" Eddie said. "I thought we were in Mexico, not some Bakersfield honky-tonk."

"Just keeping things copacetic for the *turistas*, Eduardo," Barry said. "Not to worry though, 'cause later on we got ourselves a nice little *norteño* outfit on tap. A good one too, not that jive-ass copycat shit. You guys know about that kind of music?"

We shook our heads.

"No? Well sumbitch, boys, you're in for a treat tonight. Norteño is Mexican folk music, performed by rural troubadours."

"We talkin' about mariachi music?" Vince said.

"Hell no, bro, that's purely gringo bullshit. Norteño is the real deal, the music of the people. And tonight we're getting it *narcocorrido* style. *Corridos* are ballads, and the cats who play them—*narcocorridistas* they're called—they twist it all around into tales of the drug trade, playing up the exploits of the smuggler and making him out to be larger than life. It's subversive as hell. The government outlaws it and the radio stations ban it, but the people dig it, and because of them the music lives on."

"Terrific, songs about drug dealers. No wonder they're so screwed down here," I said.

"You got it all wrong, chief. You need to realign your thinking on this one. Sure, in the States the drug lords are vilified as bad dudes. But down here they're looked upon as heroes, respected for the way they pour money into the local economy, helping out all the little towns and villages the government has forgotten about."

"What about all the violence?" I said. "They're nothing more than terrorists. Ruthless criminals taking advantage of a corrupt government and desperate people."

"Sure, they wreak a lot of havoc. And if you're dumb enough to get crossed up with them, they will surely bring down some hard rain upon your sorry ass. But they also build schools and clinics, and they pay for improvements the government takes years or even decades to get around to. In the minds of the average peasant, all that good stuff outweighs the bad. At the end of the day, it basically comes down to who's going to screw them over the least."

Barry was fully into it, painting a vivid picture in broad strokes. It sounded like textbook Marxist bullshit, all about the nobility of the poor and the need to rise up by any means necessary against the power and corruption of political machinery and bourgeois society. He seemed to believe it too, appearing to be about the right age for a hippie throwback. I wondered how the military service fit in. Vietnam maybe? He must have been a draftee though, as Barry Fitzgerald didn't strike me as the gung-ho, volunteer type. The narrative continued.

"What you have here is the last stop on the narco superhighway. Nogales is the jump point for a systematic production line of contraband that flows freely into the U.S. Some of it comes up from South America. A good chunk of it comes from right here in Mexico, the state of Sinaloa to be exact. Marijuana, meth, coke, heroin, you name it, it's all grown and produced here, and shipped north via towns like Nogales and Nuevo Laredo and Agua Prieta, and a whole lot of places that don't show up on maps.

"The Apache is a hub, a place where deals are sealed and payoffs made, and final transit is arranged. Things are wide open down here, and opportunities abound for guys with the right attitude, and the stones for taking risks."

Barry paused and raised his glass.

"Of course, this is just what I've heard. From people talking." He winked and downed the booze, the wily gleam in his eyes telling a different story.

We tipped our drinks as well, and I joined in Vince and Eddie's laughter. But my mind was elsewhere, clouded over by uncertainty. It was pretty obvious to me what Barry's game was. Although I'd never known any drug smugglers in my life, or any criminals for that matter, this guy fit every stereotype I'd ever read in a book or seen in a movie. A new image came to mind, and it featured Barry as Jimmy the pilot, from that *Miami Vice* episode with Glenn Frey.

So what about Benjie, what part did he play in Barry Fitzgerald's endeavors? And if Benjie was involved, where did that leave Kenny? Was he even in that picture? The mission was the boots, but an unexpected backstory was developing, and I couldn't help but feel it was all connected in some way to the big picture.

Then again, it could just be that I'd indulged too much film noir and pulp fiction. In those stories nothing is ever as it seems, and everyone has something to hide. But real life isn't a Jim Thompson novel and Chandler and Hammett have been dead for a long damn time, and besides, if one of them had written this story, I expect it'd be a hell of a lot more interesting.

THE WAITRESS CAME over to clear our table. Barry leaned in close and whispered something in Spanish, tipping her a handful of bills. She let out a flirty laugh as she walked away, and Barry shook his head, chuckling under his breath. "So you fellas going to head on down to Hermosillo?" he said.

The three of us exchanged ambiguous glances, and it was a long moment before anyone spoke.

"Why don't you tell us some more about it," I said.

"Sure thing, boss, whatever I can do to help smooth the way. Hermosillo's a big town, a lot bigger than Nogales, and it's the capitol of Sonora, which is the state you're in right now. It's about a two-hour drive south of here. Benjie went down there looking for a guy named Davey something or other, maybe it was Butch. Anyway, that part doesn't matter. All you need to know is he's down there.

"Now, when you get to town, you set yourself up at the Hotel Presidente, and stake out the El Burro Bar. That's where you'll most likely find Benjie, and pretty much anything else you might need when you're down there. The owner's a friend of mine, a fella named Max Hollister. You can trust him. If Benjie isn't there, Max will know where to find him."

Barry nodded approvingly, shifted sideways into the corner of the booth and pulled an Altoids tin from his shirt pocket. His mouth curled slightly as he opened the tin and removed a fat number. He fired up and ripped a toke, and offered it around the table.

"Are we cool here?" I said, leaning out of the booth to spot potential eavesdroppers.

"Oh yeah. Just gotta keep it mellow, baby."

Barry's voice sounded weird as he spoke through a lungful of smoke. He held it for a few seconds, before releasing a mushroom cloud over his head. He passed the joint to Vince, and Vince passed it to Eddie, both of them partaking. I waved it off, wanting to stay sharp, keep my wits about me. Even though I'd settled down after my shaky introduction to the Apache, I still didn't trust the place, nor its dubious patrons, and I wasn't about to let my guard down.

"So you guys have your papers, right?" Barry rasped through another huge toke of the pungent weed. I was getting a contact high just sitting there.

"What papers?" Eddie said.

"Passport, birth certificate, something that says you're legit."

"They didn't ask for any of that when we crossed over," I said.

"That's because here at the border you're in the free zone, so you don't have to mess with it. But if you want to travel to the interior, you got to comply. There's a checkpoint about ten miles south of here where they issue car permits, visitor's visas, all that bureaucratic bullshit."

"I guess we missed that part of the tourist guide," Vince said with a laugh, his face obscured by a haze of smoke. "I got nothin'. How 'bout you guys, *do you have your papers?*" He said it with a mock-German accent, like some kind of Gestapo stooge, cracking himself up.

"So what's up with that?" I said. "I thought this country was pretty much a lawless free-for-all. You know, anything goes."

"Well that's partially true," Barry said. "They are seriously backwards and corrupt as all get-out down here. But they got law too, and when it comes to foreigners they don't mess around."

"We've got driver's licenses, is that good enough?"

"Sorry, bud, that don't get it."

We fell silent, Barry's meaning clear. After a minute he laughed out loud.

"Don't look so down about it, boys. Remember, there's a way around everything down here. You just got to improvise a bit."

Barry gave a quick look-see around, and he leaned into the table, speaking low, like some kind of covert operator.

"So here's the deal. Just outside of town there's a bypass, takes you way out in the sticks, to the west of the checkpoint. It joins up with the main highway about twenty miles south of here. It's unpaved and rough as hell, but if you take it slow and easy, it's a piece of cake."

He leaned back in the corner of the booth, gauging our reaction. Johnny Cash blared from the speakers, *Folsom Prison Blues*, the story of shooting a man in Reno just to watch him die. Visions of hard time in a Mexican jail filled my mind, and the walls closed in.

"Am I hearing you right?" I said. "Are you suggesting we sneak past Mexican immigration?"

"It's not as bad as it sounds. People do it all the time."

"Sure, criminals do. But we're not criminals. Not yet at least. This is the nuttiest thing I've heard since—" I instantly flashed back on the feeling I'd had at Smitty's, when Vince and Kenny first pitched this crazy scheme. "Since...well, it's just crazy, that's all. It's crazy and it's stupid. And it's going to land our asses in jail."

I waited for some backup from Vince or Eddie, but none came. They just sat there with blank expressions, likely too stoned to process simple information. Barry went on.

"Here, I'll draw you a map. You'll see how easy it is."

He took one of the paper place mats and flipped it over. A few minutes later he handed me a detailed map, complete with landmarks to help guide us along. He assured us again how simple it would be. As long as we laid low and stayed cool, we'd be cool.

"There is one other thing you guys need to know about," Barry said, his tone serious.

"Yeah? What's that?" Vince said.

"The cadejo."

"The cujo?"

"Naw, that's Stephen King. I'm talking about the *cadejo*."

Vince looked at me confused. Eddie sat upright, and the three of us turned to Barry like Cub Scouts huddled around a campfire, listening to ghost stories.

"The locals call it *'pasar el perro'*. Roughly translated, it means crossing the dog."

"You sayin' there's dogs out there?" Vince said.

"Not dogs, spirits. That's what I'm talking about. The gatekeepers of heaven and hell."

"You're bullshitting us." Eddie said.

"No, I'm not. This is the real deal, straight from the old country. The cadejo is an apparition, one that appears only at night, along the path of travelers. It looks like a big shaggy dog, with gnarled goat hooves and burning red eyes. There are two kinds, white ones and black ones. The white one is your friend, and he brings you good fortune on your journey. But the black one, well he's got the eyes of the Devil, and he's a real bastard. He'll stop at nothing to curse you and damn you to the depths of Hades."

"Like a hellhound," I said.

"Hellhound?"

"Yeah, like in that Robert Johnson song, *Hellhound on My Trail*. It's all about running from the Devil, and you can't get away, no matter how hard you try."

"C'mon, man, you guys are creeping me out," Eddie said, his eyes turning beady in their little slits. "Goddamn hounds and shit. Knock it off, for Christ's sake."

"Shut your pie hole, Eddie, and listen to the man," Vince said. "Go on, Barry, what's the deal with these dogs anyway?"

"Well first off, I don't know anything about hellhounds. What I know is, when you're out there and you cross that dog, you better hope it's the white one. And whatever you do, don't turn your back to either one, because that'll make you go stone crazy."

Barry eased back, cocktail in hand, the slightest gleam showing in his eyes. I couldn't tell if he was being serious, or just jerking our chain.

"Of course, they don't always show up," he said. "That's the bitch of it. You never know for sure when they'll be there. It's like one minute you're cruising along and everything's good, and the next, you're staring into them nasty eyes and hearing that evil growl. That's when you know you're screwed. But if it's the white one, well then it's all good, and you just keep on truckin'."

Barry slugged back his drink and broke out laughing.

"But I really wouldn't let it bother you too much. Chances are you won't ever see one of them dogs anyhow."

Vince and Eddie huddled over the table, slack-jawed, while Barry took a half-slouched position in the corner of the booth, his eyes closed and his head swaying. I honestly didn't know what to make of that story. Barry told it straight, at least up until the end there, when his laughter made me wonder if the whole thing wasn't just a figment of his stoner imagination.

Barry Fitzgerald would regale us with many stories that night, tales so outrageous they had to be either completely made up or highly embellished. He claimed involvement in everything from Iran-Contra to the takedown of Manuel Noriega, and he dropped names like Pablo Escobar and Amado Carrillo and the Arellano brothers, all heavyweight drug traffickers. He made a few obscure references to his military service, and I got the impression that Barry was some kind of black ops guy, one of those shadowy characters you hear about but are never quite sure if they exist in real life.

He told us he was retired now. Sure, he snagged some freelance work occasionally, but that was mostly for kicks, since he claimed to have a pile stashed in some offshore accounts. To hear Barry tell it, he was just another happy gringo living out his golden years in laid-back, sunny Mexico. Before all was said and done, that happy gringo would pull our asses out of the soup big time.

AFTER A WHILE I needed a break from it all. The room was too loud and the scene too crowded, and my head swam from too many drinks and the close proximity of Barry's dope. I told the others I was going to the restroom, and then I ducked out the door and sat by myself on a bench out in front of the Apache. A steady stream of people poured into the bar, no doubt to hear those narco songs Barry mentioned. I heard the band tuning up inside, the buzz of anticipation from the packed room bleeding through the walls and out into the night.

It was almost nine o'clock and the moon was on the rise, the air cool going on cold. The street was quiet, most of the businesses closed for the day. I leaned my head back and shut my eyes, attempted a brief recharge of my batteries. It's a good thing I did that too, because when I went back inside, all hell broke loose.

Nineteen

Back inside the Apache the band was going at it hard, the room crowded and claustrophobic. The air felt charged with raw energy and booze-fueled reckless abandon. The combined heat of all those bodies jacked the temperature by at least ten degrees, resulting in a humid funk rolling off the dance floor as an undulating sea of humanity got its freak on to music best described as a frenzied polka beat rave-up.

The band was a four-piece fronted by a Ricky Ricardo look-alike decked out in a gaudy western suit that was equal parts Nudie and thrift-store Nashville. He sang in a high-pitched squeal with an odd, hiccupping vocal inflection interspersed with dog-like yelps, and his manic stage manner and awkward gyrations were completely out of sync with the music. To top it off, he sported a pair of pearl handled revolvers that he pulled randomly, firing blanks into the low-slung ceiling. It was the most bizarre spectacle I'd ever seen. The crowd was eating it up.

The men far outnumbered the women, an element of danger flowing through the room like a current, one of testosterone and pent-up aggression. That bad feeling I'd had when I first entered the Apache came back in spades, and I very nearly turned and walked out, but decided to at least talk to my partners first. I wasn't about to do them the way they did me.

I found them at the bar, throwing back shots with Barry and a pair of young women. As I approached, Barry grabbed my shirt and pressed in close, grinning wildly and talking directly in my ear, his breath hot and smelling of gin.

"Ain't this shit the scene, Jackson? Are you digging the *musica*?"

"Is that what you call it? Sounds like a train wreck to me," I shouted above the din.

"Hell no, slick. This here's the real deal, the music of the people. The song he's singing right now is called *El Ladrón de Caballero*. It's a classic of the genre. It's about a dude they call the Gentleman Thief. He's a nightrider and a liberator, and he spreads riches among the poor, his bounty stolen from the *jefe*, the boss man, you dig? The women love him and the men want to be him. He's goddamn Robin Hood, brother!"

Barry was a real gone cat, grooving to the sound of manic accordion accompanied by a syncopated gut-string guitar, the beat held down by drums and electric bass, driving a rhythm that pounded your brain into submission. A whole night of that shit would drive you insane. The crowd thought differently though, and one look told you they were completely into it, singing and yelping like rabid dogs. Barry turned and shuffled off toward a group of young dudes standing near the stage, partners in crime no doubt. I joined my friends.

Vince and Eddie leaned back against the bar, smoking cigarettes and messing with the two girls. They were average in looks and on the wrong side of heavy, and they wore too much makeup, but they were friendly in a timid sort of way. They didn't speak a word of English, making up for it with constant giggling and lots of flirtatious body language that was more embarrassing than enticing.

The whole deal was lame, and I was ready to drag Vince and Eddie out of there when four guys walked up to us in a rush, their manner openly hostile. They must have known the two girls because one of the guys, a short dude wearing ridiculous stacked-heel boots in an obvious attempt to appear taller, jabbed a finger at them and grabbed one of them roughly by the arm. He yammered angrily in Spanish, while alternately staring us down with lifeless eyes.

The other three said nothing; they simply glared in the same menacing way as their stunted companion. They spread out and hemmed us in, making a quick getaway difficult. I felt bad for the two girls, their pleading eyes seeming to apologize for the situation.

All four aggressors wore the same outfit; pressed blue jeans and exotic-skinned boots, leather belts with big buckles, gaudy silk shirts opened to show off gold neck chains and ornate crucifixes. Short Guy and another one wore stiff white cowboy hats, while the third guy sported a trucker cap with a marijuana leaf logo on the front; the fourth guy was bald and he wore no hat.

Short Guy was a lit fuse. He kept up his tirade, showing no signs of slowing down. He was hassling both girls now, while his partners slowly closed in on us. One of them, a tall, thin dude with a vicious scar running down his face, crowded in close to me, his heat strong.

Vince looked pretty cool about things, but Eddie was getting fidgety. He took a nervous step back, accidentally bumping the guy with the trucker cap. Short Guy noticed and he stopped in the middle of his rant, staring Eddie down. Then he launched into another diatribe, spitting violently on the floor.

Everyone froze then, pairs of eyes darting back and forth in anticipation of what would come next. The music and the crowd grew insanely loud, and my heart jackhammered with adrenaline as the Mexicans stared at us with an intensity that said this was about to turn ugly.

It was Vince who set it off.

He smiled at the two girls—that goddamn Vince Taylor shit-eating grin—and he looked right at Short Guy and gave him a wink, just a quick little thing. And because that wasn't good enough, he blew him a kiss. Violence erupted.

"*Qué chingados! Puto pinche gringo cabron!*" Short Guy screamed, throwing a wild haymaker at Vince, missing him by inches.

In a blur of motion Vince was on the guy, knocking him to the floor and pummeling his face. The two girls let out a scream and disappeared into the crowd. I caught a glimpse of Eddie collapsing into a sea of legs, while at the same moment I was thrown up against the bar, the jolt knocking the wind out of me. A free-for-all ensued as fists and chairs and bottles went flying, the entire room joining in the melee.

I spun around and caught my breath, my back to the bar. The skinny scar-faced dude came at me fast. I stepped into him, throwing a roundhouse. Scar Face dodged the blow and grabbed my shirt, giving me two quick shots to the face. The first was a glancing blow, but the second connected solidly, knocking me sideways onto a table. I rolled off onto the floor, feeling a sharp pain in the right side of my ass when I landed.

Scar Face got on me quickly, savagely punching at my head, and it was all I could do to cover up and protect my face. The dude may have been skinny, but he was relentless and strong too, and my efforts to buck him off failed. I caught a break when the guy fighting next to us lost his balance and fell onto Scar Face, knocking them both over. I crawled out and stood up, and in that moment the full extent of the madness inside the Apache Bar came into view. Absolute chaos reigned, and I found myself standing in the middle of Mexican Armageddon.

The band had stopped playing and people were screaming, running in every direction. It seemed like every man in the room was fighting someone, not to mention a few women mixing it up and giving as good as they got. Two wiry bartenders jumped over the stick, swinging billy clubs wildly into whatever moved, and a couple of massive coolers lumbered into the action and started picking up brawlers and throwing them out the front door as if they were twigs. I saw one poor bastard groaning in the corner, lying in a pool of his own blood. I had no idea about Vince or Eddie, and could only assume they were lost somewhere in the bedlam.

Reality refocused when Scar Face came at me with a knife, and a look to kill. My brain went numb and my heart pounded wildly as the crazed assassin slashed and swung his blade in a slow-motion dance of death. I shucked and jived, barely avoiding being sliced, before I was finally able to grab the fool in a bear hug, locking him up tight and holding on for my life. He tried head butting me and cutting me and stomping my feet, but I held on.

Just as my arms turned to rubber and I feared losing my hold, I spotted an empty tequila bottle lying on the floor. In a mad, desperate move, I released my grip and took a rolling dive, coming up with the bottle as the killer charged with the knife held high. I prayed to God and closed my eyes and swung as hard as my spent arms would allow, feeling the weight of the bottle as it connected with a sickening thud. Scar Face went down in a heap and I dropped the bottle on top of him, and turned for the door in a dead run.

I hit the swinging saloon doors hard and fell across the wooden sidewalk, rolling into the street like a Hollywood stuntman. Sirens echoed in the distance, louder with every second, and I heard whistles and rapid-fire bullhorn commands bellowed in Spanish. I got to my feet and took off running, making only a few steps before I was whacked hard across the back and sent sprawling head first into the asphalt. I turned over; saw a cop with his nightstick poised for another swing. Shots rang out then, a half-dozen or more quick pops from somewhere inside the bar. This wasn't the sound of Ricky Ricardo's cap guns. This was the real deal.

The cop turned when he heard the gunfire and I seized the opportunity, getting to my feet and running like hell straight for a narrow dirt alley two doors down from the Apache. When I reached the mouth of the dark passageway I dove for a pile of bricks, rolling off onto a pair of feet. I strained to focus in the dim light, nearly stroking out when I saw Vince's face looking down at me.

"J.T., thank God you made it," he whispered, out of breath but calm. "Eddie's around the corner. Let's go."

Vince pulled me up and led me to the end of the alley, where we joined Eddie, the three of us running silently into the night, the pandemonium inside the Apache Bar growing more distant with every step.

"DAMN, THAT PLACE went *off*."

Vince blew out his breath as he dropped onto the couch. He turned and peered through the window of our room at the Ranchero Hotel, scoping the alley outside, the sound of sirens audible in the distance. "Talk about a fuckin' riot."

"Those spic bastards were all over me. Like death," Eddie said vacantly. He was sitting down against the wall near the front door, staring at his feet. He'd dropped in that spot the minute we came through the door, and hadn't moved since.

"I had to crack that fat dude with a damn bar stool. Christ, he was a tough mother to get down. I think I hurt him. Bad." Eddie looked up at us, his expression doubtful. "What a shitty deal."

Vince nodded and turned to me. "How 'bout you, Jackson? You doin' all right over there?"

"Yeah, sure, I think so," I said slowly. "I got nailed pretty hard."

I sat on the bed, propped against the headboard, rubbing my chin while feeling for loose teeth. My arms ached from fending off all those blows, and surely by morning I'd be sporting some serious bruises. My ass hurt too, from falling off that table, and worse, my cell phone was broken; it was in my back pocket when I hit the deck, and now it wouldn't even turn on.

I wasn't in too bad of shape, considering what I'd just come through, and Vince and Eddie looked no worse for wear. All in all, I'd say we did pretty well for ourselves.

Vince got up and handed me his flask. "Take a jolt." He gave me an uncertain look. Maybe it was fear. Maybe it was regret for dragging me into this fiasco.

I took a hit from the flask, just like those tough guys do in the pulps. That's the thing, right? When bad shit goes down you hit the hard stuff to straighten out your head. The burn felt reassuring, and I hit it again for good measure, and handed the flask back to Vince. He took a pop, and sat down on the couch.

"Either of you see what happened to Barry?"

"I thought I saw him bail out the front door right before the cops showed up," Eddie said. He turned and flashed me those squinty eyes of his. "How about you, Jackson, you see anything?"

"I'm not sure what happened to him. Last I saw, he was up near the stage grooving to that narco jive. Once the shit hit the fan, I lost him. After that, I was preoccupied with that scar-faced asshole trying to carve me up."

The full impact of those words hit me hard. That guy really *did* want to kill me. Seriously. Yet I came through it. I prevailed, while the asshole failed, and with any luck he was sitting in the back of a paddy wagon right now, chained up to the rest of his asshole friends. Sure, I'd had some help, and if that dude hadn't knocked Scar Face off me who knows how it would've turned out. But that part doesn't matter. The only thing that matters is I survived.

I retraced each step of the fight, feeling no fear, or regret for my actions. Instead, I felt alive, and for the first time in a long time I had a moment of clarity. Sitting there at the Ranchero Hotel that night, after fighting for my life, I had the overwhelming feeling that no matter what else happened; from that point forward *I* was going to be okay.

"I'm sure Barry found his way out of that mess," Vince said. "He's a cagey one. It would take a lot more than a barroom brawl to sink that guy's ship." He let out a laugh, but there was no humor there; it took a lot to rattle Vince Taylor, and that night he was showing it.

"So what's the plan?" Eddie said. "We going to do like Barry says and head for Hermosillo?" He got up and went for a beer.

"Depends," Vince said.

"On what?" I said.

"You."

Vince kept it loose, but I could see the anxiousness in his eyes. He clearly wasn't ready to pack it in yet. I hesitated with my answer, while I ran it down in my mind.

It made no sense to continue. In fact, it was shaping up dangerous as hell. But there was something else at play, and it wasn't just the money. It was the pull to break out of what I'd become, the life I'd made for myself, all of it predicated on the foolish notion that my role as a husband and a father obligated me to taking the safe road. After all, I was a provider and people counted on me, and grownups don't do stupid shit, and they most certainly do not gamble with other people's future.

But Lucinda blew that all to hell. And because of her, everything I'd ever lived for was gone, and the things I believed to be true turned out to be lies, or worse, just not important anymore to the one person I thought would never let me down.

Well to hell with her, and screw playing it safe. It was all right there in front of me, clear as day. Life was about taking chances, and if you weren't risking something—if you weren't *living*—then all you were doing was taking up space.

So for the second time in a week I made a decision that was entirely unlike me. It was a decision there was no turning back from, and it would change me forever.

Twenty

We split for Hermosillo before dawn on Wednesday. Barry had said the bypass was best traveled at night, and we took him at his word. I'd managed just a few hours of sleep before leaving and fatigue dogged me, my body aching from the beating I took at the Apache.

Since leaving Orange County late on Monday night, we'd been on the road for barely thirty hours, although it felt like it'd been a week. Sleep deprivation took hold, my senses seriously out of whack. It seemed like a hundred years ago that Lucinda dropped the boom on me, sending me on this crazy journey. I thought about her and the kids and it made my heart hurt. Did they miss me? The kids, I mean. I knew Lou didn't miss a damn thing about me, or our old life. How do you do that, anyway? Just flip the page on what was. I wondered if I would ever come to understand it.

I forced those thoughts away, focused instead on what was in front of me. The Jeep rattled and bounced on the dirt road. The route through the desert was desolate and just short of treacherous, but Barry's map was a good one; surprising, when you consider he was stoned when he drew it. Vince kept it slow and steady and we had a good moon to guide us, and soon we came upon *La Roca de Cristo,* The Rock of Christ. It was some kind of stone marker signaling the end of the bypass was near. I didn't quite get the Christ thing; it looked like a big pile of rocks to me.

The marker topped a modest hill with a clear view of the immigration checkpoint in the distance. Vince parked the Jeep behind a barrier of low desert scrub and we got out, stretching stiff limbs and shaking off the cold. Daybreak broke over the horizon, blanketing the land in pale light. A thick band of thunderheads gathered in the west, the wind blowing in choppy waves; portentous signs of bad weather ahead.

I retrieved Vince's high-powered binoculars from the back of the car and made my way to the pile of rocks, positioning myself like a sentry, scoping out the situation below. The checkpoint looked deserted, the lanes leading up to the booths clear. I saw movement through the window of a small outbuilding, wondered if they were looking up at us.

"Y'all don't see any of them dogs out there, do ya, Jackson?"

Vince smirked over his shoulder while taking a piss in the weeds. His words were immediately drowned out by a stiff gust kicking up a billowing dust devil. The swirling funnel rapidly circled the Jeep, raking it with grit and small pebbles, before tracking straight for a distant ridge. Vince's eyes widened as he jerked around.

"That was straight bullshit Barry was dealing," Eddie said, his voice tense. "He was only trying to get a rise out of us." He fumbled with lighting a cigarette, the smoke curling around his face.

The dust devil disappeared as quickly as it had arrived, leaving an eerie silence in its wake. Out of the corner of my eye I sensed movement, the faintest blur of motion, and I turned with a start. Vince mocked me with an offhanded laugh.

"Got some heebie-jeebies there, bro?" He walked up and took the binoculars from my hand. "I wouldn't sweat that ol' cujo too much. Remember what Barry said?"

"What?"

"That dog only hunts at night. Take a look around. It's daybreak, the dawn of a new day and all that kinda jive." Vince guffawed. "Besides, Jackson, I'm feelin' extra lucky today."

I shrugged off his words with a dismissive wave, and I glanced over at Eddie sitting inside the car, smoking his cigarette. He stared back at me with those expressionless eyes, and a thought seized me—*what if Eddie was the cadejo*?

What I mean is this; what if that black devil dog from hell took on the form of a human and was hitching a ride with us right now, biding his time until the perfect moment to strike? Yeah, I know it sounds crazy, but I'm telling you, Eddie's empty stare could unnerve the sanest of men.

Again I felt that sense of motion just outside my peripheral vision, and I turned to my right, my subconscious tingling. Something was out there. I could feel it.

When I turned back to Eddie, I saw Vince standing close by. I caught a laugh and some whispered words passed between them. They were talking about me, the same way they did back at Vince's house. I felt resentment, Eddie's presence an intrusion, his enigmatic manner a catalyst for too much negativity.

All at once I was aware of the cold, the breeze driving it straight into my joints. I pulled my arms across my chest in an effort to ward off the feeling. My nerves burned and my breath felt unnatural, and a massive surge of energy coursed through me, my chest tightening. It was a familiar and frightening feeling.

I turned away from Eddie and Vince and their bullshit talk, focused instead on the black ribbon of highway that would lead us to Hermosillo. I stared hard at that long arc of road, out to where it disappeared into the horizon, as if by sheer force of will I could predict what lay ahead.

A SHORT TIME later we merged easily onto the highway and began our run south to Hermosillo. I stared out the window, my mind blank as I watched the desert scenery roll by. I'd settled down after experiencing one hell of a panic attack up on that hill, next to that pile of Christ-like rocks; a condition likely brought on by a delayed reaction to my near-death experience at the Apache, and further fueled by Barry's absurd tale of the cadejo.

It was a ridiculous idea—Eddie Dowd as a demonic interloper sent to torment and destroy? I could laugh about it now, the warmth of the car and the soothing sense of motion on the road working to ease my mind. Sure, he was a weird dude, and sneaky and ambiguous and all that, but so what? He was still just a guy. A flesh and blood human like you and me, and six billion others occupying this planet of ours. I'd just have to try a little harder to get along.

I stretched out on the seat, closing my eyes. We were making good time on the nearly deserted highway, and so far Barry's little scheme was working out for us. All we had to do now was keep a low profile, pass ourselves off as some of those expats Barry was telling us about, and it'd be smooth sailing all the way to Benjie Cole and the boots.

Still, Hermosillo remained the question. All we had to go on was some guy named Max Hollister and a place called the El Burro Bar. Pretty thin. And what if Benjie wasn't there, exactly how far would we take this thing? Knowing Vince, he'd chase that dude all the way to South America if it came down to it.

There were a lot of variables, and far too many ways to go wrong with the law. There was the gun still nestled in the glove box, and Vince had augmented Barry's plan by stealing some Mexican license plates from an abandoned Chevy parked near the Ranchero and swapping the Jeep's plates with them, the better to blend in, he'd said. It seemed we were fast on our way to becoming genuine gringo banditos, outlaws on the lamb from the infamous Apache Bar Melee, on a quest for James Dean's missing boots. Maybe someday an up-and-coming young musician will write one of those narcocorridos about our exploits, turn us into regular folk heroes. Hell, maybe the Loose Screws could add an accordion player and write one themselves.

Now *that* would be a kick in the ass.

Twenty-one

It was just after nine o'clock when we rolled into the outskirts of Hermosillo. The trip took longer than the mileage indicated, mostly because we'd bypassed the toll roads in favor of the rural back roads through the small towns and dusty pueblos of the Sonoran Desert. We saw no law along the way, and with every mile passed, my confidence level was boosted significantly. Until we hit town, that is.

Hermosillo is about four times as big as Nogales, and spread out, which meant a lot of ground to cover. Once we hit the city proper, the feeling of being in over our heads returned. Unfortunately, Barry had drawn no maps for this leg of our journey, so it was up to us to figure out how to find Max Hollister.

We approached from the north, through grass-covered plains, the area agricultural in appearance. Rolling green hills framed the city, backdropped by jagged peaks jutting sharply along the horizon. I noticed right away that the drivers down there didn't pay much attention to speed limits or rules of the road, and we found ourselves swept up into a flowing artery of cars and trucks and taxis jockeying for position, darting in and out of lanes while incessantly honking their horns as if they were paid to do it. Every so often we'd hit large speed bumps—*topes* they were called—out in the middle of the road, the Jeep's undercarriage bottoming out violently each time, until Vince got the hang of things and started easing over them.

After a few miles we sought out a less congested route, one that took us east of downtown, past a large reservoir and into a mixed commercial and residential area. Vince peeled off the wide boulevard and followed a railroad spur into an old warehouse district, the likelihood of finding what we were looking for in *that* part of town pretty slim. After a few minutes I let him have it.

"What the hell, Vince?" I said. "You got some kind of radar that leads you straight to the shitty parts of town?"

"Easy there, we'll find our way. You just gotta have faith, brother."

He started singing the chorus from that lame George Michael song. I kid you not. That Vince, he's a goddamn barrel of laughs.

"You know, Jackson's right, maybe we should stick to the tourist district this time," Eddie said from the back seat. "Last night was enough slumming for one trip, you ask me."

"Yeah? Well who asked you, guitar man?" Vince looked into the rearview mirror. Then he turned and gave me a crooked smile. "And they say it's the drummer who's the problem."

Eddie mumbled something about a shitty deal. Vince ignored him, lighting a cigarette as he studied the side of the road. After a few minutes he accelerated and cut diagonally across an empty parking lot, bounced across a narrow lane and eased up to the front of a shabby café set back from the street.

"How's this?"

I stared at him. "For what?"

"Food. I don't know about you guys, but I'm straight famished. I say we get some eats, recharge our batteries, and get on out there and find this Max Hollister dude, see what's what."

"So you want to eat. Here."

"Sure, why not."

"Damn, Vince, can't you find a Denny's or something?" Eddie said. "This joint looks like a goddamn health inspector's wet dream."

"Eddie, my man," Vince said. "Don't you know the adventure is where it's at?" He grinned and swept his hand toward the café. "What more do you want? We got location, ambiance, and best of all, no crowd."

"And the Apache wasn't enough adventure for you?" I said, putting a little extra something behind it. Then I turned to the back seat. "Remember, Eddie, he comes from the South. Joints like this are high living down there." I laughed and gave Vince a wink. What I didn't do was blow him a kiss. Too many bad memories there.

Vince ignored my jibes and exited the vehicle. I shrugged at Eddie and did the same, following Vince to the side door of the café. The place was dark, with a crooked sign on the door that read *cerrado*. I assumed that meant closed, because the place sure as hell looked closed. Or condemned. I was about to say something smart when Eddie shouted for our attention. He'd lagged a few steps behind, and now he was pointing down a debris-strewn alley running across the rear of the café.

"Hey, you see that, down there?"

"What the hell you lookin' at?" Vince said.

"Over there, that rundown building to the right."

"Dude, they're all rundown," I said. Eddie shot me a look.

"Whatever, Jackson. I'm talking about the one over there, with the crazy donkey painted on it."

Vince stepped out for a better view, surprise crossing his face as he turned and motioned me over. "Well damn it all to hell, will you look at that? C'mon, let's check it out."

We walked down a short block lined with ancient brick buildings and piles of trash and a couple of abandoned cars, came up on the rear of a craggy two-story wood structure, its identity revealed by a huge painting of a bucking burro with crazy eyes, and scrolled lettering above and below.

The El Burro Bar & Cantina.

"Impossible." I whistled loudly. "Like finding a needle in a haystack." Vince smiled at me and shook his head.

"No, Jackson, not impossible. It's called luck, and I'm cloaked in it, brother." He laughed then, that Southern boy guffaw he slips into when he thinks he's being clever.

Vince led us through a narrow passageway threading between the El Burro Bar and the adjacent building, and we emerged onto the next street. It was nearly deserted, save for a few scattered vehicles and a handful of pedestrians. We walked to the front of the El Burro and stood at a polished wood door set with an oval piece of beveled glass, embossed lettering on the transom that read: *Est. 1989, Max Hollister, Proprietor*. A sign affixed to the red-lacquered wood siding indicated the bar opened at seven o'clock. As I stared at a smaller version of the crazy burro etched into the beveled glass, I couldn't help but wonder at it all. Maybe Vince did have some kind of good luck mojo.

Meanwhile, Eddie had wandered out into the street and made another discovery. He was a regular explorer that day. "Hey, guys. Check this out," he said.

We joined him in the street. He pointed to a tall, square building standing a block away on the street corner, with large billboard-style letters on the roof.

"This is just dumb luck, you know that don't you?" I said to Vince, gazing in amazement at the Hotel Presidente.

"Whatever you say, Jackson. But I'll sure as hell take dumb luck over no luck any day of the week. And twice on Sunday."

I looked over at him and smiled; luck or not, things were definitely improving.

"YOU ALL RIGHT there, partner?"

We were holed up at the Hotel Presidente, waiting for the El Burro Bar to open for business later that night. Our third floor room—a suite of sorts—was threadbare but clean. It reminded me of countless dead-end hotel rooms I'd seen in those old movies I kept in a box back home. It was the kind of room where dreams died and losers reached the end of the line, and they killed time drinking whiskey and listening to the sounds of the city, while solemnly waiting for the inevitable knock of fate on the door.

"Yeah, I'm okay," Vince said. "Just thinkin' is all."

His tone was somber. It wasn't one he took very often, and it was a little unsettling to see him like that. He seemed to have emotionally nosedived as soon as we checked into our room. I hesitated making too much out of it, seeing how we were all pretty much fried by that point.

Still, I sensed something more than tiredness in Vince. Maybe he was homesick for his girls. Maybe it was simply the events of his life catching up with him. It was coming up on two years since his wife had passed, and even though we didn't talk about it as often, it was always there, hovering in the background, the open wound that refused to heal.

I let it unfold, and gave Vince time to say what needed saying. Eddie was in the other room with the door shut, doing whatever it was Eddie did when he was by himself. Vince and I lay stretched out on twin beds in the front room. My lumpy mattress felt like a million bucks. I wanted to hear Vince out, but I was fading fast.

"You ever think, Jackson, how things turn out all wrong sometimes?"

He started out slowly, seeming to be a little unsure of himself.

"They just fall apart and there's nothin' you can do about it. You plan it all out, set up your little house of cards so it's just right, and when you least expect it a nice little breeze comes along and knocks the whole thing down. Right on top of you." He yawned and rubbed his eyes. "Damn if I ain't so tired I could sleep for a year."

He grew quiet again and I let it pass. Faint street noises seeped in through the closed window. From another room a transistor radio played, one of those booming, reverb-laden announcer voices that you only hear on Mexican radio stations.

"You miss her," I said, "and the girls too."

"More than you'll ever know."

Vince sighed deeply, seemed to collect his thoughts. When he continued, his voice was unsteady.

"When Leslie died, the whole thing just fell out, you know? I mean overnight it just *changed*, and that house of cards came down so hard it liked to kill me. I tried to figure it out, tried to comprehend how a beautiful young woman, the picture of health, just drops dead from a heart attack. Forty years old, can you imagine that? That's just about as wrong as anything ever gets in this cruel goddamn world.

"It ain't easy, doin' it by myself. Sometimes I don't believe I can. Leslie was the one who held everythin' together. She loved those girls of ours, and she loved me, as purely and honestly as a woman can ever love a man."

Vince turned to me, his face drawn.

"What the hell was she doin' with a cat like me?"

He fell back onto his pillow, eyes closed. Silence passed between us. I'd known Vince for a long time, but never like I did that day. He was always so unaffected, playing it off cool and casual, like nothing was ever a big deal. But I knew differently, and for a long time I'd suspected a cover-up going on, sensing in my friend a deeper truth. Vince Taylor was a lot more vulnerable than he ever let on, and that day in Mexico he finally showed it.

"You wishing you hadn't come down here?" I said.

"No, I'm not. It needed to be done. I'll admit, when Kenny first came to me with this deal I thought he was plain crazy. But the more we talked about it, the more it made sense. Or maybe I just wanted it to make sense. Anyway, none of that matters. This ain't about findin' Kenny's damn boots, Jackson. It never was.

"This is about two broken guys lookin' for spare parts. I'm tired of feelin' the way I do, tired of how things are. And you know somethin'? I think you are too. So whatever happens down here, we're turnin' a page, startin' fresh. This is step one."

Vince's words hit home. He was right. I *was* tired of the way things were, only I didn't know what to do about it. Or maybe that was just a convenient excuse. Either way, it was up to me to make the changes, no one else was going to do it for me.

I've always been a believer in events taking place for a reason. Call it fate or Karma, or destiny if you choose. But the point is life isn't random. Sure, random stuff happens. But I believe there's an underlying purpose to it all, a method to the madness, if you will, and it's all interconnected and tied into a larger plan. Most times we never get to see the big picture; we simply experience the twists and turns along the way, moving through our lives one day at a time. And that's okay, because ultimately, I don't think we're supposed to know. We'd probably just screw it up if we did.

"You remember the garter?" Vince said, laughing quietly to himself.

Sure, I remembered. I laughed along with him.

"You did that on purpose, you devious bastard."

At Vince and Leslie's wedding reception I caught the garter and Lucinda caught the bouquet, and the next year, almost to the day, we were married. Lucinda and Leslie had been childhood friends.

"That was a good day, wasn't it?"

"It was a great day."

"You ever think about it, Jackson."

"Yeah, I do. All the time."

Vince paused a moment, staring at some imagined point on the ceiling.

"Me too," he said.

Then he turned and faced the wall, and we both fell asleep.

Twenty-two

I sat by the window, gazing down at the street, taking in a snapshot view of our little slice of Mexico. Vince and Eddie were asleep. I'd woken a few minutes earlier, restless with anticipation, the restlessness pushing me forward like an unseen hand at my back. Toward what I couldn't say. Life, I suppose. The future. Good, bad, or indifferent, it didn't matter; it was coming whether I wanted it or not.

The neighborhood seemed to come alive with the afternoon, a steady stream of cars moving down the boulevard, the sidewalk teeming with pedestrians. I pulled up the window sash and let in the sounds of the city. That nearby transistor radio was going strong, the reverb-soaked announcer spewing his gas.

After a few minutes I got up and went into the bathroom, took a long look at myself in the mirror. I needed a shave and a haircut. I looked old, felt older, the lines of fatigue showing at the corners of my eyes. At least the sleep had rejuvenated my senses, my mind feeling clearer than it had all week. A nice hot shower and a shave would go a long way toward wiping that old man look from my face.

I thought of something my dad used to tell me, by way of imparting some of the wisdom fathers seem to be born with.

He'd say, "Son, life comes at you fast, and it's not easy dodging bullets. At the end of the day it's a break-even proposition, and if you can look in the mirror and see an honest man looking back, well then you've done all right for yourself."

I'd have to say Dad was right about that.

And while the man looking back at me in the mirror may have felt old and beat down, at least he was honest. And that's a fact.

With several hours to kill before the El Burro opened, I was feeling adventurous, recalling long-ago Caribbean vacations from back in the days when life was all about traveling. I'm talking about the prehistoric days, before marriage and kids, and divorce.

Back then I was enamored with pirate lore and tales of the New World, the exotic lure of West Indies locales drawing me off the beaten path and into the pubs and cafés, and the secret places that only locals knew, where I'd soak up the rhythms and the ways of life. I possessed a hopeless romantic's sense of adventure and an insatiable hunger for new experiences. I was a fool for it.

And then one day it all stopped, like flipping a switch, and I moved on to something different; namely marriage and fatherhood. I went all-in too, fully embracing my new life as much as I did the wandering, free-spirited one that came before it. Indeed, I played my role to perfection. Or so I thought.

Looking back, it's easy to see how I let my spirit fade, one little piece at a time. Before long I wasn't *living* my life anymore, I was merely watching it from the sidelines. And believe me when I tell you I kept a real good eye on it, making sure everything important to me stayed safe and secure. Like that house of cards Vince talked about, I built mine high and proud, and admired myself for the accomplishment. I was some kind of builder, all right.

Yet all that hubris only served to suck the life right out of me and Lucinda and our marriage, and damn if that wind didn't come along and knock it all down anyway.

I suppose I couldn't blame Lucinda for what she'd done. Her execution may have sucked, but the play was solid; something had to give, and I wasn't exactly lining up to make any changes. So that left her to pull the plug and set us all free. At least that's what she told me; on the few occasions she was willing to say anything at all about it. She never really said much about the *why*, leaving me to figure it out on my own. But from what little she offered I knew the truth; it was mine to lose all along.

I pulled away from the mirror, the disappointed face looking back at me becoming a drag. I resolved to head out and explore the town, have a little fun, maybe reconnect with something I'd lost long ago. I started the shower and let it warm up, checked on Vince and Eddie. They were still out. Good. I needed to go it alone for a while.

Stepping under the water, I let the warmth wash over me. I closed my eyes, trying my best not to think. About anything.

THE GUITAR CAUGHT my eye for only a second, and I nearly missed it while walking by. I was exploring a downtown marketplace reminiscent of countless others I'd experienced down-island. The flea market atmosphere was a little too touristy for my tastes—kind of like a swap meet or one of those bazaars that spring up at cruise ship ports—but the narrow cobblestone walkways and old-Spanish vibe held just enough allure to scratch that itch from long ago. I took my time with it, lazily walking the labyrinth of pathways, my spirit unburdened by troubles both real and imagined.

The fat salesman started in on me before I'd even reached his stall. He was short and blustery, in a jovial sort of way, and he was determined to sell me *something*. "Hey, amigo. Let me show you some very special things I have here in my shop," he said with an inviting grin.

I was about to brush the guy off when I spotted the guitar hanging on the back wall. I made a beeline for it, the salesman following, yakking his spiel.

"Oh yes, my friend. You have found something you like? Something very special you must have from your visit to Hermosillo?"

I pulled the instrument down and turned it in my hands. It was a three-quarter scale acoustic painted a sweet sunburst color, with intricate lettering around the sound hole that spelled out the words *Hermosillo, Sonora, Mexico*. The backside featured a very cool sunset over a desert landscape. I strummed the strings lightly, adjusting the tuning. Nice.

"You like the guitar, amigo?"

He pronounced it *geetaro*.

The fat man crowded in close to me, forcing me back a step to keep some space.

"It is genuine," he said, "made by Mexican hands from Hermosillo. And today is a special day for you. Because I am willing to sell to you my beautiful geetaro for only fifty dollars. No finer instrument you will find in all the land."

He stood back and folded his arms, proudly admiring his pitch.

"Fifty dollars?" I feigned shock. "I think you're charging me too much. Forty bucks sounds more like it. Maybe even thirty-five. But fifty?" I shook my head. "Fifty is too high, amigo."

I smiled assuredly. The fat man didn't miss a beat.

"Perhaps you are correct, señor," he said, shaking his head thoughtfully. "I can see the point that you have made. Perhaps fifty dollars is *muy excesivo*."

His face clouded over and he put his hand to his chin, tapping his index finger lightly on his cheek. As if on cue, he brightened and clapped his hands together loudly.

"I know what must be done, mi amigo. Today, I will make the special price of forty-five dollars for this fine geetaro. This is good?" He laughed out loud, convinced that he had the upper hand.

To be honest with you, at fifty bucks the guitar was a steal. But I was having fun haggling with the guy, and he seemed to enjoy it too. I turned the instrument over and scrutinized the detail, more to keep him hanging than anything else. But then something caught my eye, right there on the back of the headstock. It was a small sticker that read *made in China*. While it wasn't a deal-breaker for me, I knew I had the guy.

"Hey, wait a minute," I said, winding up for the kill. "This guitar isn't made in Mexico." I pointed to the sticker. "This guitar is made in China. Fifty dollars? No way, pal. I think fifteen is more like it."

The fat man's face registered astonishment, and he took the guitar from me while apologizing profusely.

"No, my friend, this geetaro is not made in China." It came out sounding like *cheena*. "This is an original Mexican geetaro, it does not come from that other place. You must believe me, señor." He awkwardly peeled the sticker from the back of the instrument, as he desperately tried to salvage the sale.

"It sure looks like a cheena geetaro to me," I said, playfully mimicking his speech. "I think maybe this thing is only worth ten bucks." I was really jerking his chain now.

"No, my friend, please, I tell you the truth! It is no cheena, no cheena, mi amigo!"

He was practically pleading with me, sweating heavily, his face bright red. I was afraid the guy would go coronary on me, so I let him off the hook.

"Hey listen up, it's okay. Really. I'll tell you what. I'll give you forty bucks for this Chinese-made Mexican guitar. What do you say?"

"It is a deal, señor," the fat man said gratefully, breathing an audible sigh of relief as he turned and pulled a sturdy case from behind the counter and carefully placed the instrument inside. That was a nice touch. I smiled as I handed over the cash.

I gave the guy fifty anyway, and a ten-dollar tip just for brightening my day. He was so thrilled he hugged me. Then he tried to interest me in some genuine Mexican fireworks, the very best in all the land. I politely declined and left his shop, stopping long enough in front to take it all in. I smiled, and laughed out loud as I turned to go on my way.

***

I TURNED MY attention to finding a pay phone to call my kids; it felt like a million years since I'd last heard their voices, and I desperately needed to make that connection.

After some luckless wandering I opted for help, stopping in front of a small shop filled with curios and tourist souvenirs. An old woman stood up front, tending to a table covered with ceramic figurines. Further back in the shop, a girl sat behind a counter, reading a book. She was strikingly pretty, and I stared at her, mesmerized.

"*¿Cómo le puedo ayudar?*"

The old woman's words startled me, and I turned to face her.

"*¿Cómo le puedo ayudar?*" she repeated in a girlish voice.

I felt embarrassed to be caught staring at the girl. The old woman smiled, as if she hadn't noticed. I asked about a telephone. The woman just smiled.

"Telephone?" I said loudly, as if shouting would make my meaning clearer. I mimicked holding a receiver to my ear. The old woman just shook her head sadly, as if she wanted to help, but didn't know how. The pretty girl came to her rescue.

"My grandmother doesn't speak English," she said, smiling beautifully. "Can I help you?"

Her voice had a pleasant lilt to it, almost lyrical. She came out from behind the counter holding a small dog in her arms, and instantly I was smitten. After a brief moment where I blanked out, I suddenly remembered why I was standing there.

I explained my predicament. The grandmother looked on with interest, nodding and grinning in the way of those stymied by a language barrier. The girl gave me directions to an Internet café nearby, one with a pay phone. As we spoke, the little dog grew agitated, squirming and nipping at the girl. She tightened her grip and admonished it to behave. It was kind of cute, even though I can't stand lap dogs.

We finished our business and I thanked them both. As I turned to leave, the dog broke free of the girl's arms and darted out of the shop. She gasped and the grandmother laughed, and I played the hero, breaking into a mad dash after the little mutt, the girl hot on my heels.

I turned left out of the curio shop and in seconds the girl pulled even with me, keeping a steady eye on her fast-moving friend. We dodged pedestrians in a human obstacle course, and at the next corner she overtook me.

Momentarily distracted, I looked to my left, and I was stopped dead in my tracks as I clipped a large object on the edge of the sidewalk. I spun around and fell hard to the ground. Stunned, I looked up at the outline of a hulking figure clad in black leathers standing over me. The sun was behind his back, casting him in silhouette. The guy reached down and grabbed my hand, pulling me upright.

"Sorry, bro, I didn't see you."

"That's cool," I said. "I wasn't exactly watching where I was going."

The guy stared at me and something clicked in my brain. Then he turned and walked away quickly, and I crouched down and opened my guitar case, checking for damage, a nagging thought tugging at the back of my mind. As I snapped the case shut it hit me.

That was the guy I saw yesterday, at the border.

Energy coursed through me as the connection was made. I recalled the two bikers sitting in the middle of the street, the big one pointing at me. Sure, it was the same guy. A lot of weird ideas flooded my mind then, but before any of them stuck, the curio shop girl reappeared, her little runaway tucked safely in her arms.

"Thank you so much for your help," she said, slightly out of breath, a thin bead of sweat across her forehead. She looked wonderful. "I don't know what I would have done had I lost her."

"You're welcome," I said. "But I'm not sure how helpful I was, falling on my ass like I did. At least I tried, right?" I smiled nervously, trying to act cool. I was seriously out of practice with cool.

"No, you were perfect, mister, uh…"

"Jackson. Mr. Jackson Thomas," I said, holding out my hand.

"Well it is very nice to meet you, Jackson Thomas. My name is Milena."

She laughed in the way girls do, and when she took my hand I felt a tingle. She had long black hair and flawless brown skin, and stunning green eyes that were clear and full of life. She was so beautiful I found myself giggling like a schoolboy.

"So about that phone," I said, breaking the spell.

"Oh yes. The Enchanted Cup is that way." She pointed down the street. "It is a very cozy place, with good food and excellent coffee. They have books and magazines, and computers connected to the Internet. And of course, they have a telephone too."

She smiled again, her eyes pure in their innocence and sincerity. I nodded back dumbly, completely absorbed in the moment. I wanted to hold every detail of that beautiful face in my memory, record the sound of her voice into my brain. And later, when this trip was over, I would recall all of it, and I would remind myself that there is a whole world of opportunity out there, for those willing to take it.

I snapped out of it long enough to thank my new friend, and I turned and floated away on a cloud of bliss.

Twenty-three

A few minutes later I entered the Enchanted Cup. I ordered a large coffee and a pastry, bought a prepaid phone card and went to make my call. I sat down at the pay phone and sipped some coffee. It tasted excellent. Did I mention how much I love good coffee?

After two more sips I read the instructions on the phone and dialed the number. I stopped after the area code, finger poised over the keypad. I held that position as a terrible awareness came over me.

I didn't know the number.

What I mean to say is, Lucinda had recently changed hers and I hadn't memorized it. Sure, it was programmed into my cell phone, but my phone was broken, thanks to that scar-faced asshole at the Apache. I spent the next few minutes trying to shake the number loose from my memory, but to no avail. The absurdity of the situation galled me. It got worse when I realized Lou had never given me the details of her trip to San Francisco, and in my anger and self-righteousness over learning of her plans I never bothered to ask. I hadn't spoken to her since that morning outside the courthouse, and I literally had no idea where she was or how to reach her. Yeah, I showed her all right.

I took several gulps of the coffee and lit a cigarette, the nicotine rush a nice compliment to the caffeine. Anxiety spiked at the realization I was completely cut off from communication, and the thought of my poor kids wondering why daddy wasn't calling broke my heart. I hit the smoke again, just to numb myself.

Then I thought of email; maybe they'd tried to reach me that way. I paid for an hour of Internet time and logged onto one of the coffeehouse computers, my heart thumping as I waited for my inbox to load. My hope sank when I saw a box full of spam, two messages from my shithead attorney, and nothing from Lucinda. I didn't know Lou's new email address so I checked the trash folder, hoping desperately for a deleted message from her. A click of the mouse and it was strike three, and now I was officially the biggest loser on the planet. Unbelievable.

I smoked my cigarette and finished my food, just going through the motions. Then I got a refill on my coffee and returned to the computer. After a few minutes spent staring at the screen, I started thinking about the guy I ran into on the street, the one I was sure I'd seen at the border. It got me to thinking again about Kenny Lopez, why he didn't send one of his biker pals down here to get the boots. Strange ideas filled my head about that. Was there something else at play here?

On a whim, I Googled Kenny Lopez. The results loaded as I sipped my coffee. The fifth hit down was an OC Weekly article with the headline: *Kenny Lopez. The antichrist?* When I opened the link, this is what I read:

> *Kenny Lopez, the head of South Coast Financial Partners, is expected to be indicted next week on Federal corruption and racketeering charges. Lopez is notorious for his involvement in the Orange County bankruptcy scandal in 1994. His firm at the time, Triad Securities, was accused of setting up many of the dubious investments made by the county treasurer, resulting in the loss of over 1.7 billion dollars of taxpayer money.*

> *Lopez stood as a key figure in the County's dealings with Triad, and many people consider him the mastermind behind the risky investment strategies used by the treasurer. Although charges were never brought against Triad or Lopez, the stench of corruption has remained. Since that time, Kenny Lopez has rapidly ascended the ranks of the County's top political and financial movers and shakers, and he continues to...*

I stopped reading and stared blankly at the smoke curling up from the end of my cigarette sitting in the ashtray. What the hell was Kenny doing, screwing around with a pair of boots when he had something like this hanging over his head? Shouldn't he have bigger fish to fry, like keeping his ass out of the penitentiary? It made no sense.

But maybe it wasn't the same Kenny Lopez. I kicked that idea around, decided the likelihood of it being the same guy was pretty high. Not that it made a whole lot of difference to me now; I wasn't going to split for home just because I found out Kenny was a crook. If anything, the article merely validated my assessment of him as a total fraud. I considered if I should tell Vince about what I'd read, but quickly dismissed the idea, figuring he'd just laugh it off as no big deal.

I looked at the big clock on the wall, saw that it was almost time to head over to the El Burro Bar and find Max Hollister. Hopefully, he'll point us right to Benjie and we can end this thing quickly. I had a thought then, about Kenny and the implications of what I'd read. The article was a week old, and it said an indictment was likely to be handed down next week, which meant *this* week. If true, then it would seem we were in a race against time. If we didn't find those boots and get them back before Kenny landed in jail, my thirty grand was going to end up in the wind.

Twenty-four

The El Burro Bar had the look and feel of an old New Orleans drinking establishment; all Deep South and southern gothic to the core. It was a fairly large place that felt intimate, with flocked burgundy wallpaper and mahogany wainscoting softly illuminated by Pullman-style lamps, and a stamped-tin ceiling with wide-bladed fans circulating air that smelled strangely sweet for a saloon. The concrete floor was painted red, cracked and faded from use, the tables, chairs, and leather-trimmed booths sturdy and comfortable in appearance. Potted ferns and gilt-framed mirrors rounded out the affair.

The vibe of the El Burro was classy and warmly inviting, in notable contrast to the Apache Bar, and it didn't seem very likely that we'd find any trouble there; a welcome change indeed.

We walked through the room, taking it in. Music played over a sound system—the Neville Brothers classic album *Yellow Moon*. It set the scene perfectly. In a corner near the bar sat a vintage Wurlitzer jukebox, and directly next to it an antique upright piano, its wood creased and aged to a mellow hue. I closed my eyes and pictured Jelly Roll Morton riffing on that old piano. Sweet.

"This place is the shit," Vince said with a wide smile. "I used to play joints like this down in the Quarter." He approached a massive mahogany bar, topped with a thick slab of white marble trimmed in brass, his attention drawn to something on the back wall. "Take a look at that."

Vince pointed to a framed portrait of a young black woman, her strong features and wide eyes looking down at us, focused in a steady gaze. A blue shawl covered her shoulders, her head topped with a brightly colored fabric wrap. In her hand she held a rooster, the table in front of her covered with an odd assortment of items. The painting was mesmerizing in its detail.

"Who the hell is that?" Eddie said.

"That's Marie Laveau. The voodoo queen of New Orleans."

Hailing from Lake Charles, Vince had an affinity for New Orleans, and over the years he'd shared many stories of his exploits in the French Quarter, and of his fascination with voodoo. Creepy tales of midnight visits to the ancient cemeteries out on the edge of Storyville, hanging out with his buddies on the crypts at St. Louis #1, drinking absinthe and rattling bags of chicken bones in an attempt to draw out the souls of the departed. Vince swears that one night a lone apparition chased him all the way down Rampart Street and straight into Louis Armstrong Park. He never went back after that.

"Marie who?" Eddie said.

"Laveau. C'mon, dude, pay attention."

"I've heard of her," I said. "Isn't there a shop named after her, on Bourbon Street? A place where they sell all kinds of voodoo potions and paraphernalia?"

"Sure, the House of Voodoo. That's where I got this." Vince pulled back his sleeve, revealing a beaded bracelet. "It's my good luck charm. A genuine Haitian trouble bracelet. It wards off all kinds of evil spirits and bad juju. I never go anywhere without it."

"Really?" I said dubiously. "And the Apache last night, you call that protection?"

"Yes. But just think, Jackson, how bad it *could* have been."

Vince guffawed, lightly rubbing the colorful beads. The funny thing is I don't ever remember seeing him wear that bracelet.

"YOU ADMIRING MY painting, are you?"

A strong voice drifted into the room, followed by a tall, well-built man entering through a rear door. A full head of gray hair cut military-short framed his handsome face, his eyes thoughtful and steady. He appeared to be in his sixties.

"I got that at a gallery on Toulouse Street. It was painted by a guy named Dimitri Fouquet. That particular painting was used on a Dr. John album." The man set a crate of beer on top of the bar and began pulling bottles, feeding them into a cooler behind him. "I'll tell you what," he said over his shoulder. "There's no place quite like the Crescent City, nothing like it in the whole world."

The man continued with his work. After emptying the crate he walked to the end of the back bar and took the tone arm off a record player, cutting off Aaron Neville as he crooned Sam Cooke's classic *A Change Is Gonna Come*. He turned on a satellite radio tuner, the sounds of *Purple Haze* filling the room, and he casually went about his business. He said nothing more as he moved around the room, offering only an occasional glance our way. After a few minutes I broke the ice.

"You're Max Hollister?"

The man turned slightly and eyed me with a considered stare, his soft blue eyes reflecting a sort of world-weariness, the kind you acquire when you've seen some things. He wore workingman's clothes, and on his left wrist was one of those Vietnam era nickel-plated POW bracelets. I took note of it because I had one when I was a kid.

"I suppose it depends on who's asking," he said, his tone firm but cordial. He spoke in a lazy drawl. The man resumed his puttering around. Vince nudged me and pointed at the guy, encouraging me to go on. I cleared my throat.

"Barry Fitzgerald told us to look you up. When we saw him last night, at the Apache Bar."

The man stopped and looked at the three of us. Something in his eyes said he was assessing the situation, balancing his scales. Slowly his expression changed, and he broke into a wide grin.

"Barry Fitzgerald, you say?" He shook his head and laughed. "Yes, I'm Max Hollister. And you gentlemen are?"

He held out his hand and we introduced ourselves in turn. His grip was strong and unwavering, the kind you rarely see anymore.

"Why did Barry send you down here to see me?"

"We're looking for Benjie Cole," I said. "We expected to find him in Nogales, but we missed him. Barry told us Benjie came down here. He said we should look you up when we got to town. He seems to think you know where to find Benjie."

Max Hollister's face brightened at the mention of Benjie's name. "Yes, I know Benjie. Used to be he'd come around here four or five times a year, and we'd always make a point to get together. We were close." He paused, seeming to reconsider. "What I mean to say is, back then we were. The last year or so things changed."

Max went silent and the brightness clouded over. He let out a heavy sigh.

"Benjie was in here a few days ago, looking for a man named Butch Davey. I don't know anyone by that name, so I couldn't help him. I suggested he stay a while but he nixed the idea, said he had business to attend to. He said…"

Max's voice trailed off and he began wiping down the bar, making no effort to elaborate any further on Benjie or his whereabouts.

So once again our target was in the wind, and we were left chasing a ghost. On top of that, it would appear Benjie was chasing a ghost of his own. Ghosts chasing ghosts, deep in the Third World. You couldn't make this stuff up. It was Eddie who spoke next.

"Where'd he go, Max?"

"He took off for Concepción, down in Sinaloa."

"Where in Concepción?"

Eddie was acting like he had a dog in this race. It was there in his tone of voice, in his body language. His sudden interest in Benjie seemed off to me. Max took a few measured breaths, and he carefully folded his bar towel before answering.

"I can't say exactly where Benjie was headed. But I'll tell you this: Concepción is a small town, and it's rural too. You won't find it on any maps. If you boys head down there, you watch yourselves, you hear me?"

I stole a glance at Vince. The Doors played on the radio, *L.A. Woman*, the musical intro sounding a spooky backdrop to Max's ominous warning, like a car ride to a bad place.

"Why the concern about Concepción?"

It was Eddie again, taking on the role of inquisitor. Max leaned in, resting his forearms on the edge of the bar, his rolled shirt sleeve revealing a Special Forces tattoo on the inside of his right forearm.

"Concepción is east of the capitol, Culiacán. Like I said, it's out in the sticks. The thing of it is, she's right smack in the middle of the *despoblado*."

"The what?" Vince said.

"The badlands. The kind you don't want to know about. Understand this: Sinaloa is the cradle of the Mexican drug trade, and Culiacán is its heart and soul. It's a place where fools pay a high price. If you head down there, you watch out for yourselves. And stay away from the cowboys."

"The cowboys?" Eddie said.

"Sinaloa cowboys. And I'm not talking about goat ropers either. These are badass drug cowboys. S*icarios*. Assassins. They're the foot soldiers of the cartels and they're bad news, and you'd do best to steer clear."

"So you're sayin' we shouldn't go down there?" Vince said.

"I wouldn't, unless there was no other way around it. But if you choose differently, you watch your backs, and keep a weather eye out."

"One more question," Eddie said. "When did Benjie head down there? What day was it?"

My intuition pinged; Eddie was fishing now, for specifics. Vince wasn't having it.

"What gives, Eddie, why all the questions? Max already told us Benjie was in here a few days ago. Ease up. You're startin' to annoy me."

Eddie's face turned a shade of red and he dragged hard on his smoke, his eyes narrowed. Several minutes passed where no one spoke. The opening bars of *Sympathy for the Devil* played and time slowed, my head filled with visions of marauding Sinaloa cowboys hell-bent on wiping out the gringo intruders, swarming like Hells Angels at Altamont while the Stones played on. Let the good times roll, baby!

Real time resumed when the front door creaked open, spilling into the bar the sounds of laughter and loud voices. A group of young Mexican dudes strutted in like they owned the place, heading straight for the pool table at the far corner of the room, shucking and jiving each other while eyeballing the three of us sitting at the bar. I looked at Max.

"That's not them," he said. "You'll know the cowboys by the way they dress, all duded-up in pressed jeans and silk shirts, wearing those fancy-skinned boots they prefer. The real tipoff though is their headgear, those expensive white cowboy hats and trucker's caps with embroidered insignias, marijuana leafs and AK-47s and such. Trust me. You'll know them when you see them."

I turned to Vince. "You thinking what I'm thinking?"

"You mean those fools we tangled with last night?" he said. I nodded. Max whistled and let out an ironic laugh.

"You fellas mixed with some of them at the Apache, did you? Can't say I'm surprised by that. The Apache Bar is a little rough around the edges, to put it mildly. It's got a reputation for that sort of thing. But I'll tell you what, if you danced with the cowboys, count yourselves lucky to be in one piece." Max shook his head gravely. "Those bastards are meaner than a sack of rattlesnakes."

He moved to the rear door then, held it open and yelled out back. "Enrique, get your ass in here and give me a hand, we've got customers!" Max let the door swing shut as he walked over to the cooler and took out three beers. He slid them over to us. "Here you go, gentlemen. On the house."

Max smiled amiably, and he disappeared through the rear door. Vince took a long pull off his beer, lit a cigarette, and then he lit into Eddie.

"What the fuck, are you in charge now? Whatever business I have with Benjie doesn't involve you. You're just along for the ride. So cool it with all the questions, or else you and me are gonna have some big problems."

Eddie seemed to shrink into his bar stool, and for a few seconds I actually felt bad for him. But Vince was right, Eddie had asserted himself a little too strongly and it didn't add up. Outside of his words to me by the pool at the Ranchero, he hadn't said a damn thing about Benjie this entire trip, and now he wants to get inquisitive about it?

"Goddamn, Vince, you don't have to be a dick about it. I was only trying to help out," Eddie said weakly. He shifted in his seat, muttering under his breath about what a shitty deal it was.

Vince stared Eddie down, holding it long enough for Eddie to start fidgeting. Then he busted out laughing, and he slapped Eddie hard on the back.

"You're right, guitar man. I don't *have* to be a dick, but I choose to be. Do you see the difference? So you just let us ask the questions from now on. All you gotta do is sit back and enjoy all that sweet Mexican sunshine."

Vince checked Eddie with his beer and drained it in one pull. Eddie retreated into himself, dragging on his smoke, staring at

Vince through those squinty eyes. At that moment, I would've given a bundle to read that guy's mind.

A FEW MINUTES LATER a young guy sauntered in through the rear door, looking like Rico Suave's lost twin. He wore a checkered bandana do-rag over long black hair pulled into a ponytail, along with numerous rings, bracelets, and earrings. His western-style shirt was open, revealing a heavy gold cross hanging on a thick chain, his ripped jeans tucked into scuffed black boots.

"Sorry, boss, I was waiting out back for Felipe to bring some more discs. He was—" the kid stopped talking when he realized Max wasn't behind the bar. He looked at us eagerly.

"Americans? Right on, my bros. How would you like one of my music discs? For free, of course. But not for long, because one day they will be of great value, when I am a bigger star than Julio Iglesias."

The kid pulled a disc from the box tucked under his arm, held it out for us to see. The sleeve featured a photo of him dressed like 70s-era Elvis, complete with flowing cape, aviator glasses, and a greasy pompadour. The track listing was eclectic, with songs like *Rebel Yell*, *Daydream Believer*, and *I Want It That Way*.

"You have quite a diverse selection of music," I said, trying not to laugh.

"Yes, you are correct. This is because I am a very diverse artist. I will sing anything that touches my heart." The kid tapped his chest emphatically, looking upward with doe eyes.

"Shut your trap, Enrique, and go see if those boys shooting pool want something to drink!"

Max was shouting from the back room, and he nearly knocked the kid over as he came through the door.

"That guy and his music. It's nothing but cheesy karaoke tracks with Enrique's out-of-tune warbling slathered over the top. You couldn't give that shit away at a Tulsa truck stop, for crying out loud." Max paused and shook his head with a bemused laugh, an affectionate gleam in his eye. "He's a great kid though, and good with the customers too. That is, when he's not daydreaming about stardom and laying his rap on folks."

"Speaking of music, you ever get any bands in here?" Vince said.

"No bands. Too much trouble. They get the locals all riled up. Especially those narco bands. I'm happy to make do with that old juke over there, and the satellite radio. The piano's just for show. Every now and again I lose my mind and let Enrique do his thing, but only for an hour or so. Much more than that, he starts driving customers away."

Max reached for a bottle and some shot glasses. He came around to the front of the bar.

"Rico, take over while I talk to my friends."

He led us to a corner booth and we slid in. Max set the bottle and the shot glasses on the table, and he pulled some papers from his back pocket.

"I wanted to give you fellas some information, in case you decide to head on down to Concepción. I still advise against it, but if you choose otherwise, I at least want to point you in the right direction. First though, let's drink ourselves a toast."

Max poured four shots. The smell of tequila hit me hard. I'm a whiskey man, and my previous experiences with the devil blue agave have been memorable, for all the wrong reasons. But alas, I let peer pressure get the better of me.

"Here's to good fortune and clear weather for all ye brave wayfarers," Max said heartily. He downed his shot, and we followed suit.

The rush to my head was immediate, the warmth spreading from my chest inviting. Instantly I craved a cigarette. Vince obliged, sliding me the pack after lighting one of his own. Eddie took one, and the pack was offered to Max.

"No thanks, I gave that up years ago," he said.

Max unfolded a map of Sinaloa and spread it out on the table, along with a blank sheet of paper. He carefully outlined in red marker the route from Hermosillo to Culiacán, pointing out the general area where Concepción was located. On the blank sheet of paper he sketched out the rest, this map even more detailed than the one Barry drew. When it came to drawing maps, those dudes were aces.

The whole time Max was doing his map thing, Eddie was intently watching him, as if trying to commit every detail to memory. He was completely plugged into what Max was doing.

When Max was finished, he folded both maps together and handed them to Vince. Then he refilled the shot glasses. When he got to the fourth one, Eddie put his hand over the glass.

"Not for me," he said. "Where can I get some smokes around here?"

Max raised an eyebrow, glancing at the nearly full pack of cigarettes on the table. He gave Eddie directions to a market located around the corner. The neighborhood was safe, so walking there should be no problem. As Eddie slipped out of the El Burro Bar and into the Hermosillo night, those familiar suspicions came roaring back.

"So what's up with him?" Max said.

"Who?" Vince said.

"Your friend Eddie. Something about that boy isn't right. I picked up on it the minute I saw him. It's his eyes." Max downed his shot, chased it with beer. "You can always see it in the eyes."

"Eddie's all right," Vince said. "He just takes some gettin' used to."

"Whatever you say. But I'd keep an eye on that one, if I was you."

I looked at Vince; he flashed me a *not now* glare. Enrique rushed up to our booth then.

"Here you go, boss, I brought you some beers." He placed a bucket filled with ice and bottles of Corona on the table, and he stood there for a moment, an anxious look on his face. "Hey, boss, you mind if I put my disc in the player? Get some *musica* going?"

Enrique did a little ass-wiggle. Max scowled as he pulled three bottles from the bucket and passed them around. "Ease up on the floor show, kid. And turn off that damn radio. I told you, when the customers show up, we've got to make them feed the juke."

"Sure thing, boss, I'm all over that. No worries for you, okay?" Enrique smiled broadly, primping like a rock star.

"Sometime *today*, Rico?"

The kid took the hint and split for the bar. Max poured himself a shot, and he proposed another toast. "Remember this, boys. It all works out in the end. And if it doesn't work out, well then you just haven't reached the end yet."

We shot the booze and slammed our empty glasses down on the table. The tequila mainlined straight to my brain, a one-way ticket to a major drunk. Max lined up three more shots, paired each of them with a bottle of beer. It looked like he was settling in for a long one.

Twenty-five

"What's your interest in finding Benjie?"

Max looked at us, his eyes clear, lacking reproach. It was an honest question, and I sensed a direct answer was in order. "We're looking for a pair of boots," I said. "Benjie has them."

Max did not respond. We downed the shots and sipped our beer. Max poured three more, showing no curiosity about my statement. Finally I said, "Do you want to know why?"

"Why what?" Max said.

"Why we're looking for the boots?"

"No sir. If that's what you say it is, well then so be it. Your motivations are none of my business, Jackson, and as such, they don't concern me. I was just curious about what brought you down here. Now I know." Max raised his beer and chuckled. "Believe it when I tell you I've heard far stranger things come out of the mouths of men."

"It's actually a favor we're doin' for a friend of Benjie's," Vince said. "A guy named Kenny Lopez. Do you know him?"

"Never heard the name," Max said.

"The boots belong to that dude Kenny," Vince said.

"It makes no difference to me. Now if the two of you meant Benjie some kind of harm, well then it'd be a different story. But if that were the case, I doubt we'd be sitting here right now."

Max smiled assuredly, and I thought, Damn I like this guy. You just don't encounter many straight shooters nowadays. It seems everyone is working an angle or off on their own trip, and the simple courtesy of giving and receiving respect has become a lost social skill.

"It's like this, fellas." Max leaned forward, his face cast in shadow from the overhead lamp. "A man has to know his place in things, and he's got to learn to stay out of another man's business. That's just the way of it. Besides, most folks will tell you just about everything you need to know without a question being asked. Least none they'll ever know about."

"So what can you tell us about Benjie?" I said, my head fuzzy from the liquor.

Max drained his beer and slid the bottle next to the other dead soldiers; we'd polished off quite an army there. He seemed to collect his thoughts before speaking.

"I first met Benjie Cole in Nicaragua, back in the eighties. At the time, Benjie was an idealistic Marine cajoled into service by an asshole operator named Terry Stone. Stone had a special knack for picking out young recruits and spinning them into his web, playing on their insecurities while filling them with false notions of patriotism and an inflated sense of purpose. Once he had them fully indoctrinated, Stone would farm those boys out to various covert operations."

"You're ex-military?" Vince said.

"Army. Three tours in Southeast Asia."

"I had a brother killed over there," Vince said.

"Sorry to hear. What year was that?"

"Sixty-nine."

Max hesitated a moment, seeming to consider this fact while staring curiously at Vince. "Where did you say you were from?" he said.

"Lake Charles, Louisiana."

153

"That's a nice town."

"I suppose for some people it is," Vince said. "I had my fill a long time ago."

"Yes, I know the feeling. So anyway, I met Benjie down there in Central America. I was Army Intelligence at the time, having been lured out of my retirement from military service. I planned on being a career soldier, but after the politics of Vietnam I'd had enough, so I pulled the plug. I went to college and got degrees in political science and philosophy, set out to conquer the world. But damn if I didn't end up working the rigs down in the Gulf." Max sighed deeply. "Turns out you can't do shit with those kinds of degrees, except maybe teach or write books, neither of which interested me much."

"So how did you become a spy?" I said.

"I wasn't exactly a spy," Max said with a chuckle. "I was more like an independent contractor, as the term goes. Hired to share my vast wealth of knowledge in the art of war." He laughed ironically, and paused to drain his beer. "By the way, that's where I met Barry Fitzgerald, down there in Nicaragua. He's former Air America, and a solid man in a pinch. We fell right in from the moment we met, did quite a bit of work together.

"But to answer your question, it was an old Army buddy who roped me back in. They needed experienced players to work with the Contra rebels in that nasty little business with the Sandinistas. It was a plum gig, and an opportunity for me to get back in there and kick some commie ass. Remember, these were the days before radical Islam was all the rage. Mother Russia was still the enemy and the Cold War was going strong, and Central America was ground zero in the fight to stop the spread of Communism.

"Benjie was hooked up with a group of military advisors working with the Contras, providing training and logistical support. At least that was the cover story. The truth is they were engaged in actual missions. I got to know Benjie real well down there, found him to be a solid kid with a good head on his shoulders. He told me about his life, some pretty rough stuff growing up in the barrios of Santa Ana. It seemed to me he'd had more than his share of hard knocks.

"When he first got down there, Benjie bought into the indoctrination full-tilt, one hundred percent Semper Fi straight down the line. He truly believed all that horseshit about honor and fighting for the greater good, right versus wrong and other such nonsense. Hell, there was a time I bought that nonsense too."

Max laughed deeply, and as his humor faded, he quietly sipped his tequila.

"Yes sir," he said, staring into his shot glass. "We were true believers all right. A whole lot of us. Benjie included."

"So what changed?" I said.

"The lines got blurry, that's what changed. Turns out the Contras were no damn better than the Sandinistas, and it got to Benjie, started eating at him down deep. Once that happens you can't turn it off. Simple fact is, you can't be a fighting man if you've got a guilty conscience."

Max Hollister told of Benjie's declining state of mind, his intense moral conflict over the things he saw, and was ordered to do, and the small ways he tried to help those caught in the crossfire of a no-win situation. He also told of the day it all blew up, the botched recon mission and the innocents killed, with Benjie unwittingly playing a key role. In the aftermath, Benjie suffered a complete breakdown, and he was shipped back to Camp Pendleton, deemed unfit for service. A series of violent, alcohol-fueled incidents ensued, which led to an eventual dishonorable discharge from the Corps. Max lost contact after that, until the day in the early 90s when Benjie walked in the front door of the El Burro Bar and ordered a beer.

"A voice from the past," Max said. "And a man I didn't recognize sitting there at my bar. It hit me hard, the shape he was in. The years hadn't been good to Benjie Cole. He was purely a lost soul."

There were sporadic visits over the next few years, always followed by long periods with no contact, and each time Max feared the worst. Whenever he was here, Benjie would just sit at the bar and drink all day, listening to the same songs over and over on the jukebox; his eyes vacant in what Max called the thousand-yard stare. Max tried his best to help, but each time Benjie begged off, insisting on going his own way.

And then one day Benjie Cole arrived reborn. He pulled up on a fine spring morning, riding a shiny new Harley and looking fit and filled out in ways Max hadn't seen since their days in the service. Benjie told of a new business venture he'd started with a friend of his, and he flashed a fat bankroll as proof of his success. He laid a satchel full of cash on Max and insisted he take it, payment for the years of unwavering friendship and loyalty.

The visits grew more frequent, and in time Max realized it wasn't simply leisure that brought Benjie south. He'd seen enough in his time to know when a man was operating out on the fringes of the law, and in Mexico that usually meant contraband. He never pried though, and Benjie never brought any of his activities into Max's world.

Max went on to tell of what he called Benjie's second decline. How over time, the lure of money and the trappings of success were no better cure for the soul than simply sticking your head in the sand and wishing it all away. Benjie's demons hadn't gone away, they'd merely taken a hiatus, and lived to fight another day.

"The last few times he was in here he seemed burned-out," Max said. "I got the impression things weren't working out too well back home, even though he claimed business was better than ever. He talked a lot about selling off everything but his bike and heading south to Bolivia, disappearing like Butch Cassidy and the Sundance Kid. I had to remind him about what happened to those two, but Benjie wasn't swayed. He said it'd be a helluva way to go. Honorable he called it, being shot down in a hail of bullets like that." Max shook his head and sipped some beer. "Benjie Cole always did have a flair for the dramatic."

"You know, there's some who claim they got away. Butch and Sundance," I said.

"No shit," Vince said, lighting a cigarette. "Imagine that. I'd say the movie had a better ending though."

"Well whatever the case, Benjie was fixated on some idea he had in his mind of…"

Max's words trailed off, and he closed his eyes and rubbed his chin.

"Look, fellas, enough of all that. The business of the past should stay there, in the past. My dad used to say there's no profit in talking about things that can't be changed, and I tend to think he was right about that. All you need to know about Benjie Cole is this: he's a good man, and he's got a good heart. In a way, life's been beating him down from the get, and when I think of it in those terms, I feel a hurt for my friend that can't be healed. And I fear for him too. Far too many from the old days are gone now, and I pray to God that Benjie doesn't go that way."

Max excused himself to go take care of some business. Our night should have ended there. I was tired and drunk, and it didn't seem likely that we'd learn more information about Benjie. But our night didn't end there. Max Hollister would soon return with another story to tell, this one the most improbable of all.

Twenty-six

At the time of our trip to Mexico I had known Vince Taylor for fifteen years, and in that time we'd grown as close as brothers. We played music together and drank to excess on occasion; enjoyed family vacations, kids' birthday parties, and Sunday afternoon barbecues; and when the bottom fell out of our lives, we leaned on each other and shared our pain. Yet despite all that, I was unprepared for what I heard that night. For his part, Vince was visited by a truth he'd only guessed at, one that cut so deep he was never the same upon knowing it.

It started out innocently enough, when Max Hollister returned to our table and engaged in some meaningless small talk, the whole time focusing on Vince as if searching for some lost detail or fact known only to him. The conversation turned to talk of family and the shared experiences common to us all. Then, in a moment of pure serendipity, it was revealed that Max Hollister and Vince Taylor came from the same hometown, the same neighborhood in fact. Max knew of Vince's older siblings, and he knew of Vince's brother, the one killed in Vietnam. He knew Ray Taylor because he served with him, and he was there when it happened.

"Recognize anyone?" Max said.

He put a framed photograph on the table, one he'd retrieved from his office; a group of soldiers gathered around an anti-aircraft gun, posed in the way of young men full of piss and vinegar, firm in the belief that they alone held the world by the balls. Vince studied the photograph.

"That's you," he said. "And Ray. I'll be damned, Max. It's you and my brother together."

Vince held the photograph gently by the edges, as if it were a fragile artifact unearthed from the sands of time. When he spoke, his voice was small, like it was on the day he told me Leslie had died.

"Tell me what happened."

IN 1969, RAY TAYLOR was a twenty-three-year-old Army sergeant on his third tour of duty in Vietnam. His Special Forces unit was attached to the 101st Airborne, and they were tasked with special reconnaissance in preparation for a late-spring offensive. Operating near the Laotian border, Ray's squad ran mostly low-risk daylight forays, probing enemy lines and gathering intelligence, fairly routine stuff for a war zone.

But nothing in Vietnam was ever routine, and on a day that should have been a milk run for Ray Taylor, the bottom fell out big time. On their return to base camp his squad was ambushed and a hellacious firefight broke out. The men took cover in a rock shelter cut into the bank of the river they'd been traversing.

The shelter had an oblique angle of approach advantageous to defense of the position, and Ray's squad was able to fend off several attacks before the enemy fell back to regroup. For the next few hours, sporadic gunfire was traded back and forth, and a standoff ensued.

While the squad suffered no fatalities in the initial ambush, they were torn up pretty good, with two of the men seriously wounded. Their radio was shot to hell and their ammunition was low, and with nightfall just a few hours away, the situation was dire.

The cut where they hid was actually a narrow cave, twisting some fifty yards back, and at the end there was a hole showing daylight about six feet up. An hour of work with bayonets widened the hole large enough to slip a man through, and a quick recon indicated the area above was clear of enemy soldiers.

A plan emerged, whereby the men would wait until nightfall and then creep out through the hole, in hopes they could steal away undetected. It wasn't much of a plan, but it was all they had, and they'd have to find a way to make it work.

Ray Taylor didn't like it, and he insisted on insurance. He told his men he would stay back and provide covering fire, keeping up the illusion they were still hunkered down, when in reality they were escaping out the back door. The men balked, calling the plan suicide, and they argued over it. Eventually Ray gave his men a direct order.

Ray collected as much ammunition as his men could spare, and he rigged up a couple of claymores that he planned on detonating upon his escape. He wished his men good luck, joking that he'd be along shortly and they'd all share a laugh about it over cigars and whiskey back in the comfort of base camp. It was not to be.

As the men put distance between themselves and Ray, fierce gunfire erupted, and their hearts sank at the inevitable truth. They made it back safely by dawn, and immediately a team saddled-up to search for Ray, but they were turned back a half mile from the river by a massive NVA force that had mobilized in the area.

Ray Taylor was eventually listed as missing in action. He was credited with saving the lives of his squad and was awarded a posthumous medal of honor. He was three weeks shy of his twenty-fourth birthday.

VINCE'S FACE REVEALED nothing. Max refilled the shots and raised a toast to Ray Taylor. After, there was no slamming of glasses on the tabletop; this was a somber affair.

"Thanks, Max," Vince said, his eyes downcast as he fingered an unlit cigarette. "My mom used to keep that medal inside a little wooden box on the mantle. My old man made that box. He did that as a hobby, workin' with wood and whatnot."

Vince paused to light his cigarette, his eyes watery pools of emotion.

"I never knew what it was about. I was just a little kid when Ray died. Shit, I barely remember him. Ain't that a bitch? Whenever I'd try to talk to my dad about it he'd get all uptight and just shut down, brush me off. Thing is, he'd get pissed off at me just for askin'. My poor old mom could only cry. She'd get about two words out and then she'd be gone, dropped into a funk that'd last for weeks."

Vince dragged on his smoke. He studied the smoldering tip, a look of resignation set in his eyes. "After a while I stopped askin'. It was just easier that way."

"I know all about that," Max said, his voice reassuring. "You've got to talk about such things, enough to where you never forget, but not so much that you hurt yourself in the process. It's a tough one to balance."

Max drained his beer and stared at the empty bottle for a long minute, his intelligent eyes losing none of their clarity, despite his excessive boozing. He placed his palms on the table and hoisted himself out of the booth, stood at the edge of the table and reached for our hands with his steady grip. As I took Max's hand, I wondered what it would be like, going into battle with such a man.

"I think I've jawed enough for one night," Max said. "I'm going to leave you fellas alone for a while. Good luck finding Benjie. When you do, tell him to stop by here. Tell him there are people who care about what happens to him."

"Will do, Max," I said, my tongue thick from the booze.

"It's been a real pleasure sharing the evening with you gentlemen. I'll try and get back over here shortly, but if you need anything at all, just flag Rico down. And feel free to slap him around a bit, if the situation warrants it."

Max smiled graciously and gave us a wink, and he turned to leave. He stopped after a step, turned back and placed his hand on Vince's shoulder.

"Your brother was a fine man and a helluva soldier, Vince. I'm sorry for your loss. I want you to always remember, he died doing what he believed was right. That's the kind of man he was, and it was a real honor to know him."

Max turned and walked away. I eyed Vince warily, wanting to say something profound, but my booze-addled brain wasn't working right. Instead, I sat back and waited for him to speak.

"My brother Ed used to talk about Ray all the time," Vince said. "The way I heard it, Ray was my dad's favorite. Ed always seemed bitter about that, like he could never measure up. Ray was the oldest, followed by Ed and then my two sisters. I'm the baby of the family. I was little when Ray first went overseas, and I might've seen him a few times between tours, but honestly I can't remember. I think I was seven when he died. Anyway, after Ray died I think my old man felt like he had no true Taylor left, you know, chip off the old block and all that."

"What about your sisters?"

"They were my mom's favorite for sure. For my dad, they were just his daughters. I don't think he related to women very well. I always wondered what my mom saw in him, because my old man was a rough dude. He never got over what happened to Ray, and in the end I think that's what killed him. That, and a fifth of Beam a day, behind two packs of unfiltered Pall Malls.

"I was twenty-two when my old man died. I was gettin' set to head out to L.A. for my music. My dad never cared for me bein' a musician. I ever tell you about that? Son of a bitch used to go on all the time about pussy guitar players this and longhair faggots that, how musicians didn't work for a livin' the way a real man does. I never had the nerve to ask him if that's the way he saw me."

Vince sighed, a lifetime of truth in it.

"The year Ray died it rained a lot, more than usual. Lake Charles is a wet place anyway, but this one year it was out of control. I remember thinkin' that somethin' was up. I could *feel* it. But no one ever said anything to me about it. So this cloud was hangin' over our lives, and the whole time it was rainin' like a son of a bitch, big fat drops of that Louisiana rain fallin' down like tears from heaven. Storm after storm blew in off the Gulf that year, drownin' everything it its wet goddamn misery. And here I am, this little kid, and all I want is to go outside and play and have some fun, but I got all this sadness around me and I don't know how to stop it.

"It was a long time before I put it all together, that the year of all that rain and all that sadness was when my brother died. Ever since then I've hated the rain, and I told myself that as soon as I was old enough I was gonna get as far away from the Gulf as I could, away from all that swampy Southern gloom. Nowadays I can hardly stand to go back."

The next few minutes fell wordless, an awkward silence that couldn't be filled. Vince stared absently into the throng of people crowded at the bar, while I stared at the side of his head, feeling the weight of his sadness in my heart. I began to speak, but Vince cut me off with his eyes.

"Let's get out of here, Jackson."

"What about Eddie?"

"Screw that guy. He can take care of himself."

Vince got up slowly and started for the door, and I followed a few steps behind.

Twenty-seven

T *he dream returned.*
   I'm on that hill again and I'm riding a motorcycle. The bike has a sidecar and there's a guy sitting in it, dressed in jungle fatigues. The guy isn't moving and he has no face. He's in bad shape. I think he's Ray Taylor.

   The hill is very steep, the surface slick with mud from a recent rain, and my bike fights for traction. I push my machine hard. The powerful vibration between my legs feels strangely sexual as I throttle for more power. Gravity fights me like a bitch, but I fight back. Ray just sits there. I think he's dead.

   The engine whines and the tires slip, but still I push on. I need more power!

   And then I fall, Ray tumbling out next to me. We fall together, into the deepest, darkest black I've ever known. Falling...falling...

I WOKE UP COLD with sweat, immediately aware of a breeze blowing through the open window, billowing the sheer curtain. The air smelled of ozone and impending rain. My head throbbed and my vision blurred horribly, and I was gripped by a woozy seasick feeling. I heard an engine rev from somewhere outside the window, faint yet recognizable, and I wondered, *Am I still dreaming*?

The sound grew louder, undulating in rhythmic intensity as it neared; it was a motorcycle, the exhaust rattling through the tailpipe in a hollow echo. I checked the time—just after two in the morning. Then I heard voices, two of them arguing, the low rumble of the bike drowning out the detail. I staggered out of the bed and over to the window, missed the chair completely and fell awkwardly onto the floor.

Shit, I was drunk.

I pulled myself up onto the chair, breathing hard at the effort, and gazed out the window in time to see the bike's taillights vanishing like tiny red orbs into the night. The street below was empty and eerily quiet. I sat there for a few minutes, taking in the silence. When I stood to close the window, a feeling like vertigo came over me, and I dropped onto the bed in a heap.

Goddamn tequila.

I heard footsteps in the hallway, and a key inserted into our door. My heart jumped and I rolled to my side, facing the door, burying my face in the pillows and pulling the covers over my head. Slowly the door creaked open. I peeked through the covers. *It was Eddie.*

He stepped inside the room and quietly closed the door. He turned and looked straight at me. I held my breath, tried to stay perfectly still. Could he hear my heart pounding in my chest?

Eddie moved across the room and disappeared from view, his door clicking shut. I exhaled slowly and threw off the covers, and stared at the ceiling, unable to comprehend what had just happened. The room gyrated crazily and I gripped the edges of the mattress, trying desperately to make it stop.

Goddamn tequila.

THE RAIN CAME at dawn, at first a gentle patter against the window, hypnotic and soothing, then a steady downpour. Peculiar light crept into the room, and all at once my head felt like jackhammered concrete. I focused on the space directly in front of me, trying to concentrate through the fog. Where the hell was I, and how did I get here?

I rose slowly, bracing for the dizziness. My equilibrium was off and the room slanted left, so I went right. I made it to the window, sliding it open to breathe in the air. Rain peppered my face. After a few minutes I closed the window and flopped back down on the bed, cursing my stupidity.

Goddamn tequila.

THURSDAY WAS A lost day.

We'd decided to wait out the weather before pushing south. It rained like a mother all day, thunder and lightning, the works. It seemed like it would never stop. Whatever Vince may have felt about all that rain I couldn't say, for he hardly spoke. He was lost in his private world, surely processing the things he'd heard last night.

This was a version of my friend I'd never seen before, even back when Leslie died and it seemed nothing worse could ever befall one man. He lay on the bed and picked out blues riffs on my guitar, staring into space, while Eddie and I steered clear.

Speaking of Eddie, that guy was enigmatic as ever. He never said where he went last night and we never asked. It was the pink elephant in the room. I thought about my dream, the bike, and Eddie's return, how they had all happened at once. My head began to hurt from dwelling on it.

A few hours of that and I started going crazy, a severe case of cabin fever settling in. My drunk had worn off and my stomach had settled enough for food, and I was hungry and ready for a break from the funk that would not go away. My head still hurt like it was stuck in a vise, but constant aspirin dulled it enough for me to think straight. I told the others I was going down for some food, maybe a walk to clear my head. They didn't ask to come along and I didn't suggest otherwise.

Tomorrow's another day, I told myself. Just write this one off and move on. That's something my mother used to tell me.

She'd say no matter how bad things got, you could always start over. Thanks, Mom.

I'D JUST FINISHED eating when Eddie showed up at the hotel coffee shop. He wasn't hungry though, he just wanted to talk. It made me uncomfortable at first and I wanted to slap him silly for his weirdness and demand that he explain his actions, but I didn't do that. Instead, I bit my tongue and listened. Besides, it's not like I had anywhere else to go.

"I appreciate what you said, Jackson."

Eddie got right into it, with no preamble. His voice was raspier than usual, like maybe he'd been yelling recently and wore it out. The strange thing was his eyes; he actually had them open, and for the first time I saw they were green. It struck me as odd that I didn't know what color his eyes were.

Eddie seemed unsettled, jumpy. I thought about last night, wondered what the hell he'd gotten himself into out there on the mean streets of Hermosillo.

"Back at Vince's house," Eddie went on, "that thing you said about me and my girlfriend. I'm sorry I blew you off. I've had a lot on my mind lately."

Haven't we all, I thought regretfully. I looked at Eddie and he averted his eyes. I felt crappy about being so hard on him. The guy looked honestly hurt, the sadness obvious in the lines on his face. God knows *that* was a familiar feeling.

"Look, Eddie, I realize we hardly know each other, and I don't know the full story about you and your girl. But the thing I *do* know is the pain of loving someone and losing them. All I was trying to say is that it's okay to be hurt and to feel like shit about it. And it's also okay to be mad as hell. It doesn't have to mean anything more than that. But if you deny it, it'll eat you alive."

As my words tumbled out I looked for a sign, anything to indicate I was getting through. Eddie sighed and stared out the front window, at the rain falling steadily. He gave a slight nod.

"It's been tough, dealing with it. It seems like I can't catch a break these days. Like that rain out there, shit just keeps coming down on me."

Eddie looked at me, his face drained of color. There was panic in his eyes, and it spooked me.

"I got this feeling, like a premonition." He gulped and licked his lips, started fiddling with the saltshaker. "It's telling me something is gonna happen. Something bad. It's this place, the things that go on down here. Think about it, Jackson. You could die here and no one back home will ever know about it. I mean, we're nobody to these people. We're less than nobody."

His words sent a chill through me, like a cold steel blade cleaving my soul. I shuddered.

"You feel it too?" Eddie said.

I didn't answer. Great, now we had two paranoid people on the crew. Vince would get a real kick out of this. Eddie lit a cigarette and he spent the next few minutes quietly smoking. It seemed to calm him a little. There was a long stretch where neither of us spoke, Eddie's eyes turning squinty again as he turned inward, smoking incessantly. I grew weary of the scene but I didn't know how to end it, so I just sat and waited for him to make a move. When he crushed out his final cigarette he obliged me. He stood suddenly, told me that he had to use the restroom, and he turned and walked away. I did not see him again until much later that day.

Where Eddie went during that time I cannot say. But throughout that whole afternoon I thought about what he'd said, about having a feeling that something bad was going to happen. Eddie Dowd would prove to be a prophet of epic proportions.

Twenty-eight

Conceptión is a desolate and lonely place, exiled far beyond the fringes of civilization, dropped like an afterthought into a flat desert wasteland of cactus and sagebrush and wind-swept emptiness; just one more stop on the road to nowhere.

We approached from the west, the town's outline distorted grotesquely in the road thermals. The sharp rise of mountains loomed in the distance; ominous thunderheads piled high against the peaks. The asphalt ended and we turned onto a dirt-road main street, and ran headlong into an apocalyptic, washed-out scene.

Buildings of crumbling adobe lay baking in the sun, their roofs in various states of disrepair, some with thatching so dry it would surely collapse in a strong wind or ignite into a fireball at the mere flick of a butt. The whole town was caked in dirt, with no green to be found anywhere, the few trees lining the street nothing but bleached-out skeletons, their jagged branches extending like broken arms pointed in odd directions. It was as if we'd stumbled onto an abandoned set from a Sergio Leone film, and I imagined the whistling theme from *The Good, The Bad and The Ugly*, announcing our arrival.

Vince drove steadily to the end of the street, turned around and came back. There were no hotels, gas stations, or viable business concerns of any kind, no earthly reason why any sane person would ever venture out to such a godforsaken place.

"Nice town," Vince said.

I looked at him dubiously. "You thinking about investing?"

"Jesus, where the hell are we?" Eddie said.

"This is what you call out of the way." Vince said.

"Out of the way my ass. This place doesn't even exist."

Vince pulled to a stop halfway down the street and we exited the car, working out the road cramps. I lit a cigarette and tossed Vince the pack.

"Who turned up the heat?" I said. The air was stifling, the breeze hot. I noticed a mangy black-haired dog eyeing me from up the street. "Remind me again, what it is we're doing here?"

"We're havin' fun. I keep tellin' you guys, it's all a state of mind." Vince let out a booming guffaw. He'd done a complete turnaround after his all-day funk yesterday, his good-humor demeanor firmly back in place. As annoying as it was, I was glad to see it.

"Did you guys know today is Friday the thirteenth?" Eddie said, his eyes skittish.

"Shit, don't pay that black magic nonsense no mind," Vince said with a laugh, while fingering his voodoo good luck charm.

I turned my gaze up the street, staring down the black-haired dog as it inched closer, hobbled by an arthritic gait. I was gripped by a surge of nerves as I recalled Barry's story of the cadejo. What was it he called it? Crossing the dog? I held my ground against the demonic stray, flicking my burning cigarette at its evil eyes. It snarled viciously and limped away.

That's when the full measure of our situation hit me. All I'd wanted was a little fairness from that hanging judge back home, and now look where it got me, staring down scabrous mongrels in a Third World village left over from the Stone Age.

"What now?" I said.

"I'm not sure," Vince said, his attention directed at the far end of the street. "What about that place over there?"

He pointed to a building standing off by itself in a patch of weeds. We started walking. When we got closer I saw it was a cantina, the curved roof parapet painted with a crude rendering of the Devil pitchforking an angel, gothic lettering spelling out *El Diablo de los Muertos.*

"The Devil of the dead," Eddie said.

"You know Spanish?" I said.

"A little," Eddie said, pushing through the front door.

I glanced at Vince. He rolled his eyes and followed Eddie into the El Diablo bar. Passing through the doorway, I noticed bullet holes arrayed in a perfect little arc over the front window.

THE PLACE WAS empty when we entered, the room smelling of dust and disuse. Like everything else in Mexico, the Diablo seemed about fifty years behind the times and in no hurry to catch up.

"Anybody home?" Vince called out. "Hey, amigos, you got customers here."

I noticed him rubbing his voodoo bracelet. "You work that thing any harder, you'll wear it out," I said.

"Easy there, Jackson, don't be doubtin' the power of Marie. She's got our back, jack, and that's a fact."

"This place is a dry hole," Eddie said. "There's nothing here for us." He stood by the front window, holding back the ratty curtain and looking out at the street through glass streaked with a lifetime of residue.

We poked around the room, just getting our bearings while waiting for the next thing to happen. Vince lit a cigarette and offered me one. I was reaching for the pack when I heard the sound of shuffling feet coming from the other side of the room. I turned and saw a boy pop his head out of a doorway. "*Hola*," he said.

The boy stepped through the doorway and went behind the bar. He switched on a transistor radio and tuned in a station. He was short and skinny, with dark skin and jet-black hair. He might have been twelve years old. He turned and smiled at us with a toothy grin.

"You like?" the boy said.

"Yeah, we like." Vince smiled. "What's your name, kid?"

"Lupe is my name. And you are?"

"Vince. And this is Jackson. The guy over by the window is Eddie."

"It is my pleasure to meet you," Lupe said. He came around to the front of the bar and shook our hands. He had almond-shaped eyes, probing yet friendly, and he seemed unusually self-assured for a child. I thought of my own son then, and a lump grew in my throat.

"Would you like some refreshments?" Lupe said.

Vince nodded and Lupe darted off. Eddie walked over and snorted loudly.

"Shit, what the hell is a kid doing in a place like this? That's just a shitty deal."

"Ease up there, guitar man. Maybe his pops runs the place. Sure, the joint's a dump, but that don't mean nothin'."

"Damn, Vince, you can put a shine on anything," I said.

"You got that right, brother. I call it my secret to good livin'."

Lupe returned, carrying a tray with beers and shot glasses, a saucer of sliced limes, and a dark-colored bottle with no label. He set the works on a table near the front door and waved us over. We sat down and Lupe poured three shots from the bottle, set one in front of each of us, along with a beer. The beer was very cold and it went down nicely. The shot smelled like tequila.

"This is my grandfather's very special mescal," Lupe said proudly. "It is the best in all of Mexico. The first one is on the house."

He stepped back, anticipating our reaction. I had no interest in reliving my El Burro Bar experience, and I eyed Vince and Eddie warily. But they were off to the races, already shooting the booze. I quickly threw mine back, telling myself that just one wouldn't hurt. It went down easy, the warmth in my gut pleasant.

What the hell, maybe a little buzz right now wouldn't be such a bad thing after all. I sucked on a lime and drank some beer. Lupe stood there smiling. He was exuberant as hell, and clearly pleased to have strangers visit his little corner of the world.

"Lupe, where you at, boy!"

A voice boomed from behind the bar. Lupe hunched his shoulders and giggled, and he ran out the front door. A middle-aged fat man waddled into the room. He wore a dirty apron tied around his bulging gut. He looked like he just woke up.

"I'd be careful if I was you," the fat man said. "I'm not sure that shit's safe to drink. Ain't nothin' but fermented cactus Lupe cooks up in an old washtub out back. I ain't shittin' you one bit about that."

The guy's expression was dazed as he swayed on his stubby legs. A sour odor came off his dingy clothing, and I casually eased my chair back to clear some space.

"The name's McGovern, by the way. Gus McGovern."

Gus didn't offer his hand.

"I'm Jackson. This is Vince, and that guy is Eddie."

Nods were passed in lieu of handshakes. Gus stared at us, seemingly lost. This went on for a minute or two before he finally spoke.

"So what brings you to our fair town?" He mumbled something incoherent as he swatted at a fly, tracking it with crossed eyes.

"I was gonna ask you the same thing," Vince said with a chuckle. "How does a Yankee end up in a place like this? You're American, right?"

"You think that's funny?" Gus said gruffly. "Shit, brother, you don't know the half of it. I came down from Deadwood, seeking my fortune. You ever seen that movie *Treasure of the Sierra Madre*?"

"Sure," Eddie said. "Bogart was in that one, right?"

"Oh yeah, he was great too. Anyway, those mountains out yonder are the Sierra Madres. They say there's still gold up there, but I'm here to tell you that's pure bullshit. And I know gold too, because I come from the Black Hills."

"No luck, huh?" Vince said.

"Ha! I'll say. Damn if I didn't come up aces and eights from the get, didn't even find me one single nugget. That's the dead man's hand, by the way. They call it that because ol' Wild Bill Hickok was holdin' them cards when he caught one in the back of the skull, sitting right there in saloon number ten, back home in Deadwood. Ain't that a bitch?"

Gus paused a moment, laughing spitefully. Then he grew quiet, his face pinched as if he were concentrating on something.

"No sir, I ain't had one bit of luck since I came down to this godforsaken hellhole. I had to take a job in this fine establishment just to make ends meet. But this is only temporary. Fact of the matter is, it's about time for ol' Gus to ramble on outta here, find myself some greener pastures."

Gus collected our empty bottles and said he'd be right back. He disappeared through the back door, shouting for Lupe.

"Man, that dude is *baked*. He's lost his goddamn mind for sure," Vince said with a laugh.

"Let's split this joint," I said. "This guy isn't going to help us find Benjie. Hell, I don't think he even knows what day it is."

"Jackson's right," Eddie said. "This place creeps me out. There's nothing here for us but trouble." He had that look in his eyes, the same one as when he told me of his premonition.

Lupe came in through the front door then, his face lit up with excitement. He had three more bottles of beer and a plate of tortillas with salsa. He set the food and drinks down on the table, scampering off just as Gus re-entered the room.

"Well I'll be damned. Where in the hell did that kid go?" Gus approached our table, a look of surprise crossing his face when he saw the beers and tortillas. "What the hell?" he said, his eyes crossed severely.

"What's up, Gus? Somethin' the matter?" Vince had a devious gleam in his eye, like he was getting set to wind the dude up. I kicked his shin under the table, just to cool him out.

"So anyway, Gus, we need some help from you. Information about a guy we're looking for," I said.

"What kind of information?"

"It's about a friend of ours, a guy named Benjie Cole," Vince said. "We heard he came down here and we need to find him."

Gus thought about it. Lupe peeked his head around the end of the bar, giggling and waving at us. The kid was a real joker, a miniature Vince Taylor.

"I don't believe he's been in here," Gus said vaguely. "Hell, we ain't had no customers in weeks."

"It's the off-season?" I said.

"Ha! There ain't no season around here. It's the same thing all the time. Emptiness, surrounded by a vast desert of nothingness. Shit, there's hardly any people even live around these parts, goddamn drug cartel scared all the honest folks off."

"So about Benjie, you haven't seen him?" I said.

"Ain't that what I just said?" Gus screwed up his face, his eyes bugging out under bushy brows. "Your friend's a little deaf, Vince?"

"Maybe it slipped your mind or something," I said, my tone defensive.

"Well goddamn it, man, I know what I seen. And I'm telling you, your friend ain't been in here." Gus's face turned red as he swatted at the fly buzzing around his head.

"Hey, we're all good here," Vince said. "Jackson meant nothin' personal by it. We've been out on the road a while and I guess we're a little wore out, that's all. You know how that is, don't you, Gus?"

Vince laid it on thick, and it started the fat man back around.

"Sure, I know all about that. I done quite a bit of traveling myself. I got me a wandering spirit. Least that's what the ladies tell me." Gus winked and laughed out loud, his belly jiggling at the effort. "Hey listen, fellas, I got to be headin' out right now. I wish I could help you, but just the same, it's been a real pleasure. If that kid ever shows up, you tell him I'm lookin' for him."

Gus smiled and turned to leave. He stopped after a couple of steps, looked over his shoulder at us. "You boys take care of yourselves. And keep your eyes open. Things ain't always what they seem around here."

He laughed on his way out the door. A car door slammed and a rough engine coughed to life, the rumble of a busted muffler sounding through the room. I looked out the front window and caught a glimpse of Gus driving past, behind the wheel of an old pickup truck.

"Goddamn weirdo," Eddie said.

"You try living in a dump like this and see where you end up," Vince said.

I thought of the movie, how old Fred C. Dobbs lost his mind out there in the Sierra Madres, greed and isolation slowly eroding his sanity. Life imitating art. Now that's a trip.

"EXCUSE ME, Mr. Vince."

It was Lupe, standing over by the bar. He wasn't giggling anymore. In fact, he looked concerned.

"You are correct," he said. "Gus is loco. And he is dishonest, about the man you are looking for. Your friend was here."

"How do you know?" I said.

"I was here. I saw Benjie. He gave me this."

Lupe approached our table and held out a large coin. I took it from him and turned it over. It was a twenty-dollar gold piece, a *Double Eagle*. This one was dated 1906, and it was in pretty good shape, maybe worth a grand to a collector. I knew this because my son was going through a serious coin-collecting phase, and it was all he talked about lately. We'd spent a lot of time down in Old Towne Orange, perusing the cases of coins in the antique shops, looking for whatever it is that catches a young boy's eye. I handed the coin back to Lupe, feeling a big hole in the pit of my stomach. This was hitting too close to home for me.

"That's a nice piece," I said softly.

"Si, it is, Mr. Jackson," Lupe said. "And Benjie was very generous to give this to me. He said he wanted to take me from this place, back to the United States. I like this idea very much."

"What about your family?" Eddie said.

A cloud passed over Lupe's face and he looked down at his feet. "I am an orphan," he said.

The room went quiet. After a moment Eddie said, "I'm sorry to hear that."

Lupe nodded, hands clasped in front of him.

"So what about Benjie?" Vince said.

"He was here a few days ago," Lupe said eagerly, taking a seat at the table. "He was looking for a man named Butch. Benjie was very tired from traveling. I made him some food and gave him some of my special mescal. I like Benjie very much. He was very nice to me."

"Where'd he go?" Vince said.

"When Benjie was here, Gus was watching him from behind the door. I heard Gus call on the telephone to Vicente, the police captain of the town. After it was dark, Vicente came to the Diablo, and he snuck up on Benjie and hit him on the head. He took Benjie to the jail, and Gus and Vicente stole Benjie's motorcycle and his money."

Lupe paused, out of breath from telling the story. Vince whistled loudly. "Now *that's* a shitty deal," he said.

I recalled what Gus said when he left, about things not being as they seemed. Yeah, sure they aren't, you bushwhacking son of a bitch. "Can you take us to Benjie?" I asked Lupe.

"Si, I can take you there."

I looked at Vince and Eddie. They nodded back.

"Let's go," I said.

Twenty-nine

Vince pushed along at a steady clip, the Jeep's worn shocks useless on the washboard road. The desert hardpan spread out before us, giving way to the foothills of the Sierra Madres, the afternoon sun hugging the horizon and bathing us in golden light. We rounded a rocky turn and came upon a lone shotgun adobe standing in the middle of a clearing, the surrounding area thick with saguaro and ironwood. Lupe announced our arrival.

Vince pulled up close and killed the engine, and we took a few minutes to check things out. The jail was maybe fifty feet long and about the width of a trailer. It had a tile roof, windowless side walls, and an overhang shading the front door. The building looked abandoned.

"You sure this is the place?" I said to Lupe.

"Si," he said.

We got out and approached the front door. Vince pointed to a thick chain and heavy padlock looped through the door handle. "I guess no one's home."

"Follow me," Lupe said.

We walked single file to the back of the building and stood under an opening. It was high up in the wall, about two feet square and protected by steel bars. Twenty yards away a wide arroyo cut through the desert, and I gazed up to its point of origin in a narrow gash at the base of the mountains. Roiling black storm clouds shrouded the peaks, and I thought of a flash flood barreling down on us. It was a hell of a spot to build a jail, you ask me.

"This is it," Lupe whispered. He pointed up at the opening. We listened for movement inside the cell but heard only silence, and the sound of the breeze blowing through stiff desert scrub.

"You sure he's in there?" Vince said.

"Si, Benjie is here," Lupe said, nodding his head earnestly.

The opening was too high to reach from the ground. A quick search turned up an old wooden bench lying in the weeds, and we positioned it underneath the opening. I tested it for sturdiness, and once satisfied I wouldn't tumble off and break my neck, I stepped up for a better look.

The cell was small. A man lay sprawled on a bunk bolted to the far wall, his back turned.

"Lupe, get me some rocks," I said over my shoulder.

Vince crowded up next to me, the bench rocking precariously under the added weight. "Is he in there?" he said. I shoved him off the bench.

Lupe returned and handed me some softball-sized rocks. "Damn, kid, when I said get some rocks, I didn't mean boulders. Can't you find some pebbles or something? I want to throw them at this guy and wake him up."

My voice came out sharper than intended, and Lupe's eyes watered. Then his demeanor changed to one of surprise. Vince stifled a laugh, and Eddie had a goofy look on his face.

"What's with you guys, you think this is funny?" I said.

"Turn around, Jackson," Eddie said, pointing to the opening.

I turned slowly. A pair of hard eyes stared back, and I nearly fell off the bench.

"Who are you?" the man whispered through crushed gravel.

"Uh...a friend."

"A friend, huh? Well listen, friend. If you don't have a key to the front door of this shit box, then all you're doing is taking up space, so scram."

"What are you, like eight feet tall?" I asked, wondering how it was he could see out through the opening when I had to stand on the bench to see in.

"No, you dumb-ass, the ground is higher on the inside. So once again, what are you doing here?"

Lupe giggled and I shot him a look. I turned to face the man.

"I already told you, I'm a friend. In a manner of speaking. A friend of a friend kind of thing. You *are* Benjie Cole, right?"

"Listen, pal. I don't have any friends of friends. So again, what's your gringo ass doing outside my window?"

I took a deep breath. "Me first. You're Benjie Cole, right?"

I gave him my best tough-guy face, feeling pretty confident with that thick adobe wall and those steel bars separating us. He stared at me for a long minute, before finally giving some ground.

"Yeah, I'm Benjie Cole, so what. Who the hell are you?"

"I'm Jackson Thomas."

"Well nice to meet you, Jackson Thomas. Now what the fuck do you want?"

"Kenny sent us."

Benjie's eyes narrowed. "Kenny who?"

"Lopez. You know him, right?"

"Yeah sure, I know Kenny Lopez. So does half of Orange County, so what?" He paused a moment. "Are you saying Kenny sent you down here to get me?"

"Not exactly. He sent us for your boots."

"My what?"

"Your boots. Or should I say, *Kenny's* boots. He says you took them by mistake."

Benjie seemed confused at first. Then a look of recognition crossed his face, and he laughed out loud. "Well I'll be damned, no wonder these things don't fit." He had a deep, full-throated laugh, and in it I sensed a lot of irony.

"Huh?" I muttered dumbly.

"Never mind. You say Kenny sent you down here to get his boots?"

"Yes, that's what I'm saying."

"Tell him why," Vince said.

"Who is that? Are there others?"

"Yeah, I've got a couple of friends with me."

"Move out of the way so I can see their faces."

I stepped off the bench. Benjie stared down through the steel bars for several seconds. He saw Lupe and smiled. "Hey, little amigo, how are you?"

"I am very well," Lupe said. "I have come to help you."

Benjie nodded affectionately, and almost instantly his expression turned intense, his eyes narrowed to a glare. "You've got to be kidding me. Vince Taylor?"

Vince's face flushed. "Hi there, Benjie," he said awkwardly. "How ya doin'?"

"You guys know each other?" I said.

"Hell yeah I know him. For the worthless son of a bitch he is. I'm gonna kick your ass, Vince, like I should have a long time ago."

Vince shrugged and smiled sheepishly. "He'll get over it," he whispered.

"The hell I will." Benjie stepped out of view, mumbling to himself.

"What's he talking about?" Eddie said.

"Maybe Mr. Benjie has turned loco from the jail?" Lupe said innocently.

"Or maybe Mr. Vince is the loco one," I said, my voice tight. I stared at Vince. "Come on, give. What the hell is going on here?"

"You guys just keep on talking. I've got all day," Benjie shouted.

"Well?" I said.

"Look, it's no big thing, okay," Vince said. "I went out with his sister, that's all."

181

"That's what you call it?" Benjie shouted. "Goddamn it, man, she *loved* you. You broke her heart."

"I can't believe this," I said, throwing my arms up. I stared into Vince's eyes. "You said you barely knew this guy, met him once. You remember that? Why'd you lie to me?"

"Because he's a goddamn liar," Benjie shouted.

"Hey now, you're just pissed off 'cause you're all locked up inside that jail there, ain't that right, stumpy?"

"Only my friends call me that, Vince, and you aren't one of them. I'm telling you, man, I'm going to square this thing just as soon as I'm out of here."

"Ha! We'll see about that, tough guy."

"Christ, Vince, why didn't you tell me about this?" I grabbed his arm and forced him to look at me. Eddie moved in a few steps, his eyes tense, fists clenched. Vince shot us both a hard look.

"Would it have made any difference, Jackson?" he said defiantly, jerking his arm away. "Get real. You tellin' me you'd have said no to this deal had you known the truth? That's bullshit, and you know it. Nothin' changes here just because I know this guy, so get off it already."

"That isn't the point. I'm your friend, and you should've been straight with me."

"He's right, Vince," Eddie said firmly. "Lying about it is bullshit."

"Yeah, Eddie? Well who the hell asked you anyway?"

"Hey guys, remember me?" Benjie laughed. "I'm the dude with the boots. You let me know when you're ready to take care of some business."

"So what now, genius?" I said.

"What do you mean? We get the boots and leave, simple."

Typical Vince. It was no big deal. Nothing was ever a big deal, as long as there was someone else around to handle it. He brushed past me and stepped up on the bench, pressed his face to the steel bars. "Say, Benjie, maybe we can work out some kind of—"

Bam! Instantly Vince launched backwards and fell on his ass.

"That's for Rosie!"

"Goddamn! What'd you do that for?" Vince held his nose, his breathing ragged.

"Because you had it coming, that's why. And there's more of that waiting when I get out, so be ready."

"Shit. Does it look broken?" Vince turned to me, his eyes watering.

"You'll live," I said sarcastically. "Now, what the hell do we do?"

"I dunno. I guess we gotta bust him out or somethin'."

"What? Are you out of your mind?"

"Sounds like a plan to me, Jackson." Benjie laughed. "The only way you're getting these boots is with me attached. Think of it as a package deal."

"Man, I don't think this is a good idea," Eddie muttered nervously.

"Really? Well thanks for stating the obvious." I glared at Eddie. "Kiss my ass," he shot back.

"Come on, Jackson, don't be shitty with Eddie. He's just tryin' to help."

"Sure, Vince, whatever you say. Everyone's just trying to help. It's one big helpful world out there, with you sitting in the middle, the king of helpful."

We went back and forth like that for a few minutes, arguing over what to do, while Benjie kept up with the verbal jabs at Vince. In the middle of it all, Lupe spoke up.

"I know a way," he said timidly. The bickering stopped and the three of us turned to him.

"How?" Eddie said.

"I have some things, back in town."

"Some things?" I said.

"Si," Lupe said. "Some things."

"And these things can free Benjie?"

"Si. I believe they can. But we must hurry."

"I'd listen to the kid if I was you," Benjie said. He was looking down through the opening, his face close to the steel bars. "We're burning daylight here, and when the sun goes down that goddamn sheriff's coming back to check up on me. Then you're screwed. It's now or never, boys."

I kneeled in front of Lupe. "Can you really do it?"

"Si, I believe so. But we must go, now."

And that's what we did.

Thirty

We returned a short time later, arriving at the jail just as the sun dipped in the west and the moon rose simultaneously in the east, full and bright like a beacon. The ride was tense, Vince's deception hanging out there like a crushing weight about to fall. I wanted details about his relationship with Benjie, but Vince blew me off. The more I pressed him, the more he dug in. I finally let it go, vowing to settle it eventually.

We approached the jail slowly, on the lookout for the sheriff. The coast was clear and Vince pulled around to the back of the building, and he parked a short distance away. We got out and gathered under the opening.

"Benjie, it's me," I said, keeping my voice low.

"Well hey there, Jackson, how ya doin'?" Benjie's voice echoed inside the cell. "You get everything worked out?"

"Yeah, I think so." I turned and looked at Lupe. "Okay, kid, what's the deal?"

Lupe had not yet revealed his plan for freeing Benjie. We'd taken him to the El Diablo Bar where he lived in a back room; he came out carrying a backpack, two large duffel bags, and several woolen blankets rolled and tied with twine. It seemed like a lot of stuff for a jailbreak. Little did I know, Lupe was planning his own escape.

"My plan is simple." Lupe unzipped his backpack and held it open for us to see. "I will use these to set Benjie free."

I gaped in disbelief. "Is that dynamite?"

"Si."

"Your plan is to blow up the jail?"

"Si, this is my plan," Lupe said calmly.

"Right on, Lupe!" Benjie shouted. "Let's light this joint up."

"Where in the hell did you get dynamite?" I said incredulously.

Lupe giggled. "I stole it from Gus."

"What the hell is that lunatic doing with dynamite?"

"He uses it for the gold mining."

"Man, this ain't right," I said to Vince. "This is how guys like us end up wasting away in a Third World shithole. You ever see *Midnight Express*? That's what's waiting for us if we go through with this."

Vince shrugged. "I say we do it."

"Don't be a pussy, Jackson," Benjie said. "Take a look around you. We're in the middle of nowhere. We do this now, we get away clean."

"I'm with Vince," Eddie said. "Let's do it."

"Listen, Jackson," Benjie said. "I'm sure Kenny offered you some kind of reward for the boots. The only way you're getting it is by busting me out. Otherwise you're shit out of luck, and you've wasted a trip down here for a big fat zero."

My brain froze in indecision. My gut said to get the hell out, the money wasn't worth the risk. But my head said we couldn't just abandon Benjie to an uncertain fate at the hands of a corrupt asshole with a badge. I looked down at Lupe. "You aren't going to kill us, right?"

"I would never think of such a thing."

The mental gears cranked up as I weighed it one more time. Five days on the road and it came down to this, a kid and his sack of dynamite. I laughed inside at the absurdity of it. And then, for the third time in a week, I made a completely irrational decision. God help me if I chose wrong. I sucked in some air, exhaled it slowly.

"Do it."

IT TOOK LUPE a few minutes to prepare the charge. He removed three sticks from his backpack and twisted the fuses together, stuffed them into a chink in the adobe. He assured us it was just enough to make a hole in the wall. It looked to me like it was enough to knock the whole damn building down. Vince and Eddie took positions at opposite sides of the jail, on the lookout for the sheriff. Benjie was a cool customer.

The full moon illuminated the desert in ghostly light. The sky was clear and sharp, filled to overflowing with stars, each one of them looking down on us as we prepared to head down a road of no return. Lupe finished his work. "It is ready," he said.

"Last chance to back out." I said.

There were no takers. I said a silent prayer, and nodded at Lupe.

"I think perhaps Benjie should step back," he said. "I do not wish for him to be hurt."

Benjie backed away from the opening, said he was ready to rock and roll. Lupe grinned, a faint glimmer of mischief in his eyes. Of course, what kid doesn't dig blowing shit up?

Lupe looked at each of us and nodded. He lit the twisted fuses and we scrambled back behind the Jeep for cover. Sparks flew off as the flame inched its way to Benjie's freedom. And then it happened.

There was an ear-splitting boom, the ground shaking violently as a ball of flame shot upward and a concussive wave washed over us. Debris rained down from the sky, chunks of dirt and adobe and steel bars landing in a metallic thud on the hood of the Jeep. It took several minutes for the dust and smoke to clear enough for us to see the full extent of the damage. The entire rear wall of the jail and a portion of the side walls were gone, and the roof was partially collapsed, forming a pile of rubble in the middle of the cell.

"Damn, Lupe, you think you used enough of that shit?" I said, dumbfounded at the kid's handiwork.

"Perhaps one stick would have been perfect," Lupe said. "I think Vicente will be very angry." He suppressed a giggle, his eyes wily.

"Is he alive in there?" Eddie said, moving forward cautiously.

"Benjie, are you okay?" I shouted.

There was movement, and Benjie stood and dusted himself off, coughing loudly. He walked toward us, a shadowed figure in the blown-open cell. I met him halfway.

He was my height, built solid, dressed in black. He looked like Kenny Lopez, but with a lot more miles on the odometer. I stared at the boots on his feet, at the object of all this madness, and stifled a laugh.

"Jackson Thomas," I said, extending my hand. "I've heard a lot about you, Benjie Cole."

"I'll bet you have." Benjie took hold of my hand firmly, just like Max Hollister. "Thanks for getting me out."

"Thank Lupe, it's his show."

Benjie kneeled down in front of Lupe, looked the boy in the eyes. "Thanks, little man. That's some serious ordnance you've got there. I'm just glad you didn't add one more stick, otherwise you'd be picking up body parts."

"I am truly sorry, Benjie. You will forgive me?"

Benjie smiled at the boy, rubbed the top of his head. "You still have that lucky coin I gave you?" Lupe nodded proudly. "Good. You ready to go home with me?"

"What the hell?" Vince said. "We're taking him with us?"

"I'm not leaving him behind."

"What about his family?" I said.

"Cartel killed his family. He's got no one left here."

Lupe stared at the ground, hands clasped in front of him as if he were awaiting punishment for some misdeed. Benjie looked at Vince, then Eddie, and finally me. His eyes were green and focused, holding no ambiguity.

"This is non-negotiable. You guys don't like it, you can take a hike. I'll find another way out of here."

After a moment Vince nodded his approval. Eddie said, "What the hell, let the kid come. This place fucking sucks." They both looked at me.

"I guess it's settled," I said.

Lupe grinned and hugged Benjie, tears on his cheeks. Benjie looked at the bombed-out jail, a sly smirk crossing his face. "It's time to roll," he said. "I know a shortcut through the mountains. It'll take us to the highway. If we get moving, we can make Nogales by morning."

"And then what?" I said.

"Then we go home, Jackson."

Part Three

The Double-cross

Thirty-one

Three hours later the car broke down.
We were pulling a steep grade through the foothills along the eastern edge of the Sonoran Desert when the engine let out a harsh grinding and the transmission lurched violently. Benjie goosed the accelerator, coaxing the Jeep over the crest of the hill and coasting down the other side. We came to a stop as the road leveled out, the smell of burning oil seeping through the dashboard vents.

Benjie got out and popped the hood. Smoke billowed out, along with a sharp hissing. After a few minutes he walked to a rock outcropping about fifteen yards past the front of the Jeep. He stood at the edge, seeming to gaze at the desert below. Then he walked back and hung his head through the open window.

"You guys have a map?"

I fished it out of the glove box and handed it over. Then I had a thought, and I looked over my shoulder. "Hand me the binoculars," I said to Vince.

I got out of the car and walked around to meet Benjie, gave him the binoculars. He walked back to the outcropping and unfolded the map; spread it out on a flat boulder. The wind was up so he placed small rocks on the corners of the map to hold it down. Moonlight was plentiful, eliminating the need for a flashlight.

Benjie scanned a point far off into the distance, toward a cluster of lights shimmering in the surrounding blackness. He consulted the map several times, seemed to mentally calculate something in the process. He glassed the desert once more while I stood by, waiting for some indication that this dude had a plan. When Benjie was finished, he folded the map and handed me the binoculars. I followed him back to the Jeep, where he motioned for the others to join us outside.

"It's not as bad as it seems," Benjie said firmly.

"Yeah? How do you figure?" Vince smirked. It was more of a challenge than a question. Benjie glared at him.

Since our escape, a truce of sorts had been called, with Vince's ass kicking shelved for another time; in the aftermath of the jailbreak, we had far more pressing concerns to deal with. But the tension never left, and it threatened to spark at any moment.

Benjie stared daggers at Vince and I figured this was it, time for retribution. It was probably best, to get it out of the way now and be done with it. The moment lingered before Benjie finally broke his stare, and he drew a measured breath.

"You see that radio tower down there?" He pointed to a flashing red light hovering over the desert floor. "If I'm right, that's the tower at Agua Sienna. There's a garage there with a good mechanic, the kind who doesn't ask questions. He can get us back on the road. We'll make camp here tonight and hike down in the morning."

"And if you're wrong?"

Benjie turned, his jaw set, cold eyes on Vince.

"Look, music man, you want to start wrenching on the Jeep, be my guest. I'm waiting for morning and going down for help."

Vince elbowed me, rolling his eyes. "I guess he's in charge now," he whispered.

"Dammit," I said, "why the hell don't you give it a rest? We've got limited options here, and being a smart-ass isn't one of them." I looked at Eddie, challenged him with my eyes.

"He's right," Eddie said, picking up my cue. "We should listen to what Benjie says."

Vince waved us off and walked away, his shoulders hunched, the heat of defiance radiating. I'd never seen him like this, and I passed it off to stress, maybe an emotional reaction to the things he'd heard about his brother. Regardless, I needed to cool him down and ease the tension with Benjie. I walked over and put my hand on his shoulder.

"Let it ride, man. We'll lay low until morning, and then we'll get the hell out of this lousy country. Go back home to our kids."

Vince stared at a grove of trees in the distance. He lit a cigarette, hitting it deeply. Then he turned his head and gave me a small nod. It was good enough, and I walked away and let him be.

We went to work on our camp, clearing rocks and building a fire pit alongside the Jeep. Benjie dragged over a length of fallen tree trunk and he positioned it in front of the fire pit for us to lean on. Vince had a dog blanket in his car and Lupe had the blankets he'd brought from the El Diablo, along with several woven ponchos. He'd also brought along tortillas and beef jerky and a large block of cheese, all of it packed inside his duffel bags. I'm telling you, that kid was a regular Boy Scout, prepared for anything.

After we finished our work and we got settled, we had ourselves a nice little setup. The fire gave us warmth and the food was filling, and we had plenty of water to drink from the case of it we'd bought after leaving Hermosillo. Lupe pulled out a bottle of his grandfather's special recipe mescal and we took a few nips, just to take the edge off.

From our camp we had a clear view of the valley below, and our destination come morning. It was almost easy to forget our circumstances, and I tried to keep that mindset, that things weren't as bad as they seemed. It worked pretty well too. At least until morning came.

Thirty-two

T he Devil gained on me.
I ran hard through the open desert, dodging cactus and rattlesnakes, the red bastard poking my ass with his pitchfork and laughing like a freak. My feet felt burdened by lead boots, each step a monumental effort. I spotted a doorway in the side of a mountain and I went for it, the Devil hot on my heels, spewing his mangled non-sequiturs and disjointed stream-of-consciousness musings. And the really weird part? The Devil sounded like Eddie.

I made it to the door and crashed through, falling onto the floor of the Apache Bar, at the feet of Max Hollister and Barry Fitzgerald. They were laughing and dancing spastically like court jesters, lyrically repeating the same line: "we told you so, we told you so..."

You told me what? I don't understand.

I turned to face the Devil. He was different now, everything about him changed. He was a Sinaloa cowboy, his pitchfork morphed into a gun, an enormous Dirty Harry magnum. In his other hand he held a pair of boots, and he was licking his thin lips with a pointed tongue, grinning madly as he taunted me.

"Come and get them, gringo," the Devil said. "Come for the boots and fulfill your destiny."

Over the Devil's right shoulder I saw Lucinda and the kids, and standing next to them was Benjie. Off to the side, Kenny tended bar. He was laughing and winking at the Devil while throwing back shots of tequila and puffing on a foot-long cigar, blowing perfect smoke rings at Lupe, who sat tied in rope on top of the bar. Music played loudly through massive speakers suspended from the ceiling, Slow Ride *in an endless loop, accompanied by a mind-numbing psychedelic light show.*

The whole gang was here. Except for Vince. I asked the Devil what he did with my friend, I pleaded with him to tell me. Kenny laughed hysterically, his perverse grin and perfect teeth clenched on his stinking cigar. The Devil's mouth curled upward as he spoke, some indecipherable jive about choice and truth and fate.

"It makes no sense!" I screamed. "Please, God, help me. It makes no sense!"

"Stupid gringo," the Devil said, his voice a conciliating purr. "There is no God. There is only you and me, and what you choose."

I closed my eyes and wished it all away. And then a cruel awareness came over me, and when I opened my eyes I understood what the Devil meant. It was the boots for Vince. It was mine to choose or to lose. I could have the money or my friend, but not both.

The Devil dangled the boots like baubles as he transformed back into a pointy-tailed bastard, a blood-red vision of pure evil. The room gyrated and the lights flashed in rhythm with that damn song, and I heard Vince singing along. In between the verses he begged me to help him.

"Slow Ride, take it easy...please J.T., save me from this evil red bastard. Slow ride, take it easy...help me please!"

Laughing bled into singing and singing into flashing lights, the room spinning wildly as all the faces melted into one. The Devil howled great peals of laughter, his gun turning back into a pitchfork as he poked at me, pricking my flesh with each violent jab.

And then all at once it stopped, in one great flash of white-hot light. And in that flash, all that I was, and all that I would ever be, was gone.

"JACKSON, ARE YOU okay?"

I rubbed my eyes, tried to focus through a deep mental fog. Benjie sat across from me, his face obscured by smoke. "Are you okay?" he repeated.

"Damn, that was wicked," I mumbled.

"Dream?"

I nodded, gazing around the campsite. "Where are the others?"

"Vince and Lupe are sleeping in the Jeep. Eddie's rolled up in the blankets over there. You turned in a couple of hours ago." Benjie laughed. "The last few minutes you've been putting on a hell of a show."

"Have I? Man, this ordeal has me dreaming up some weird shit." I glanced at my watch; it was nearly three in the morning. "What about you? Don't you sleep?"

"Sure, I sleep. But someone's got to keep watch."

I studied Benjie's face through the haze of smoke and considered what he'd said. A rush of nerves pushed away the last vestiges of sleep, leaving an empty chill in its wake. "So what kind of trouble can we expect, when they find out?" I said.

"Hard to say. If we're lucky, that old sheriff will let it go. If not, he might bring in some help and come after us. Either way, we should have enough of a jump on them to make the border before any trouble starts."

"That's assuming we get the car fixed."

"Trust me, Jackson. One way or the other, we're driving out of here tomorrow. In *someone's* car."

The way Benjie said it left no doubt in my mind. We grew silent after that, the crackling fire and stiff breeze the only sounds. The gusts had a bite to them, and I pulled my blanket tighter, staring unfocused into the flames.

"So how'd you get roped into this shit anyway, Jackson? Did Vince talk you into it?"

"He isn't so bad."

"Says you. I see it differently."

"Did you know his wife died? It happened a couple of years ago. He's got two girls, and it's been a rough road ever since, raising them by himself. I'm not saying it excuses bad behavior, but it's something to consider."

Benjie looked off into the distance for a long minute. "We've all lost someone," he said, kicking at the fire, sending up a spiral of sparks and smoke.

The moment settled between us.

"Back to you, Jackson. Why the hell did you agree to this thing anyway? Did you just get bored with your life?"

"I need the money," I said.

"Ah yes, the pursuit of the filthy lucre. The downfall of all good men." Benjie chuckled sardonically. "So Kenny's offered you some cash, has he?"

"Thirty grand. Vince was giving me his half."

Benjie studied me, an odd, almost calculating look on his face.

"That's a lot of bread. Did he say why he wanted the boots so bad? I would've brought them back eventually. What's his hurry?"

I told Benjie the story Kenny gave me, feeling pretty foolish about it. That calculating look on Benjie's face intensified and I had the strong sense of something deeper at play. When I finished, Benjie said nothing, and every doubt I'd had for the past week came down on me at once, and I felt like the world's biggest fool.

"The fact is, I'm getting divorced," I said, feeling a strong urge to explain myself to this man I'd never met before, a man I'd likely never see again after this was over. "I need the money for a custody fight. Kenny's story might sound goofy as hell, but the money is real. At least the down payment he gave Vince is."

"How many kids do you have?"

"Two. A boy and a girl. How about you?"

"I was married for a while, but kids were never a part of that picture."

Benjie sipped from the bottle of Lupe's mescal. I held my hand out and he corked the bottle and tossed it over the fire. I took a hit, and tossed the bottle back.

"So yeah, I guess you could say I fell for the lure of easy money."

"A lot of men do, Jackson."

"My turn now," I said. "What's the deal with you and Kenny? And how the hell did you end up with his boots anyway?"

Benjie laughed. "Let's just say the boots involve a drunk redhead and a swimming pool, and leave it at that." He poked at the fire with a stick.

"And Kenny?"

Benjie stared impassively at the fire for a long moment. I studied his face, the resemblance to Kenny striking. They really did look like brothers, although Benjie clearly showed the wear and tear of harder miles. Physically he was a little bigger than Kenny, yet Benjie's demeanor exuded something much more substantial. Whereas Kenny had the look of carefully manufactured refinement, Benjie reflected a more honest and human quality. Let me put it this way. Kenny struck me as the kind of guy who *says* he'll stand by you. Benjie is the one who *will* stand by you.

"We ride together," Benjie said.

"You mean the Satans."

"Yeah, the Satans."

"I met your crew the other night at Weeds. Some of those dudes are weak."

"Nice, huh?" Benjie said dryly. "Those are Kenny's friends. Bunch of lawyers and financial types. None of them are worth a shit, you ask me."

"Fakers." I laughed under my breath.

"You got that right."

"And the others?" I was thinking about the big dude I ran into in Hermosillo.

"Those guys you don't want to mess with. That was Kenny's idea. Mix in some hard cases to give his club some street cred. It's all a big circus, you ask me."

"So what're you, the recruiter for the convicts?"

Benjie eyed me evenly. "I've done some time," he said coolly.

"So we're talking about guys you did time with?"

"Some of them. A few I know from the service."

Benjie didn't elaborate. I wanted to know more, but Max Hollister's words came back to me, about a man's business being his own. I held the silence and waited. After a long while, Benjie spoke.

"Let me tell you a story about that," he said. "After I got out of the service I stayed with my mom for a while, just to get my bearings. I'd been through some heavy shit and needed time to decompress. I hadn't seen or spoken to her for over two years.

"So I moved in with her and her boyfriend. This guy was a real piece of work. He drank all day and didn't work for shit, fancied himself some kind of Latin lover, running around town disrespecting my mom. He and I had major friction from the start. I didn't like him and he couldn't stand me, because he knew I saw right through him. I told my mom this guy was trouble, tried to drill it into her goddamn head. But she didn't want to hear any of that. She said she loved the guy.

"One day I came home and found this fool beating on my mom. He was drunk out of his gourd and spun way out of control. Man, I tore that bastard up. It took three neighbors to pull me off the guy. The cops got called and they rolled with four squad cars, guns drawn, the works. And you want to know the kicker? My mom had me arrested. She laid some bullshit rap on the cops about a simple domestic dispute that was under control until I came along and started beating the crap out of her helpless boyfriend. Can you believe it? And the dude pressed charges. My mom testified on his behalf, the jury felt sorry for both of them, and I ended up doing three to five for aggravated assault."

Benjie paused a moment, and took a deep breath.

"So off I go to the slammer. Meanwhile, my mom stayed with the loser, and you know how he repaid her? He broke her arm for letting me live with them in the first place. I found this out the one time she came to see me in the joint, right after I was sent up. She was a mess. I know she felt like shit for what she did to me, but she just couldn't say the words. And I would have forgiven her if she had. She made that one visit to ease her soul, and I never saw her again."

"But you saw her when you got out, right?"

"No, I didn't. And you know why? Because her boyfriend killed her two months after she visited me. No one told me anything about it either. I didn't find out until after I was paroled."

"What happened to the boyfriend?"

"He was killed making a drug buy three weeks after he capped my mom." Benjie stared at the fire, kicking at the embers. "I guess in the end, the situation took care of itself. Like most things in life."

Benjie hit the bottle. I stared at the fire, at the flames dancing in the breeze. I felt an emotional weight pressing down on me. A combination of shame and indignation, and a sense of pure helplessness.

"I'm sorry I asked," I said quietly.

"Don't be," Benjie said.

I signaled for the bottle. Benjie tossed it over and I took a long pull. I savored the burn in my throat, the immediate jolt coursing through me. I tossed the bottle back, watched Benjie take a hit. I thought about Kenny as I watched Benjie, and I knew intuitively that there was one hell of a story between those two, and that I'd been pulled into something far bigger than I could have ever imagined.

Thirty-three

The next day I woke up hard, my body aching from sleeping on the ground. A deep chill seeped into my bones, wrapping itself around every fiber of my being. It'd been a long time since I'd spent the night outdoors, long enough for me to forget how unpleasant it can be if you're not prepared for it.

The sun rose from behind the mountains, the eastern sky cloudless and colored a deep blue-black, golden light firing the silhouette of the Sierra Madres. A light breeze blew from the north, the morning air chilled. The others slept. I looked around for Benjie and saw that he was gone. I made a feeble attempt at stretching my knotted muscles before rising unsteadily and walking to the rock outcropping, slumping onto a sloped boulder and leaning back on it like it was a recliner.

Gazing down at Agua Sienna, I wondered how the hell we were going to get there. In the light of day the distance looked farther and more treacherous than I'd imagined. I wanted the binoculars but I was too dazed and unfocused to go back for them. Instead, I looked at the horizon and contemplated what new adventures this day would bring.

After a few minutes I heard footsteps behind me, and I turned to them abruptly. "Morning, Jackson," Benjie said as he neared.

"I thought you'd left already. Where were you?"

"Reconnoitering."

"Find anything?"

"This is desolate country we're in. Not much to find out here."

"You know it well?"

"I've spent some time down here." Benjie walked past me to the far point of the outcropping. He stood there for a long moment. Then he spoke to me with his back turned. "Wake the others and get the camp broken down. I want the car loaded and ready to go before the mechanic gets here."

"So what's the plan?" I said, easing off my recliner and stepping up to Benjie's shoulder.

"I go down alone. The fewer strangers the better."

"What about Vince?"

"What about him?"

"Am I going to have to referee some kind of bullshit between you two?"

"It depends."

"On what?"

"On how he chooses to play it."

A moment passed. I wished I had some coffee. I wished like hell I was back home. Benjie turned his head slightly; sharp features and a determined set in his eyes, the look of a man not easily swayed. He gave me a small nod.

"Don't worry about it, Jackson. I've got more important things to deal with right now, and Vince isn't one of them."

We moved through the camp then, rousing the others. Benjie went back to the outcropping, eyeballing the town through the binoculars while he consulted the map. The wind gusted and stirred up a cloud of ash from the fire pit. It was a cold wind, driving the air temperature down. Clouds massed across the southern sky, and countless birds chirped a singsong morning chorus high up in the rustling trees. I observed all of this with an odd sort of detachment, like I was there, but not *really* there. More than anything, I felt a heavy sense of anticipation hovering over us, as if something was about to blow wide open. It was that damn intuition again, sending signals for me to watch out.

In fifteen minutes the car was loaded and ready to go. Vince sat in the front passenger seat, stretched out with his eyes closed. Lupe hunted for a lizard scurrying near the front of the Jeep. Eddie just wandered about, seemingly lost as he mumbled about what a shitty deal it all was.

I was standing at the rear of the Jeep, stowing my guitar, when a distant sound echoed from above the tree line. I stopped and listened, picking out a muffled din that seemed to get louder, undulating in intensity. Vince heard it too, and he turned to me, his eyes questioning. Within seconds the sound became a steady thundering rumble. I started to say something, but never got the chance.

Three quick pops rang out. The guitar case jerked in my hand as the side window of the Jeep shattered and blew pieces all over me. At the same moment, two motorcycles bore down on us like mechanical beasts descended from above.

"Take cover!" Benjie yelled.

I dove for the ground. Lupe screamed as more shots rang out. One of the riders circled the Jeep and pointed his weapon, firing erratically as I rolled under the vehicle. The bikers swung around and disappeared. I crawled out from under the Jeep and peered around the side. Vince was frantically digging through the glove box. It took a second for it to register—*he was going for his gun*.

The attackers came down the hill for another pass, running side by side before splitting off as they neared. A quick burst of gunfire stitched the ground in front of me and I curled into a ball, making myself small. The sound of a third gun rang out, and I poked my head up and saw Vince shooting wildly through the open passenger window, using the door for cover. Out of the corner of my eye I saw Eddie running madly toward the trees, before a burst of gunfire forced me down. Ten seconds later it stopped, and the two bikes fishtailed back up the hill, obscured by a cloud of dust. It grew quiet, the breeze blowing the smell of gunpowder and dirt and exhaust heavy through the air.

"You guys okay?" Benjie shouted from his cover at the rock outcropping.

"Si, I am inside the car," Lupe said, his voice trembling.

"I'm good too," Vince said. "What the hell's happenin'? Who are those guys?"

"Jackson, Eddie, are you guys okay?"

The bikes idled up on the hill. Eddie didn't answer. About ten yards away I saw feet sticking out from behind some sagebrush. My heart thumped wildly at the sight. "I'm okay," I yelled, my voice pinched by nerves. "But Eddie's down."

"Jackson, grab the tire iron and toss it over here," Benjie yelled back. I found it in the utility compartment, a nice old school jack handle, one with some heft to it, and I heaved it over to the rocks where Benjie was hiding. Then the next wave came.

The two bikers attacked coming down the hill, firing with precision. The car windows exploded and the tires popped, and a spray of bullets peppered the side of the Jeep. It was a goddamn shooting gallery.

When the bikes were nearly on top of us, I saw Vince stand, blazing away with his pistol. One of the assailants went down, flipped off the back of his machine, his bike rolling another thirty feet before toppling over in a weed patch.

The other biker circled around and came on fast, firing as he bore down on us. Benjie timed it just right, jumping out from the rocks and swinging the tire iron, hitting the guy square in the face as he roared by. The dude sprawled off his bike, and Benjie attacked viciously. Vince came around and together we pulled Benjie off the biker.

Lupe walked over then, his face ashen. "I think Mr. Eddie is hurt. He is not moving, over there."

Vince went to investigate while Benjie dragged the bloody biker to the side of the Jeep and propped him up. When Vince returned, he was visibly shaken. "Eddie's dead, he's got a goddamn hole in his head." His eyes went unfocused. "Holy hell, what just happened?"

Benjie walked over to the fallen biker, the one shot off his motorcycle. He crouched down and checked his pulse. He stood and returned to the Jeep, shaking his head.

I looked over at the dead man; saw his jacket with the O.C. Satans insignia. Then I turned and looked at the wounded man leaning against the side of the Jeep, every nerve in my body tingling with fire as the truth hit me hard. He was the guy I ran into in Hermosillo, the one I saw at the border. I stared at Benjie.

"You know these guys," I said.

"Yeah, I know them. This piece of shit is Johnny Scoots. The dead guy is Willy Stiles, better known as Boxhead." Benjie stared at the wounded biker. "So what's the deal, Johnny, why the party?"

"Kiss my ass."

"Wrong answer." Benjie kicked him hard in the side. "Talk, goddammit."

Johnny shook his head and laughed, spitting blood. "Benjie Cole, always the badass. What's the matter, can't figure this one out on your own?"

Benjie grabbed the jack handle, swung it two-handed at Johnny's shoulder, producing a sickening sound like muscle tearing from bone. Johnny gasped and leaned over.

"Do you see us laughing?" Benjie said, breathing hard. "Why'd you ambush us?"

Johnny glared; grinning like it was some kind of game.

"Vince, toss me your piece." Benjie kept his eyes on Johnny. Vince hesitated. "Now!" Benjie shouted.

Vince tossed the gun and backed away from Benjie.

"I could say that what we have here is a failure to communicate." Benjie spoke with his back turned. He ejected the magazine from the pistol and checked the load, slammed it back in place. "But that would be a cliché. A bad one too." He looked off into the distance, tapping the pistol against his thigh.

"It's time for a little game, Johnny. I ask you a question. If you answer correctly, we're cool. If not, then I get to shoot you. What do you say, man?"

Johnny spit on the ground. "Kiss my ass, stumpy."

Without warning, Benjie spun around and shot Johnny in the shoulder, the same one he'd whacked with the tire iron.

"Goddamn it!" Johnny screamed, gritting his teeth and sucking air.

"Now that's a damn fine shot, I'd say." Benjie gave out an interrogator's laugh. "So once again, tell me what's going on here. Either you start talking, or I keep shooting, one limb at a time."

Johnny was in bad shape. Blood covered the side of his face, and he leaned to one side, holding onto his shoulder. His nose looked broken, and for the first time I noticed his leg sticking out at a weird angle.

Benjie was the picture of controlled rage. He stared at Johnny with a look so hateful it haunted me for a long time. "I'm waiting," Benjie whispered hoarsely.

"Fuck off," Johnny mumbled, his voice nearly incoherent.

Benjie shot him in the other shoulder.

"Now you have two fucked-up shoulders, and I'm losing patience. I *will* kill you, Johnny, and you know it. So here's the deal. You tell me what I want to know, and I'll send someone up here to help you. But then again, maybe you can just crawl out of here on your own. The town's only a few miles away. That's probably what I'd do, rather than wait for the wolves to take me. So what's it gonna be, cowboy?"

Benjie knelt down, putting the gun barrel up against Johnny's knee, the one on the bent leg. Johnny looked like he wanted to cry, but damn if he didn't hold it together. Benjie pressed the pistol in, and started counting.

"One. Two. Three…"

"All right!" Johnny yelled. Benjie raised the pistol and fired into the dirt a few feet away. "Kenny sent us down here to find you." Johnny shook violently, like he was having a seizure.

"What did you say?"

"Kenny sent me and Boxhead to find you. That dude Eddie was working with us, keeping tabs on your friends. We've been following them since they hit Nogales."

Johnny leaned his head back and closed his eyes, his breath ragged. When he opened his eyes, he looked at me, and tossed off a smug laugh.

"You almost made me, dude, back there in Hermosillo." He closed his eyes again, his head lolled to one side. I walked in closer and stared down at him.

"It was you, wasn't it? Wednesday night, outside the El Presidente."

"What the fuck you talking about?"

"You brought Eddie back to the hotel. It was late, I heard you ride up on your bike."

"You mean the night Eddie took off from the El Burro?" Vince said. He was lighting a cigarette, his hands shaking so badly he could hardly line the flame up with the tip.

"You were asleep, Vince. I heard this guy ride up on his bike, and a few minutes later Eddie crept into our room. We were drunk. I thought it was a dream."

"You got me. Good for you. You want a fuckin' gold star or somethin'?" Johnny said spitefully.

"Something happened between you two. Eddie was spooked as shit the next day. What'd you do to him?"

Johnny hacked uncontrollably. When it subsided, he spoke in a wet-sounding whisper.

"Eddie wanted out. Said he had second thoughts. I told him a deal was a deal, there were no outs. Kenny already paid him a pile of cash. I had to knock him around a little just to straighten his punk ass out. Freaky little twerp. I never liked that dude anyway."

Another coughing fit, harder now, the gurgling sound intensifying.

"Give me a smoke, man."

Benjie nodded to Vince; Johnny was on his last ride. Vince lit one and stuck it in the biker's mouth. Johnny took a few deep drags.

"I should've capped that punk right then. It's not like we needed him anymore. Kenny said this might happen, that Eddie would piss backwards on their deal, so he set us up with a GPS tracker. It's been on your goddamn ride since Hermosillo."

Johnny sucked on his smoke. I felt a stab of guilt over Eddie and my shitty attitude toward him. Maybe in the end he tried to do the right thing. There would be no winners in this deal.

"Why did Kenny send you?" Benjie said. "I know it wasn't just to find me. Shit, he's the one who sent me down here in the first place, to find Butch."

Johnny laughed, triggering another violent coughing spasm, shaking the cigarette out of his mouth. He didn't pick it up.

"What's so goddamn funny?"

"Butch Davey's been dead since last summer. He bought it in Santa Fe."

For the first time Benjie looked shaken. It was only for a second, but it was there all the same. He quickly regained his composure. "Finish it," he said evenly.

"Finish what?"

"Why did Kenny send you down here?"

"The boots, man. He sent us for the boots."

"Did he say why?"

"Why what?" Johnny said, his voice flat.

"Why does he want them? What's his game?"

"Like I know? You know how it is with Kenny. He said he wanted 'em, threw a sack of cash at us and said to get it done. And that's what we did. Or tried to." Johnny grimaced and convulsed into a coughing fit. "You gonna get me some help now?"

Benjie ignored him. He tucked the pistol into his waistband and walked over to the fallen motorcycles. He fired up the first one and it roared to life. He tried the second bike—the dead guy's machine—and after a couple of strokes he got it running. Leaving them to idle, Benjie walked back to us. "Let's ride."

Benjie set his gaze on a point far into the distance, his face hardened, his stance coiled tight. He turned and stood over Johnny.

"So was all of this on Kenny's orders, or did you and that dead fool over there improvise?"

Johnny stared back through lifeless eyes. "He said it would be best for everyone if you didn't come back. Me and Boxhead worked out the rest."

Benjie said nothing. He turned and gave us a nod. It was time to go. We collected our gear and moved it to the bikes. I took special care with my guitar, stuffing it awkwardly into one of the saddlebags. No way was I leaving it behind, not after all this. It was a meaningless gesture really, one I passed off to shock.

In a few minutes the bikes were ready to go. Lupe rode with Vince and I rode with Benjie. Johnny stayed behind to keep Eddie and Boxhead company. I spent exactly thirty seconds thinking about that, and then pushed it from my mind. The time for reconciliation would come later. Right now it was about survival. Survival and escape. Escape from a nightmare.

Thirty-four

We rode hard for endless hours across brutal terrain, on a dead man's bike. I lost track of time during that long ride, a non-stop filmstrip running through my brain. But to what end, all that thinking? After all, shit happens, and then you live with it.

We finally made Nogales and sought refuge at the Ranchero Hotel, in the same room we'd rented just a few days earlier, back when Eddie was still alive. I could not begin to fathom it, nor could I comprehend the utter madness we'd left behind; two people dead, a third barely hanging on, left to die in that lonely and desolate place. All for a pair of boots.

It was beyond twisted. It was a sick game orchestrated by a madman. I could logically retrace the steps that had led me here, but I completely lacked the ability to understand any of it. Why didn't I see it coming?

But that was surely an absurd thought. How could I have possibly seen something like this? This was Hollywood movie stuff, a plot cooked up in some fiction writer's head. This kind of thing isn't supposed to happen in real life. Yet it did happen. And now only one question remained; where do we go from here? The answer came when Lupe crashed through the front door.

"THE POLICE ARE on the street, and they are talking to the manager, and…" Lupe was nearly hyperventilating. Benjie calmed him down.

"Steady, Lupe. Take it slow and easy, and tell me what you saw."

"The police, they are looking for us. I hear them talking about Concepción, and they say—"

"Where are they now?"

"On the other side of the hotel. They are taking the people out of the rooms."

"Stay here," Benjie said to us.

He left the room. Vince crawled up on the sofa and peered through the window. He was draped in the cartoon curtain with a cowboy on one side and an Indian on the other, arrows and bullets aimed at his head, just like our predicament. We were getting it from all sides now.

"See anything?" I said.

"Not a damn thing."

Benjie entered the room. "They found the bikes. We've got to split. Now."

"How? We have no car."

"I'll handle it, Jackson," Benjie said sharply. "You guys just be ready to haul ass when I get back." He slipped out the door again.

From outside I heard bullhorn commands shouted in Spanish; they were getting closer. Lupe and I gathered our stuff and moved it near the door. Vince kept watch out the window. Ten agonizing minutes later we heard a car horn blare.

Vince turned to us. "He's back."

We grabbed our gear and stepped through the door. Benjie sat behind the wheel of a rusted old taxi, waving at us to get moving. We piled in and Benjie hit the gas before we got the doors shut. I looked out the rear window, saw cops turning the corner, pointing at our cab and shouting. Benjie tore across the front of the Ranchero and fishtailed around the big oak tree, reached the end of the street and turned right. He accelerated past the Apache Bar, skidding a hard left at the corner. Two police cruisers came in from the right and hitched onto our tail. Benjie floored it, cresting a small hill and catching air. We hit the pavement hard, rattling the taxi to its frame. Benjie made a quick right down a narrow dirt alley, driving with focused precision, like an experienced wheelman.

We barreled down the alley and turned left onto a paved street, the cops glued to our ass. Two more rights and a left brought us onto a wide boulevard. Benjie kept his foot in it, the speedometer hitting ninety as we nearly clipped a pedestrian, forcing the cops to slow down behind us. Benjie took advantage and gunned it, heading straight for a crowded intersection. "Hold on!" he yelled, his eyes locked on the road as he punched the accelerator, the wheezing engine about played out.

I grabbed the handle above the door and braced for impact. Vince leaned over and covered Lupe in the back seat. Benjie drilled it through the intersection, tagging the rear end of a pick-up truck and sending it spinning into two other vehicles. He righted the taxi and blew down the street, our pursuers swerving to miss the wreckage we'd left behind. They didn't make it. Nogales Demolition Derby unfolded in our rear window, confusion and chaos covering our tracks.

Benjie continued along at a good clip for a couple of miles, before slowing abruptly and making a quick turn onto a narrow side street. Dropping to low cruising speed, he scanned the side of the street, as if consulting a mental map. We were near the border now, so close to home I could feel it. Benjie turned into a dirt alley, dilapidated wood structures on the left, a small hill and the border fence to our right. He stopped after a hundred yards.

"Vince, get out and open that door over there." Benjie pointed to the right, at a wood shack built into the side of the hill. "You help him, Jackson."

We got out and forced open the heavy sliding door. Benjie eased the taxi inside and we followed, pulling the door shut, enveloping us in darkness. Narrow shafts of light pierced the uneven wood siding, and it took a few minutes for my eyes to adjust. The shack's dimensions barely fit the taxi, leaving just enough room to walk. Benjie killed the engine and it coughed roughly before dying out. After a few minutes we heard the sound of an approaching vehicle. Benjie squeezed out of the cab and he moved over to the right side of the sliding door. He motioned for silence, pointed to his eyes, then to a gap in the doorjamb, signaling for me to look out.

A police cruiser drove up the alley and pulled even with the shack, its wheels crunching gravel. The cop left his engine idling, black exhaust seeping into the shack, watering my eyes. He stepped out of his vehicle and stood a few feet from me, close enough for me to smell his rank body odor masked by cheap cologne. He was a skinny guy with a greasy, pockmarked complexion. He wore a Stetson hat and aviator glasses, and he had one of those kiddie-raper mustaches, thin and wispy. He walked up to the sliding door and unzipped, started pissing against the door, farting loudly in the process.

I didn't know if I should laugh or cry. When I looked at Benjie, I saw him easing Vince's pistol from his waistband. I made eye contact, saw nothing but coldness there, and I knew that if it came down to it, Benjie would kill the cop.

The cop finished his business and zipped up. He lit a cigarette and leaned against his dusty cruiser, quietly smoking. The guy seemed to be waiting for something. Then his car radio barked, harsh commands distorted by static.

"Encuentra los americanos. Arresto Benjie Cole inmediatamente. Él es muy peligroso, tenga cuidado."

The cop reached in and shut off the radio. I shot Benjie a look. I may not understand Spanish, but I sure as hell know what *americanos* and *Benjie Cole* mean. Benjie stared back, eyes empty as he gripped the pistol in both hands.

I looked through the gap and saw the cop staring right at our door. He crushed out his smoke and walked a few steps away, out of my sight. I prepared myself for the inevitable, reaching for a two-by-four leaning against the wall. Vince stood frozen by the front of the car, his eyes on the gun in Benjie's hand. The motionless air felt charged with the freakish energy of impending doom.

My heart beat wildly, threatening to blow right through my chest, and my legs felt like wobbly sticks ready to break. I braced myself against the wall for support. Benjie stood calm, steely concentration etched on his face. He was ready. Everything about the guy said he was born ready.

A woman's voice came into the picture then, girlish in nature, almost giggling. The cop moved into my view. He held a woman in his arms, kissing her neck and grabbing her tits. I couldn't believe it. This is what he was waiting for? The tension rolled off me as my heart rate ramped down, and I set the two-by-four aside and slumped against the wall.

The cop and the woman were going at it heavy now, panting and whispering sweet Spanish nothings. He pushed her to the rear of his cruiser and opened the door, tried to shove her in while he fumbled with his pants. I couldn't believe it. Romeo was going to try and knock a piece off right in front of us.

But the woman wasn't having it. She protested and the cop got frustrated, and in mere seconds the throes of passion turned into a full-on argument. He called her a *puta* and slapped her face. She screamed and ran. The cop jumped into his cruiser and sped off in the other direction.

"Shit, that was close," Benjie said tightly.

"What is this place?" Vince said. "It looks like there was a tunnel here."

Benjie walked to the rear wall of the shack, to the remains of an opening cut into the hillside. "It's a smuggler tunnel," he said. "It runs under the border and dumps out about fifty yards on the other side, inside an old service station. Or at least it used to. I had no idea they'd found it."

"How do you know about it?" I said. Benjie didn't answer. I moved closer to him and stared into his eyes. "Come on, man, tell us what's really going on here. We all heard that radio. They're looking for you. Who the hell are you?"

"Not now, Jackson."

"Screw that. We have to know what we're up against."

"Yeah, tell us why we shouldn't just bail on you right now," Vince said.

"Because you need me, that's why."

"Bullshit," Vince said.

Benjie laughed scornfully. "You two amateurs will never make it out of here on your own."

I stepped in front of Vince to separate him from Benjie. "Tell us the truth," I said.

The heat inside the shack was stifling, the musty smell overpowering. Lupe watched us from inside the car, his eyes wide, as if anticipating another blowup. The whole thing was futile, that much was clear. Benjie seemed to realize it too.

"Yes," he said, exhaling wearily. "There are people looking for me. That's why—"

"Who the hell are you, fucking Waldo?" I said. "Everyone's looking for you. Kenny. Those crazy bikers. Us. The goddamn Mexican police. Did I miss anyone?"

Benjie glared at me, his jaw tightening. He sucked in a breath and continued speaking in a measured tone. "That's why that sheriff waylaid me. The reasons don't matter right now. Later, after we get home, I'll tell you the whole deal. If you even care by that point."

Benjie held his eyes on mine, and for the first time I saw how tired he was, exhausted really. I glanced from Lupe to Vince, overwhelmed by it all. "So what now?" I said quietly.

"We need some different wheels," Benjie said. "And we need to get somewhere safe, where we can regroup and figure a way across the border."

"What do you mean 'figure' a way?" I said.

"Come on, Jackson, look around you. They're onto us. We can't just waltz across the border."

"But how the hell did they find us?" Vince said.

"It doesn't matter. They did, and that's all you need to know."

"Can't we explain it to the border agents?" I said. "Tell them what happened?"

"Listen you two," Benjie said, the edge back in his voice. "All we have is right now. Tomorrow doesn't exist without today, and the past is just yesterday's news. Right now we're on the run from people who do not give a shit about you or me or anyone else. Make no mistake about that. You might think they're a bunch of clowns down here, but trust me, they *will* find us, and when they do, they'll go hard on us, harder than you can ever imagine. You think that—"

"All right, we get it. Okay?" Vince shot back. "Enough already. Just tell us what to do."

Benjie's face went blank, a twitch in his left eye as a bead of sweat rolled down the right side of his face. "Like I said, we need another car. You guys stay here. I'm going out to see what I can find."

As Benjie slid the door open, Lupe spoke. "I can help," he said.

He was out of the car, standing next to us. Benjie turned. "How?"

"I know a guy. He can help us."

"A guy?" I said.

"Si, a guy. He owns a junk yard and he has many old cars and trucks, and I think perhaps I can go to him and he will give me one of the old cars for us to use. Yes, I believe he will do this for me."

"You're sure?" Benjie said.

"Si. I can get us a car."

"How long will it take?"

"Perhaps one hour, maybe less. But I must go now. You can trust me to do this." Lupe reached out and touched Benjie's arm.

Benjie responded with a crooked smile, and Lupe took off running.

Thirty-five

"He's gonna bail," Vince said.

He was sitting on an overturned wooden crate, throwing a knife into the dirt between his feet, repeatedly sticking it into the ground a little more forcefully each time. It was a pearl-handled switchblade he'd bought at a roadside stand just outside Culiacán, in Sinaloa.

The stand was some kind of shrine to a man named *Jesús Malverde*, a bandit from back in the days of the Mexican Revolution, a guy revered by outlaws and traffickers as some kind of narco saint. They sold all kinds of Malverde swag at that little roadside stand; candles and incense, lithographs and little plastic figurines formed in his likeness, cassette tapes full of that narcocorrido jive dedicated to his exploits. And knives, lots of knives, from little toad-stickers to Rambo-like man killers.

"Trust me, he ain't comin' back," Vince said again, as he folded the knife and slid it into his back pocket. Benjie's eyes bored into him.

"He'll be back. That kid has more grit than you'll ever know, and he'll stick to the end. Maybe you ought to study him, Vince, learn a thing or two."

Vince ignored Benjie, and he turned to me.

"How 'bout you, Jackson? You think that kid's comin' back?"

"Jesus, Vince. Ease up on the bullshit."

I was in no mood for games. Our hideout was barely tolerable, rife with heat and foul air, and funky body odor. The truth is Lupe had been gone for a long damn time. The waiting was excruciating. There was simply no way to stop the bad thoughts banging around inside my head. At the point I couldn't take it anymore, I heard a loud rumbling.

Benjie moved to the door, a sly grin crossing his face as he peered through. "Let's move," he said, as he slid the door open and stepped out. We collected our gear and followed. What I saw outside nearly made me fall over.

Lupe had returned driving an ice cream truck. It was a 1950s vintage panel truck, one side painted over with the faded image of a clown holding an enormous ice cream cone piled high with a dozen teetering scoops, forming a wobbly arc over the clown's head. Lupe flashed a wide grin as Benjie opened the rear doors, solid except for a pair of porthole windows, and we climbed in.

"You're something else, kid." Benjie laughed. He crawled forward and whispered into Lupe's ear, and Lupe nodded in reply. Then Benjie eased back against the side of the truck and closed his eyes.

"Where we headed?" Vince had to shout to be heard above the sputtering whine of the engine, clearly misfiring on a cylinder or two.

"Outside of town," Benjie said.

Lupe drove slowly, struggling to keep the boxy truck steady, his feet barely reaching the pedals. Benjie nixed the idea of one of us driving, said it was too conspicuous. I guess a kid driving an ice cream truck isn't. Damn, only in Mexico. After a few blocks, Lupe shouted back at us.

"Hey, amigos, I think perhaps there is a problem."

Benjie crawled up to the front of the truck. Vince slid to the rear and looked out one of the portholes. "Oh man, this ain't good."

I moved next to Vince and looked out, saw a group of kids chasing after our truck, like kids everywhere are supposed to do when the ice cream man comes rolling down the street. I scrambled up front and crowded in next to Benjie. There were kids running alongside the truck, yelling at Lupe to stop. He kicked at them through the open door, shouting in Spanish, trying to shoo the mob away.

Lupe swerved like a midnight drunk; the truck threatening to tip over, the kids laughing like it was all part of the show. We passed a side street and I saw a patrol car heading toward us. Before I could warn Benjie my words were cut short by a rock hurled through the door, sailing past Lupe's nose and shattering the window on the other side. The kids were stretched out in a line down both sides of the truck, and they were pissed off we weren't stopping. Angry voices rose in unison as more rocks pelted the truck.

"Guys, we got trouble here!" Vince shouted from the back.

Benjie ordered Lupe to stop, and he reached across, slid the door shut and locked it. The gang of kids rushed us, crowding up against both sides of the truck, pounding on the thin metal. Benjie moved to the rear of the truck and looked through the porthole. I scampered back and shoved Vince out of my way, looked out the other porthole and saw two police cruisers lined up about thirty feet behind us. The cop in front was on his radio, the one behind was standing next to his open door, staring at the back of our truck.

"What now?" I said.

Benjie reached for Lupe's backpack, pulling several sticks of dynamite out. He twisted the fuses together and looked up. "Either of you guys have a light?"

Vince tossed his lighter. Benjie laid it out for us.

"I'm going to light this shit up and toss it out the back. We bail out the front of this heap and run for that corner up on the right. We regroup there and move out. You guys got it?"

"They're coming," I said.

"I'm on it, Jackson." Benjie gathered himself. "Lupe, get over by the passenger door, get ready to open it." Benjie looked around the truck. "Grab whatever you can carry or leave it behind. We got to move fast."

Benjie lit the twisted fuses and shoved the sticks into the backpack, and in one quick movement he kicked the rear doors open and tossed the backpack. It flew in a slow-motion arc, little streams of smoke trailing its descent, landing in a puff of dust and sliding under the front of the first police cruiser. One cop looked at the other, wide eyes signaling awareness. Instantly both of them turned and dove away from their vehicles, as the dynamite exploded into a massive fireball.

The cruiser in front was lifted off the ground and thrown violently backwards, landing on top of the car behind it. The two cops were tossed sideways like rag dolls. The kids scattered as an enormous dust cloud blew through the rear doors of the truck, consuming us in choking grittiness. My ears rang like huge bells, reducing sounds to a low and muffled pitch. Benjie's voice cut through the confusion.

"Let's go! Move it, now!"

We grabbed our gear and bailed out of the truck. The street was empty, the police cars reduced to burning hulks, shooting plumes of thick black smoke straight up into the sky, a beacon for the reinforcements that were surely on the way. We scrambled for the corner, crowding into an alcove leading to a narrow stairwell. Benjie took off running, disappearing onto a side street. Agonizing minutes ticked by, an eternity before he returned. When he did, he rolled up behind the wheel of a chopped-top Cadillac Coupe de Ville. He yelled at us to get in, and we took off in our third getaway car of the day.

Benjie told us to duck down and hide ourselves. After ten minutes of fast driving he slowed to a leisurely pace, just another Sunday driver enjoying a pleasant Mexican evening. Benjie gave us the all clear, and we rose slowly. He parked the car at the edge of a quiet neighborhood in front of a large public park, a soccer game in progress. We piled out of the car. Vince lit a smoke and

I took one too, the nicotine calming my nerves. I looked at Benjie, drew down on my smoke before speaking.

"What now?" I said.

"I'm not sure," Benjie said.

Vince paced the sidewalk, mumbling to himself.

"Damn, what a scene. Can you believe it, Jackson? Outrageous, man. Fuckin' outrageous. I'll tell ya what, I could sure use some of Barry's weed right about now. Mellow my ass right out. I say we—"

"That's it," Benjie said.

"What's it?"

"Our way out."

Thirty-six

Two hours past sunset and thirty miles outside Nogales, we approached a long valley surrounded by a wide expanse of endless desert. We came from the east, skirting the high side of the valley before easing our way down a long and evenly graded road. As we descended, I saw a large Quonset hut surrounded by several smaller buildings arrayed in a lazy semicircle. The cluster of structures anchored the center point of a runway, a plane parked at one end, its fuselage shining brightly under a pair of pole-mounted floodlights standing guard on either side.

Benjie killed the headlights as we passed under an arched sign that read *Fitzgerald Aviation & Sky Tours*. He pulled to a stop and parked under a tree a short distance from the Quonset hut, near an abutment of boulders. We exited the car and walked single file, our shoes on gravel the only sound. Nearing building, Benjie motioned for me to look through a small window set into a side door, while he continued on to the front of the building. Smudged grime distorted my view, and I turned with a shrug. Benjie whispered to Vince, who was casually lighting a cigarette.

"Go check the other side. And put that damn smoke out until we're sure it's clear."

Vince flicked the cigarette aside and walked away. Benjie turned to Lupe. "You go sit in the car, and stay low. I'll come and get you when we're ready." Lupe nodded and disappeared with cat-like stealth.

"So why the sneaking around?" I said. "I thought this dude was your friend."

"He is. But I like to know what I'm dealing with before I go into something. The line of work Barry is in, you can never be too careful."

Suddenly, a loud crash like empty tin buckets falling from a shelf echoed from the other side of the hangar. Benjie turned swiftly and I froze, while at the same time a jacked shotgun sounded directly behind me, along with a lazy voice.

"Don't move, or I'll slay you where you stand."

"Barry? Is that you?" I said.

"Barry ain't here. And he ain't comin' back for a long time." The voice chuckled perversely.

Benjie looked over my shoulder, his face revealing nothing. The man with the shotgun spoke again. "Step into the light so I can see your faces. Put your hands up too, where I can see them. And tell that big ugly dude to move in closer."

Benjie stepped carefully around me, standing at my side, facing the guy who had the drop on us. I turned slowly and saw double barrels poking through a slotted opening in the side of the hangar, and two eyeballs showing from another slot above.

"I think we should run for it," Benjie said casually. "If we're lucky, this dude will miss. That's a tough shot to make."

"Are you nuts?" I said under my breath. "He'll cut us in two. My ninety-year-old grandmother could make that shot."

"Yeah, but his sight line isn't good. I think we can make it." Benjie glanced at me. "You know what they say. Nothing ventured, nothing gained. So what do you say, on three?"

"No way, I'm not moving. You do whatever you want."

"Smart choice, because I *will* shoot you," the man with the shotgun said.

"One."

"No way, Benjie."

"Two."

"I'm not doing it, man."

"Three."

Benjie leapt sideways and I closed my eyes. The man fired. My ears rang and my heart beat wildly, the shot going over my head. I heard a door creak open, and when I opened my eyes, I saw Barry Fitzgerald step out, a shotgun cradled in one arm. He hugged Benjie for a long minute.

"You guys are such assholes," I said in disgust, and turned and walked away.

"NO SHIT, YOU guys blew the jail at Concepción?"

Barry giggled as he twisted a fat number. He flashed his Buffett grin and fired the joint, passing it on. Benjie and I declined; Vince partook with a vengeance.

"Far out, man. I heard talk on the shortwave about some kind of commotion down that way. Now it makes sense why the heat's on. They got the goddamn border locked down tighter'n Nixon's ass. Benjie my man, up to his old ways."

We were in Barry's office, partitioned off in a corner of the Quonset hut, a picture window allowing for a view of the hangar interior. Out in the center sat a dismantled airplane, parts strewn about the floor. The rest of the space was taken up with workbenches and rolling toolboxes. The office was cluttered, with piles of books and files and loose papers scattered about. Faded maps and aeronautical charts lined the walls, and a stack of flight cases crowded one corner, held in place by several oversized duffel bags piled up and bulging suspiciously.

"What happened to that other dude, the quiet one with the weird eyes?"

Barry ripped a toke. I glanced at Vince and he looked away quickly. Several seconds passed. "He didn't make it," Benjie finally said.

"Bummer, dude," Barry said with no humor. He extinguished the roach, slipped it into his shirt pocket. I guess it's verboten to get high while speaking of the dead.

"So you see our predicament," Benjie said, getting back on track. "We need a ride home, and we need it now."

"Where'd you have in mind for a drop?"

"Mojave. That spot outside of Ridgecrest."

"No dice, bud. The DEA plowed it over last month. No big loss, it was too damn close to China Lake anyway. So where you been hiding yourself, brother? You split town kinda quick."

"Around," Benjie said. "Did you know they buried the Nogales tunnel?"

"The Terrible Herbst? Yeah, I heard about that, happened a while ago. Federales made a big show of it too, gonna prove to Uncle Sammy how committed they are to winning the war on drugs. What a joke. The weed they burned was bales of hay, while the good stuff got stashed in a safe house right there in town. Can you figure that? I'm telling you, the bastards running the show down here are goddamn incorrigible."

Barry reached for a bottle of Gentleman Jack and some shot glasses. He set a round for each of us. "Tell you what," he said, pouring the shots. "Now you know why I stick to air travel. Tunnels are strictly jive." He raised his glass for a toast. "Here's to good friends and good times, and a healthy dose of good luck."

Barry threw his shot down. I went for it, the liquor burning its way to my empty gut. A mellow wave washed over me, tamping down frayed nerves. Barry lined up another round.

"And here's to the ones we've left behind," he said solemnly, raising his glass. We joined him in a moment of silence for Eddie, then we shot the booze and my brain flipped out.

"How about some tunes?" Barry said.

He rummaged through a box of cassettes, reading labels and discarding casually, until he found what he wanted. He popped the tape into the player and turned up the volume. The thundering drum intro to Zeppelin's *When the Levee Breaks* descended from two overhead speakers. My whiskey-soaked brain transformed the beat into an ominous behemoth stomping its way into the valley, threatening to crush Fitzgerald Aviation and all who dared enter. I planted my feet to steady myself, gripping the arms of my chair tightly. I pictured John Bonham in the stairwell of Headley Grange, banging away at the skins as he recorded one of the heaviest drum tracks in all of rock and roll.

"So Mojave is out. What else is there?" Benjie lit a cigarette. He sounded far away, nearly drowned out by Robert Plant's wicked harmonica, locked in with the rock-steady beat.

"In California? Not a whole lot," Barry said, his voice sounding thin and stretched out. "Plenty of places in Arizona though. It's gotta be Cali?"

"Yeah, it does."

They went on like that for a minute or two, back and forth, running through their list of smuggler hot spots. Jimmy Page's guitar kicked in, followed by the demonic vocal.

If it keeps on rainin', levee's goin' to break...

Barry lit the joint and ripped a toke, passing it to Vince. My perception skewed and everything around me went into slow motion. Robert Plant wailed on.

Cryin' won't help you, prayin' won't do you no good...

Secondhand reefer smoke curled around my brain, working its way into my impaired cells, my heart pounding in time with Bonham's incessant beat. Benjie got up and walked over to a large map taped to the wall. He traced his finger across it, his face inches from the map. He tapped a spot decisively.

"How about the chicken strip?"

Barry looked up. "That's an idea. You know, they did some work on it about a year ago, sweetened it up real nice. Weather's good right now too, and with the moon out it'll be a piece of cake."

"Right. Easy money," Benjie said under his breath, as he continued to study the map. "All we need now is a ride out of there."

I watched Benjie, my vision fuzzy under heavy lids, the hypnotic groove of the music doing a number on me. More drinks followed, and because I was stupid and half-wasted, I joined them.

"What's the chicken strip?" I said.

"It's an airstrip near Panamint Valley," Benjie said, continuing his study of the map. A thought formed in the back of my mind, addled by booze and seriously goosed by paranoia. For reasons I couldn't explain, Panamint Valley sounded familiar. And then I got it.

"Hey, isn't that where they found Manson?"

The others turned and stared at me.

"You know, Charles Manson and his band of freaks," I said. "Out there in Death Valley. Shit, I heard there are still bodies buried out there."

My reaction was completely irrational, but it was spontaneous and real, borne of desperation and fear rising from the very center of my being. The room began to shrink, and I knew I was in trouble.

"What are you, some kind of historian?" Benjie said.

Vince laughed and lit a cigarette. "He reads a lot of books," he said mockingly.

The two of them passed a glance and a mumbled word that I couldn't hear, and I had the same feeling I'd had at Vince's house, back at the beginning of this thing, when I was sure that Eddie and Vince were talking about me. Barry snickered and I got pissed.

"Fuck you guys," I said, standing quickly. Benjie stepped in close to me. "What? You gonna kill *me* now?" I said. The veins in Benjie's neck bulged.

"Easy does it, Jackson," Vince said feebly. "Let's all just chill out, man."

I turned to him, my pulse throbbing in my temples.

"What are you, the peacemaker now? Mister 'let's go down to Mexico, J.T., and earn ourselves a little cash'. Well you can just kiss my ass too, Vince. I've about had it with your bullshit. Your chronic inability to be a normal human being. Your goddamn lies, man. I'm only here because of you, pure and simple. The blood's on your hands, *brother*."

My breath was choppy, the room coming in and out of focus, and my brain felt depleted of oxygen, like someone was pinching off the line.

"Why don't you go outside and get some air," Benjie said, reaching for my arm. I jerked it away and glared at him.

"Why don't you tell me what the deal is with those goddamn boots, and why your psycho buddy Kenny is killing people over them? I have a feeling you know a lot more than you're saying, so give it up, or so help me, I'm gonna do my best to hurt you."

Benjie stood there mutely, his eyes set. Barry occupied himself by pushing papers around his desk, with the occasional glance at the drama unfolding. Vince looked completely hollow, drained of fight; he was simply a bystander now. Benjie reached for my shoulder, placing his hand firmly and squeezing hard.

"Listen to me, Jackson. I don't know what's going on with Kenny. But you're right about there being more to it, of that I'm sure. I'm sorry you got dragged into his game. Rest assured one thing though, I *will* find out what he's up to."

Benjie released my shoulder and he turned to Barry, and they spoke in measured tones. I stared at them for a long time, my heart racing, pressure building inside my head. Vince tapped my arm and I jerked around.

"Let's go check on Lupe," he said. "Let these guys work out the details."

Vince spoke in a monotone, sounding like a different person. The mention of Lupe's name reminded me that we'd left him sitting in the car. Eddie would've called that a shitty deal. Poor Eddie. Poor, dead Eddie. He might have been weird, but he was still a human being, and he didn't deserve what he got.

I surrendered then, exhaling my anger. I was tired, hungry, and drunk, and more than anything I wanted to go home. I missed my kids. I missed my shitty life. Hell, I even missed Lucinda, and she didn't give a damn about me.

"Let's go," I said to Vince.

On the way outside, I glanced over my shoulder and caught an odd look from Benjie. It stuck with me until a few minutes later, when I realized what it was. It was the expression of deep sadness, and the realization of a hard truth: Kenny Lopez—Benjie's friend—had betrayed him in the worst way imaginable, sending men out to kill him in cold blood. And we'd led the way. A crushing feeling of guilt dropped on me then, deeper and heavier than any I had ever known.

Thirty-seven

The outside air felt pure and cooling. Through the open door, Zeppelin rocked on, the mandolin intro to *The Battle of Evermore* rising in a slow build, reverberating from the steel hangar to the abutment and back. I felt completely beat down, despair and guilt colliding in an emotional train wreck.

The events of the last week were irrevocably catching up with me. I believe in cause and effect, every action having its own specific reaction, and I absolutely believe there's a cost attached to the choices we make. My bill was grossly overdue, and fate's remittance man was howling in my ear, demanding payment. The enormity of what I'd done hit me all at once, the ensuing desperation overwhelming me.

"What the hell are we doing here, Vince?"

I stopped at the edge of the hangar, leaning against the cold corrugated steel in an effort to steady myself. I felt ashamed for my earlier actions and angry words. In fifteen years I'd never spoken to Vince like that. He turned to me, eyes downcast, his hoarse voice markedly restrained, nearly drowned out by the music.

"I don't know, Jackson. I…I don't know about anythin' anymore."

235

The music penetrated my skull, bled through my ears, reverb-drenched howls of doom riding waves of cascading notes, enveloping me in its mystical and musical repetition. The pressure built in my head, my nerves fired from within, tingling my skin. I felt as if I were floating up from myself, my body growing more distant as I rose on swells of music.

"This wasn't supposed to happen. Goddamn it, none of this should have happened." Vince nearly cried out, his hands shaking. "Eddie's dead, and it's because of me. I'm sorry, Jackson, for all of it. You didn't want any part of this and I made you come along. I spun it all around and played you so you'd say yes. I owe you more than this. You're my brother, man. I lied about Benjie and I wasn't straight with Eddie. Goddamn it, I'm such an asshole."

Vince's words shot through me. I reached out to him but my arms wouldn't make it. It felt like I was being pulled away from him, from the very spot where I stood. The pulsating music drove on, steamrolling everything in its path. I heard myself speak, disembodied words grossly distorted. Vince looked at me, questioning, yet at the same time knowing. A surge of energy jerked my limbs and my chest tightened, triggering that familiar feeling of panic. The music pounded relentlessly, and it felt like I was standing inside the speaker cone.

I made one last effort to reach Vince's hand, stretching my fingers to the very tips as he floated away from me, down into a swirling kaleidoscope of color. I couldn't breathe, and as the energy coursing through me peaked, I had the distinct feeling I was dying.

Suddenly, a hot flash of concentric light consumed me and collapsed upon itself, sucking me into immense darkness, blacker than the heart of Lucifer himself.

And then I felt at peace.

Part Four

The Endgame

Thirty-eight

I did not die in Mexico. I went home.
Home. Where I slept in my own bed for the first time in a week. Where I woke to the sound of a power lawnmower gnashing a two-stroke whine, the constant rev of the engine intensifying inside my head. My joints ached with the hurt of a thousand workouts and my vision blurred weirdly, brought along by a stabbing sensation centered directly between my eyes. Mercifully, the mower moved on, only to be replaced by a damn leaf blower. I wanted to scream but couldn't form the words, my parched throat constricted by a shovelful of sand.

I eased out of the bed and stood carefully, nearly knocked over by a rush of blood to the head. Balancing myself, I concentrated on the floor directly in front of me, following my wobbly steps out to the living room, my legs feeling strangely disconnected. I made it as far as the couch, where I dropped heavily onto the cushions like a sack of broken bones. The leaf blower carried on for a bit before finally sputtering to a stop. Then the gardeners moved on to torment some other poor son of a bitch.

I leaned back into the familiar feel of the sofa cushions; thank God for the comfort of old furniture. It was Monday morning, that much I knew, but everything else was fuzzy. As my mind gradually cleared, I pieced together the details of the previous thirty-six hours.

Barry Fitzgerald flew us to Death Valley late on Saturday night, dropping us into some hole in the wall located literally in the middle of nowhere. I barely remembered passing out at Barry's place, although oddly enough, I knew that a Zeppelin song was playing when it happened. We spent the night holed up in a dilapidated line shack, with all manner of desert wildlife scratching, slithering, and howling outside its ancient stone walls. Fortunately for my beleaguered psyche, our nighttime visitors did not include the haunting spirits of Charles Manson or his hapless victims.

Early the next morning we were picked up by a man named Hollis McCoy, another of Benjie's Army buddies, thereby completing the old home week trifecta of military has-beens. From Barry Fitzgerald to Max Hollister to Hollis McCoy, we were aided admirably by Benjie's own private A-team. Hollis drove us to a hunting lodge he operates in the hills outside of Lone Pine, where we hung around until late afternoon, although I'm not clear on the reason for this. Near dusk, Hollis set us up with his '72 Suburban wagon and we hit the road, taking Highway 395 straight through to Orange County. The truck had a blown-out rear window, a wobbly front tire, and a lousy radio, but given our circumstances there was no room for complaint.

We arrived at my house late Sunday night. Vince was asleep, so we didn't get a chance to talk. It was kind of a weird ending to it all, but I was okay with it. To tell you the truth, at that point I was ready for a nice long break from my good buddy Vince Taylor.

Benjie had little to say. He handed me a scrap of paper with a phone number written on it, followed by a cryptic word of caution about not having seen the last of it. I wasn't quite sure what to make of that, but I took the number and stuffed it into my pocket anyway. Then I grabbed my stuff, said goodbye to Lupe—he hugged me tightly and thanked me profusely for being so kind—and I headed for my apartment, my head hung low and my thoughts a mess.

And with that, my Mexican saga was over.

I never even asked Benjie about the boots. He drove off with them still on his feet.

As soon as I entered my apartment I dropped my stuff on the floor and went straight to my room, collapsing on the bed. I meant to rest my eyes, but ended up sleeping straight through to morning, a week's worth of stress, shitty eating, and excessive booze and cigarettes finally catching up with me. Not to mention a monstrous delayed emotional reaction to our wild escape and the violence I'd witnessed in the Mexican desert. Yeah, I had a few things to work through.

Once the mental fog lifted, my next step was clear. I had to call my kids. They probably thought I was dead. I brewed a pot of strong coffee and looked for Lou's phone number. At some point in my searching I noticed my answering machine blinking. There were seventeen messages, and I knew what they were before I even pressed the button.

My kids' voices filled the room, sadly pleading for their daddy to call, each message more frantic than the last. Listening to them, my heart dropped like a freight elevator cut loose from its cables. The calls started a week ago, right about the time I was entering Mexico, and they continued until early yesterday. The words tumbled out of that stupid machine, one after the other, landing in a lifeless thud at my feet, piling up in layers of sorrow and guilt until they finally buried me. The final message was the hardest one of all.

It was from Lucinda. A simple, heartfelt appeal for me to please call. Oh, and by the way, she never went to San Francisco. She turned down the job and decided to stay in Orange County.

The message ended and the machine beeped loudly, the jarring tone piercing my eardrums, and my heart. I walked over to the couch and sat down, my mind reeling from what I'd heard. I'd made such a hopeless mess of everything, and every lame justification I'd held onto for the past week came roaring back to me, stripped bare and exposed for the fallacy it was.

I was going to have to drive over to Lucinda's house. Now I had to get my story straight, decide what to tell them and what to leave out. I forced myself not to read too much into Lou's change of plans; *that* was a head-trip I could ill afford.

As I ran through a few plausible narratives, my eye caught the bags piled on the floor, in the same spot where I'd dropped them last night. There was a large black duffel bag and a backpack. Something seemed odd about that. I stared blankly for a minute before it clicked.

My guitar was missing.

How could that be? I knew for a fact that I'd brought it with me every step of that torturous journey home. I must've left it in the car when Benjie dropped me off, which meant either Vince or Benjie had it. A plan quickly formed. Before going to Lucinda's, I'd stop by Vince's house, and if he didn't have my guitar I'd call Benjie, using the number he gave me on that scrap of paper.

I showered quickly and dressed in clean clothes, feeling energized by the effort, and the promise of time with my kids. I still hadn't figured out what to say to them, or how I would explain my disappearance, but I counted on the right words coming to me when the time came. Unfortunately, I never got the chance.

Thirty-nine

I pulled up to Vince's house and parked alongside his truck. It was strange not seeing his Jeep out front. It had been a fixture for so long, I'd come to expect it as the natural order of things.

My mind flashed back to last Monday night, to the beginning of all this, and the part of me that felt like maybe it would be an adventure, a chance to reconnect with something I'd lost. Then I saw the Jeep broken-down and shot-up in the desert outside Agua Sienna, and I tried to reconcile those two images. I wondered about Eddie, what the Mexican cops did when they found him—*if* they found him. What'd they do with the Jeep?

What I didn't think about were those other two guys. To hell with them. After all, life is about survival of the fittest and to the victor goes the spoils. They lost. We won. Period.

Damn, that's just messed up.

I quickly pushed those thoughts aside before they gained traction. There was nothing to be gained from that kind of thinking. Besides, what's done is done, and armchair quarterbacking is for losers.

I knocked hard on the door, knowing that Vince was a notoriously heavy sleeper. There was no response, so I tried the doorbell, pressing it repeatedly. Again nothing. I switched back to the door, knocking louder this time. Surely his kids could hear me. A dog barked next door as I tried the doorknob. Locked. The dog barked again and I took note of it. I pounded on the door, getting pissed off about it. I wanted my guitar back and I wanted to see my kids, and I had no patience left for bullshit.

The dog was really going at it now, other dogs joining in, resulting in a damned neighborhood free-for-all. I moved to the front window for a peek inside, the sound of those dogs troubling me. The shades were pulled back just enough to see inside, and from where I stood, all seemed normal. So why the hinky feeling? The dogs finally ceased their nonsense, and as the last yelp faded, it dawned on me, the reason for my unease.

Vince's dogs were not barking.

They always went apeshit whenever someone came to the door. So why were they silent? I moved to the side of the house and found the gate swung wide open. Maybe the dogs got out. But if they had, they would have waited on the front porch until Vince came and got them. No, something wasn't right. I could feel it in my gut.

I worked my way into the backyard and looked through the patio slider. The house was a mess, with furniture toppled over and lamps broken and numerous drawers turned out and dumped into piles on the floor. Even the cat's litter box was tipped over and spread out in a shit-strewn mess.

The scene inside Vince's house was disturbing, and my nerves tensed at the implications. I had to get inside and find out what happened. Circling the house, I checked all of the downstairs windows and found them to be shut tight. I scanned the upstairs, noticed a gap in the master bedroom window. Now all I had to do was MacGyver my way in.

I briefly considered stacking two rolling garbage bins to use as a stepladder, but visions of a broken neck put the kibosh on that idea. At the side yard I found half of a twelve-foot extension ladder; it was bent and missing several rungs, but it would have to do. I positioned the ladder under the window, doing my best to steady the uneven legs. Then I screwed up my nerves, took a deep breath, and started climbing. At the top I stopped and listened, my ear pressed tight against the screen at the gap in the window. The house was silent, and if intruders remained inside I couldn't tell. I pulled away from the screen and considered my entry.

The shades were drawn so I was going in blind. I took a quick look around, just to make sure some nosy neighbor wasn't watching and getting all creeped, thinking I was some kind of perv and calling the cops on me. With the coast clear, I carefully loosened the screen and tossed it aside, and slid the window open. A gust of wind pushed against the shade, causing the weighted bar at the bottom to bang softly against the sill. I steadied it and pulled, holding firmly as it rolled itself up to the head of the window. For a split second I had visions of some crazed madman blasting me off the ladder. What I saw was an empty room.

I heaved myself over the sill and landed in a heap on top of a dresser drawer, the corner gouging into my side as I rolled off. Rising to my feet, I confronted a scene like the one downstairs. The bedroom had been worked over ruthlessly. Broken furniture and tossed clothes, papers scattered, framed photos knocked off the walls, a huge mirror shattered in a hundred reflective fragments embedded deep into the carpet.

Eyeballing a baseball bat alongside the bed, I grabbed it for a weapon, gripping it tightly as I made my way out of the bedroom. Out in the hallway there was more of the same destruction, and a peek inside the kids' rooms showed that even they weren't spared. Tension twisted thick knots in the pit of my stomach as I descended the stairs, slowly, easing my way along the wall and holding still at the bottom. The house appeared empty, and I eased my grip on the bat slightly.

The family room was untouched, as was the adjacent laundry room. Getting bolder I eased open the door leading to the garage, flipped the light switch and saw that it was clear. I headed for the kitchen then, stopping cold in my tracks. Amid the clutter spread across the floor I saw Vince's voodoo bracelet, the one he never went anywhere without. It was broken and bloody, and from it ran a long streak of red clear to a rear door.

I leaned back against the wall and slumped down, dropping the bat onto the hardwood floor, the loud thud reverberating in my brain. I shook violently, a wave of indignation washing over me. Like the final act in a play, the events of the last week hit me all at once, culminating in this invasion of Vince's life and the obliteration of his possessions. I felt fear and guilt, and unmitigated rage at whoever did this.

The moment passed and the shaking subsided, and I forced myself to think clearly and logically; it was up to me now to find out what happened here and make it right. I rose to my feet and methodically searched for clues. I saw it right away, and I knew beyond a shadow of a doubt the identity of the perpetrator. But of course, who else could it be? My eyes fixed on the open drawer, the same one I had looked into a week ago, in this very kitchen. It was the drawer that held a ten thousand dollar down payment for services rendered. The money was gone.

HEADING STRAIGHT FOR my apartment, running scenarios the whole way, a tide of fear rose inside me; what the hell was going on? I felt like giving up and crawling inside a hole, but I couldn't do that—not for me, not for Vince.

Back at my apartment I had a thought, a small idea that didn't seem like much, but at least it was a starting point. I located the number for my cell phone voicemail and called it from my landline. My cell may have been broken, but I could still check my messages. Maybe someone had tried to make contact.

The call connected and I keyed over, where I had to endure more messages from my kids. I plowed through each of them, feeling like the biggest loser on the face of the planet. When the final message played, the voice I heard was a familiar one, the words those of a killer. Kenny's message was simple. He had Vince, and now he wanted his boots.

Forty

The house was a single-story white clapboard cottage set on an oversized lot, located halfway down a sleepy, tree-lined street. They were old trees with thick trunks and roots that pushed up the sidewalks, and they grew abundantly overhead, creating a lush canopy of green. The quiet enclave of pre-war homes comprised one of the better neighborhoods in Santa Ana, and it evoked an earlier time, one of old Orange County and its promise of unbridled opportunity.

I arrived at dusk, the setting sun painting a shelf of clouds fire red in the western sky, the air temperature beginning its slow descent in anticipation of a cold night ahead. On my way there I got turned around in the chaos of the Second Street Promenade, and when I finally found the right street I missed the house on my first pass; Benjie had said to meet him at five, and now I was running late.

Turning off the street, I eased my car down two parallel ribbons of concrete to the detached garage at the rear of the property. I parked next to Hollis McCoy's Suburban, closed my eyes and recalled the ride home in that old truck, thinking it felt like a very long time ago. Then I turned and observed the house, dark save for a single naked light bulb centered over the back door, its dying filament flickering to strange effect.

I'd called Benjie after hearing Kenny's demands. Quite simply, I didn't know what else to do. Benjie seemed to be expecting it, that cryptic warning of his confirmed. He told me to come to this address and he'd lay it all out for me, about the boots, and about Kenny. Then we'd go get Vince.

For a brief moment I considered calling the cops, even had the phone in my hand, ready to dial. But I was stopped cold by the reality of the situation. What the hell would I tell them? There were at least two dead bodies in Mexico, most likely three, and my name was written all over it. Would it even matter that it went down in a foreign country? In the end, I decided to put my fate, and Vince's, in Benjie's hands.

I stepped out of my car and approached the back door, stood under that lone flickering bulb and knocked, my reflection in the small inset window coming back to me hollow and uncertain. There was no response. I reached for the doorbell but stopped short when I saw the frayed end of wire dangling from below. Leaning against the side of the house, I lit a cigarette, and wondered if maybe Benjie Cole wasn't just completely full of shit. By the fifth drag I heard faint footsteps from inside the house. I turned my head and saw a pair of eyes peering back at me through the lace curtain covering the window. Then I leaned my head back and finished my smoke.

I FOLLOWED HIM through a small laundry area and into a darkened sitting room at the front of the house. A car passed by out on the street, a shadowed blur diffused by the screened-in front porch and sheer curtains hanging over three evenly-spaced windows. My eyes had barely adjusted when Benjie threw dim light into the room from a table lamp.

The room was sparsely furnished, just a few old pieces set across a wood floor, the kind with a crawl space underneath so it creaks when you walk across it. My attention was drawn to a slender metal box sitting on a small table nestled between two high-backed padded chairs. The boots were on the floor, next to one of the chairs.

"Sit down, Jackson. You want a beer?"

I continued standing, my eyes going from the box to the boots. Then I looked around the room.

"Where's Lupe?"

It just slipped out like that, random, a demand more than a question. I guess I just needed to know the kid was okay. I needed to know *something* was okay in this whole stinking mess. Benjie took a seat in the chair next to the boots.

"I left him with Father Ramon," he said. "He's the parish priest over at Our Lady of Guadalupe. I went there as a kid, here in the neighborhood. The Padre's searching for a distant relation of Lupe's who lives in town. He's good at that sort of thing. Rest easy, Jackson. Lupe's in good hands."

I nodded my approval, and got down to business.

"He's got Vince. He took him because of those fucking boots." I stabbed a finger at the floor.

"I know, you told me that already. Why don't you take a seat, ease up some."

My breath felt unnatural, tweaked by adrenaline. I stood firm, boring into Benjie's eyes. But my defiance was a front, and a full minute later I moved for the other chair and fell into it, pulled down by the weight of lies.

Benjie reached for one of the boots, the left one, and he held it in front of him, examining it with equal parts admiration and scorn coloring his face.

"You know, I puzzled over this for a long time, what it was about these boots that had Kenny so determined. And then it came to me, loud and clear."

"What're you talking about? I'm done with the riddles, man, just give it to me straight. You owe me that much." I sucked in some air, my face hot. "We got you out of jail. You *owe* me."

"I don't owe you shit," Benjie said sharply. "Sure, you got me out of jail. But I got you out of Mexico, so we're even on that score. *Comprende*, amigo?"

He held my stare, his eyes a flashpoint. I didn't want it to go like this, not now; we had to work together to save Vince. "Just tell me what it's about," I said, taking the fight out of my voice.

Benjie gave me a small nod of recognition. Then he removed the boot heel, using a screwdriver he took from the table. He set the boot on the floor.

"This is what it's about."

Benjie turned the heel over, revealing a key tucked into a recess. He pried the key loose and held it up for me to see.

"A key? That's what Kenny's after?" I focused on the key, trying to grasp its meaning. Then I glanced at the metal box on the table, making the connection. "It fits that?" I said.

"It fits a safe deposit box. That was inside."

"What the hell is he into?"

"Everything. Stock fraud, shady land deals, extortion, influence peddling, Ponzi schemes, political kickbacks, you name it. If it'll turn a dirty buck, Kenny's in."

I nodded at the box. "Do you mind?"

"Knock yourself out."

I picked it up carefully and set it on my lap. The box felt heavy, the steel cold. I flipped the lid back and looked inside. The first thing I noticed was an automatic pistol and three magazines. I took those out and set them on the table. Next I found stacks of cash, hundred dollar bills, and I counted out ten of them. Under the money I found passports, birth certificates, and foreign driver's licenses issued in two different names, along with credit cards, maps and other miscellaneous documents. The last three items in the box were a leather-bound journal, a PDA, and a computer thumb drive.

"What is all this," I said.

"It's his insurance policy."

"Like if Federal indictments land on his head?" I looked at Benjie, held his eyes for a moment. "I read some interesting stuff recently in the OC Weekly. Seems Kenny has some issues."

Benjie laughed. "That's one way to put it."

"He's planning on leaving the country, isn't he?"

"That's the general idea."

The PDA caught my eye, and I picked it up. "What's this for?"

"It holds information on safe houses and overseas assets, contacts and connections. Fugitive resources."

"And this?" I held up the thumb drive.

"That's at least twenty million dollars, at last count. Could be more now. All his offshore bank accounts are on there."

I put the thumb drive back, took a moment to absorb it all. Benjie waited out the silence. Now that I knew the *what*, it was time to find out the *why*.

"So how is it you know about all this?"

"Because I'm the one who set it up."

"Why you?"

"Because he trusts me. And more importantly, he needed a straw man, a degree of separation to insulate him from the box. He couldn't afford to have his name anywhere near this thing, not officially at least, or else it might get seized if he was ever popped."

"What's he up against?"

"At least three major investigations, both Federal and local. He's under a microscope and the pressure's building. It's only a matter of time before things blow, and when they do, Kenny's going to be in a world of hurt. And if you know nothing else about Kenny Lopez, know this. The dude won't stand for a world of hurt."

Benjie looked at me gravely. I stared down at the box in my lap, alternately intrigued and disgusted by it. So this is what people died for? Well screw you, Kenny, because now I have your money and your gun and your new goddamn identity, so take that, asshole. The only problem, he had Vince. Advantage, psycho.

"How did the straw man thing work?" I said.

"It all went through me. Kenny never set foot in the bank. We both had keys, but Kenny's was strictly a backup."

"Where's yours?"

"It's on my bike. In Mexico." There was a short pause as the words sank in. "We set up a dead drop at Weeds, where Kenny would leave the things he wanted put in the box. It happened a little at a time, over a period of about six months."

"Why Weeds?"

"Because Kenny owns it. Nobody knows it of course, because it's hidden behind shell corporations, but the place is his."

"Damn, this thing has some serious layers to it."

"You got that right."

"So if Kenny never went to the bank and the safe deposit box was in your name, how was he going to get his stuff when the time came?"

"That part was mine too. He had an elaborate scheme worked out that he could trigger whenever he needed to run, and once I got the signal, I'd retrieve the box and meet him at a predetermined location."

"And the contingency plan for losing his key was to start killing people? That's insane. Why not just go to the bank and have them open the damn thing?"

"He tried that. Problem is, I set up the safe deposit box at a bank owned by a friend of mine from the service, and there was no way in hell anyone but me was getting inside." Benjie broke into a laugh. "I heard Kenny was mad as hell when he was told no. That doesn't happen very often. I wish I could've been there to see that."

I nodded and laughed to myself; add one more ex-military comrade to Benjie's A-Team. I thought it was telling that Benjie found it necessary to have his own backup plan. Clearly, he no longer trusted Kenny Lopez. Probably hadn't for a long time. All at once I felt like having a drink.

"About that beer you mentioned," I said. "You got anything stronger?"

Benjie left the room. I fanned through a stack of cash from the box, sorely tempted to take it. After all, Kenny owed me. But then I realized it was blood money, and I felt ashamed for being so callous. I dropped the cash into the metal box like it was infected.

Benjie returned with a bottle of Maker's Mark and two short glasses filled with ice. He set the works on the table, took the box from me and set it on the floor next to the boots. He eased down into his chair and poured the liquor, handed mine over. I took a long pull, relishing the warmth coursing through me. I told myself that maybe it was time to cut back on the smokes and the booze. But not tonight. Tonight I was all-in.

Benjie pulled a pack of Marlboros from his leather jacket, shook one loose. I signaled for one, and leaned in close to his flame, our faces nearly touching. I saw the stubble on his jawline, the soul patch starting to blend in. He had a small scar near his left eye, hardly noticeable from a distance, and deep lines etched into his forehead and at the corners of his eyes, eyes that were green pools of indeterminate emotion—maybe tired, maybe sad, maybe just completely indifferent to cause and effect, and all the feeble justifications for life's cruelty. I leaned back into my chair and dragged on my smoke, thinking Benjie Cole was one complex dude.

"So tie this thing together for me," I said.

"About two weeks ago Kenny sent me down to Mexico to find a friend of ours."

"Butch Davey."

"Yes. But it was a ruse, a way to get me out of town."

"Why did he have to get you out of town?"

Benjie took a drink. A few minutes passed quietly. I heard a car drive by out on the street and a dog barking, and the odd sounds an old house makes after dark. I finished my drink and poured another. We each smoked another cigarette. I held back the urge to speak, and waited for Benjie to explain.

"The box was meant for the two of us," he finally said. "At least that was the plan when he set it up. Obviously something changed."

"What are you to him?"

"I do things for him."

"What kind of things?"

Benjie finished his drink and put the empty glass on the table. He stared at me for a long moment.

"I run his drugs. That's a sideline of his, another of his 'off the books' enterprises. But he's no schoolyard pusher. *This* operation is strictly high-end. He uses the drugs to ply his business associates and secure leverage. The money he makes is secondary to the influence he gains." Benjie laughed and shook his head scornfully. "You'd be surprised at how many cokeheads and speed freaks live in those million dollar homes over in Newport and Coto. The moneyed folks have a hell of an appetite when it comes to partying."

"So that's why you're familiar with Mexico. And that thing you said, when we were hiding out in that garage, about people looking for you. It's because of the drugs."

"Yes. Unfortunately, it's the cost of doing business. The people I deal with can be unreasonable. I had a situation I was trying to work out with some suppliers down in Sinaloa. Apparently they didn't dig my methods of negotiation and decided to escalate things."

He paused, his eyes going beyond me. The room grew silent, and as I watched Benjie, I sensed reconciliation taking place within him. After a few minutes he continued.

"Anyway, I never put much stock in Kenny's plans. A life on the run doesn't sound like much of a life to me. Kenny's a smart guy and all, but eventually that shit catches up with you. I've always believed you live by the choices you make, and you define yourself by the things you do. You gotta take the bad along with the good, no matter what the cost."

"But you set up the box anyway."

"Sure, I saw no reason not to. Kenny is still my friend, for a long damn time he's been. Where I come from, that accounts for something. Where I come from, you stand by your friends. That's just how it is."

Benjie turned away from me. I looked at the side of his face, the set of his jaw, his neck pulled taut. I sighed, overcome by tiredness and the absurdity of the whole situation.

"But it's different now," I said, my voice low. "He didn't stand by you."

"No, he didn't."

"So where do we go from here?"

"We give Kenny what he wants." Benjie Cole turned and looked at me with the hardest, most uncompromising eyes I've ever seen. "And then we make him pay for it."

Forty-one

B enjie made the call, laid it all out for Kenny. It was to be a straight trade, the boots for Vince. He didn't tell Kenny that he already possessed the contents of the safe deposit box. Seems Benjie was planning his own payback for Mr. Loco Lopez. Now we waited for the callback confirming the time and place.

As we sat in the darkness and smoked cigarettes, I grew curious about the house we were in, why Benjie chose this place to meet. I asked him about it.

"I grew up here," he said. "For a while at least. I bought it a few years ago from some old lady who'd lived here for a long time. No one knows I own it, not even Kenny."

Benjie's words hinted at a deeper meaning, one I could feel yet could not bring into focus. This place was more than just a house he'd once lived in. On the surface, Benjie was like some immovable object, cold and unbending. But scratch that surface and you find a flowing river of emotion backed up behind a big stone wall, seeking any small crack to release its pressure. I first sensed it that night in the desert outside Agua Sienna, when Benjie shared the story of his mother.

"There's more to it, isn't there?" I said.

He stared at me impassively, behind the red glow of his cigarette. "What do you mean?"

"This house and the story behind it. I think you're holding out on me, about yourself, and about Kenny. I want the truth. I believe you owe me that much."

I awaited the verbal assault that said he didn't owe me shit, but it didn't come. Instead, Benjie raised his eyes to mine, and I saw it all right there, the vulnerability and the disappointment, the lifetime of regret. The truth is always in the eyes, isn't that what Max Hollister said? Benjie's could not be hidden any longer. His words came freely then, the whole story.

IT BEGAN FORTY years ago on a day when Benjie stepped into some business that was not his own. He was twelve years old, cruising his customized low-rider Schwinn—the one with the long forks, slick banana seat, and chrome sissy bar—in a foreign neighborhood. It was something he did nearly every day after school, riding aimlessly, blowing with the wind; anywhere was fine with him, as long as it wasn't home. It was the beginning of a wanderlust that would drive Benjie his entire life.

On this particular afternoon he came across a couple of wannabe tough guys terrorizing a smaller, skinny kid. Benjie recognized the skinny kid from school, although they weren't friends or anything like that. In truth, Benjie had no friends. He was on his third school in three years, which made it nearly impossible for him to have friends. The fact that he'd repeated the fourth grade and was a year older than his classmates only added to the problem.

Benjie sat on his bike and watched the altercation unfold from across the street, his blood boiling at the humiliation the bigger kids were inflicting upon the terrified boy. For as long as he could remember, Benjie had a soft spot for underdogs, and the idea of anyone leveraging their strength over someone weaker pissed him off to no end.

When he'd finally seen enough, Benjie darted across the street, pedaling full-tilt. He skidded to a stop and laid down his bike, stepping off into a wide stance, fists cocked and ready to go. He yelled for the bullies to stop. They turned and laughed, spitting at Benjie's feet. That's when he went to work, pummeling the bullies with ruthless determination.

When Benjie was finished, he saw that the skinny kid had taken off, leaving without a word of thanks. Benjie was okay with that; he'd acted as much for himself as for the kid being bullied. And besides, Benjie wasn't looking for anything from anyone. He picked up his bike, stared at the bloodied thugs lying at his feet, and pedaled on his way. The next day at school, Kenny Lopez meekly approached Benjie and offered his thanks. He apologized for leaving the way he did, blaming his fear and pleading for forgiveness. Benjie waved Kenny off, telling him it was cool. From that point on, he couldn't get rid of the kid.

At first it bugged him, Kenny always showing up at recess and after school, begging to join Benjie on his long rides through Santa Ana. Eventually Benjie warmed up to Kenny, and soon they were thick as thieves, spending nearly all of their time together. People often mistook them for brothers, the resemblance striking even to Benjie, especially once Kenny started to grow into himself.

The altercation with the bullies set a pattern for years to come. Kenny had a mouth on him, and an outsized ego to go with it. Being a year older, and bigger and stronger, Benjie became Kenny's de facto bodyguard; stepping in to finish whatever trouble Kenny had a knack for starting. Time and again Benjie saved his ass, to the point where people started to fear Kenny, *because* of Benjie.

Benjie didn't mind being the enforcer; for him, it was about loyalty, and he and Kenny had sealed theirs when they took the Blood Oath, just like they'd read about in a comic book one afternoon in Kenny's garage. They took a pocketknife from an old toolbox, cut their palms just like in the picture, and clasped their hands in solidarity, their blood becoming one, brothers to the end.

Life was hard for Benjie. His single mother was barely able to take care of herself, let alone a kid. It wasn't always that way. When Benjie's father was alive things were good. Robert Cole was a white man married to an immigrant Mexican woman, which in 1950s Orange County was a big deal to a lot of folks. They lived in the house we now occupied.

Robert worked hard to make a good life for his family, doting on his only child, teaching him to ignore the taunts and finger pointing of narrow-minded neighbors and ignorant passersby who didn't approve of mixed-race marriages. It all fell apart when Robert died. Benjie was nine, and his life afterwards spiraled out of control.

His mother couldn't support them and she lost the house. They became vagabonds, constantly moving from one cheap apartment to another, always one step ahead of the bill collectors. When the drinking started so too did a revolving door of undesirable men entering their life—bottom feeders and self-centered opportunists who only served to make life more miserable. A sister came along when Benjie was eleven, the product of his mom's back seat romp behind a barrio cantina. That's when things went from bad to worse, and Benjie started his endless rides.

By contrast, Kenny's world was comfortable and stable. Both of his parents were Mexican immigrants who'd worked hard to earn their citizenship, and they believed fervently in the American Dream. Kenny's father worked his way from manual laborer to college graduate, earning a degree in business. He took a job with a large insurance company, advancing in time to an executive position. Kenny's mother stayed at home to raise her only child, and she became actively involved in the community and the church. They lived in an upscale Santa Ana neighborhood, and Kenny always had the best clothes and the latest toys, the coolest stuff money could buy.

Kenny's attitude reflected his family's affluence, what he perceived as his superior position in life, and he honestly believed he was better than everyone else. Benjie was the only person Kenny deferred to, never once looking down on his blood brother's diminished circumstances. In time, even that would change.

Once they hit high school, it was Kenny's turn for turmoil. In the span of a few months his father went from trusted executive to unemployed outcast. Benjie was never clear on the details, but Kenny knew the score. In his mind, his father was pushed out by bigoted white men who couldn't stand a Mexican prospering in their midst.

The Lopez family struggled to hold on to their house and their lifestyle, while at the same time, Kenny's attitude turned militant, bordering on vengeful. He started talking out loud about the prejudice of all the races but his own, and he became convinced that there was a grand conspiracy designed to keep him down, simply because his skin was brown. He started scheming and cheating, cutting corners everywhere he could, determined to get an edge. To make up for lost income, Kenny started dealing dope, high-end pot to a select group of jocks and A-list rich kids who could afford his inflated prices. He soon had a nice little racket going, with Benjie acting as collector for the occasional fool who wouldn't pay up.

Benjie worried about his friend. Kenny was smart, and despite his family's circumstances, he was on the fast track to a top college. The drug dealing would end all that if Kenny were ever caught. For his part, Kenny didn't seem to care, and he continued his reckless behavior unabated, believing he was above the rules and social norms that applied to everyone else. It all blew up when a star football player got caught with a bag of weed and he fingered Kenny.

Facing big consequences, the light finally went on for Kenny, and he worried incessantly over what would happen to him. Once again Benjie came to his rescue. He stepped up and claimed to be the mastermind behind the pot racket, and no one involved said otherwise, so Benjie took the fall. Kenny kept his mouth shut and stood by as Benjie was expelled from school two months before graduation, convicted of drug possession and sent away to youth camp. Meanwhile, Kenny graduated with honors and went on to Stanford, his father mortgaging everything he owned to make it happen.

When I asked Benjie why he took responsibility for something that wasn't his, he merely said that's what friends do. I tried to imagine Kenny, as I knew him, and throwing my life away for *that*. I could only assume he was a much different person back then. Either that, or Benjie Cole was one of the most stupidly loyal guys I've ever known.

At that point the story paralleled what I'd heard from Barry and Max, about the military service and the dishonorable discharge. Benjie related some of what happened down in Central America, the shame and regret evident even after all these years. He talked about his time in prison and the isolation he felt after being paroled; the wandering years spent looking for answers, his time in the weeds he called it.

Benjie fast-forwarded to his reconnection with Kenny, who by the mid-90s was on his way to big money and big power. He'd survived the Orange County bankruptcy scandal and he was feeling ten foot tall and bulletproof. Benjie, on the other hand, was having a hard time with the straight and narrow. The fact he was a dishonorably discharged parolee was making it near impossible for him to find his footing. Kenny threw him a lifeline, enlisting Benjie into a new business venture he was cooking up.

The business was drugs, and Kenny wanted to capitalize on Benjie's experience and contacts in Central America. The operation started out small, with Kenny merely looking for a way to grease prospective clients. Benjie established a supply and distribution network throughout Mexico and South America, with the O.C. Satans acting as cover for the operation. Any reservations Benjie may have had dissipated once the money started flowing.

Kenny kept the drug operation separate from his other business activities, with Benjie handling everything from top to bottom, under Kenny's strict supervision. Things rolled along nicely for years, until Kenny's ego grew to epic proportions. That's when the cracks began to show. Increasingly, Benjie became less of a partner and more of a pawn, another of the chess pieces Kenny played in a twisted game that only he knew the rules to. Benjie found himself torn between loyalty and a growing disgust over Kenny's constant machinations, his hubris suffocating.

When the time came to put together the safe deposit box, Benjie had just about decided to shitcan the whole operation. He was feeling old and tired, and he wanted out of the life. He had more than enough money put away to live comfortably, and it had reached the point where the risk wasn't worth the gain anymore.

Benjie had managed to stay off the radar, even with all of Kenny's legal problems and Grand Jury bullshit. The drug dealing was nothing but rumors, and the Feds didn't seem too interested in following those rumors. But Benjie knew eventually that would change, and it wouldn't take long for the heat to come down. When that happened, Benjie didn't want to be the one left holding the bag.

So he agreed to set up the safe deposit box as one final act of loyalty to the guy he'd been bailing out of trouble for nearly forty years. He told himself he'd do this one thing, then he'd split for good, Kenny's offers of a big payday and a new identity ringing hollow for Benjie.

In truth, Benjie had no desire for a life on the run. He'd made his choices, and he would deal with the consequences. He always told himself that no matter how—

A cell phone rang.

Echoes of *Born to Run* filled the room, abruptly cutting off Benjie's story. He reached for the phone and looked at the number, got up without a word and left the room. The final act had begun.

A FEW MINUTES later Benjie emerged from the room. "It's on," he said.

He collected the boots and the box and disappeared again. I waited, deeply aware that I was giving myself over to this guy, placing my fate entirely in his hands. I couldn't rescue Vince on my own. Hell, I couldn't even save myself.

Benjie returned, dressed all in black, carrying a black canvas shoulder bag and holding my guitar.

"You left this in the car last night," he said, handing over the instrument.

I took the guitar case in hand and lightly touched the bullet hole up near the headstock, recalling the ambush in the desert. I closed my eyes and took in the moment, the enormity of all that had happened, the ending as yet unwritten. I looked at Benjie, and saw a different kind of light firing his eyes. We stood there for a moment, some unspoken thing hanging between us.

"It's time, Jackson," Benjie said.

I sent up a silent prayer, and resolved to be an able comrade. Vince deserved no less, and neither did Benjie. I lit a cigarette, sucked back a long drag and blew it out forcefully, my own cinematic moment.

"Let's do it," I said. "Let's take this son of a bitch down."

Forty-two

The endgame was set for Weeds, at midnight.

We crossed Santa Ana and into the city of Orange, took Santiago Canyon Road up through the foothills, driving Hollis McCoy's Suburban. The shitty radio played a top forty mix of static, competing with the irregular hum of the crooked front wheel and the wind howling through the busted rear window. An image came to mind.

Crockett and Tubbs, from the first Miami Vice episode, the scene where they're driving late at night to a final showdown at some deserted waterfront graveyard. A Phil Collins song plays in the background, spooky and cool; underscoring the wicked vibe of two cops reconciling personal demons in what could well be their final hour. The scene perfectly captures the essence of a *defining* moment.

But life seldom imitates art, and as such, our ride featured no cool soundtrack, no groovy camera angles of two slick detectives racing through deserted city streets in a sweet ride, all of it perfectly choreographed and cut in time with the music.

The reality was two middle-aged dudes driving a piece of shit truck through a dark canyon road, on their way to real danger, and possibly even death.

We made our way into Silverado Canyon, stopping at a church parking lot a few miles from Weeds. Benjie grabbed his canvas sack and checked his gear; sawed-off shotgun, automatic pistol, night vision scope, Rambo knife, flash-bang grenades—dude was outfitted. He checked his watch and started the engine, misfiring cylinders and rumbling exhaust echoing loudly in the canyon. He hesitated before putting the truck into gear.

"So what's the plan?" I said.

"The bar's closed on Mondays, so the place will be empty. Except for Kenny and whatever boys he's brought along. I'm going to drop you off in front. You'll go inside and stall until you get my signal."

I waited for the rest. Benjie just stared at the darkened road ahead.

"Seems kind of thin," I said.

Benjie said nothing as he put the truck into gear and eased out onto the road.

WE ROUNDED a curve and up ahead I saw the darkened sign of Weeds Roadhouse. Benjie slowed and killed the lights as we came out of the curve, rolling a little ways past the bar before stopping.

"You get out here. Go to the front door, tell Kenny I dropped you off and you don't know where I went. Stall him as long as you can. I'm going to circle around and shake out the skunks. Once I know our backside's clear, you'll get my signal."

I turned in my seat, uneasily watching the building. The windows showed a dark interior, the exterior lit by a couple of pole lights. I wavered just a little, but still I held it together. As I reached for the door handle, Benjie spoke.

"Hey, Jackson. Thanks for getting me out of that jail."

I turned and looked at him. He was staring out the windshield.

"Don't thank me, thank Lupe. It was his dynamite."

Benjie stifled a short laugh. "Damn, what a kid."

We both laughed.

"Benjie?" I said.

"Yeah?"

"Thanks for getting me out of Mexico."

"No problem, amigo. Glad I could help."

Benjie turned his head toward Weeds, the dash lights creating an eerie reflection of his face in the side window. He sighed heavily, a small circle of fog emerging on the glass as he exhaled.

"I'm sorry you got dragged into all this, Jackson. It's not right, none of it."

"I made my choices. We all did. No one's a victim here."

"Yeah, I know."

I stared at his reflection, felt something inside I could never fully explain. *In another time and place, I could have been your friend.* I stepped out of the truck, and as I shut the door, I knew someone was going to die tonight.

Forty-three

Benjie eased the truck back onto the road and disappeared into the darkness. I took a few tentative steps along the graveled edge of roadway, the crunching sound magnified tenfold by the stillness of the canyon. Amid the intermittent chirping of crickets a hoot owl called, a small breeze tickling the tops of the trees; it was a pleasant night for doing some unpleasant business.

It was exactly fifty steps from the road to the front door of Weeds. I know this because I counted them, in a feeble effort to slow the adrenaline rush. I made the light pole at the right side of the door and stopped, fumbled out a smoke and lit it. The cigarette did nothing for me, and four drags in, I dropped it to the ground. It was time.

I turned and faced the front door, observing a slight gap between the door and the jamb. Slowly I pushed it open and entered Weeds.

The room was dark, the smell of stale beer, cigarettes, and old sweat hitting me at once. Funny how joints like Weeds all have that same musty smell, the odors permanently embedded. It occurred to me that in all the clubs and bars and roadhouses I'd ever walked into, I'd never been inside one after closing.

Take away the people and the good times, and all you're left with is a smelly old room.

I took three edgy steps inside, gently flipping the door shut behind me. It hit with a thud and the lock engaged in a harsh metallic click. I spun at the sound. At precisely the same moment, light was thrown into the room from a bright stage spot, forcing me sideways to escape its glare. I saw the shape of a man standing in front of me, arm outstretched.

"Glad you could make it, Jackson. Where's Benjie?"

I blinked stars out of my eyes. When they cleared, I saw Kenny Lopez, pistol in his hand, an arrogant smirk planted on his face. "He's parking the car," I said, my voice strong. "Where the hell is Vince, you goddamn bastard."

Kenny laughed out loud. "No need for the attitude, J.T. It's just business."

He flipped some switches on the wall and I saw Vince illuminated up on the stage. He was tied up in a chair, multi-colored stage lights reflecting crazily off a mirrored disco ball hanging above his head, his bruised and swollen face distorted like some kind of sick special effect. I felt pure rage rise inside, fueled by a blinding desire to beat the living shit out of Kenny Lopez.

"Jesus, what the hell did Vince ever do to you?"

Kenny laughed at me, patronizing and disdainful.

"All you had to do was find Benjie and bring my boots back," he said. "Simple. But instead, you two clowns had to go and get all clever, and in the process fuck everything up."

"What the hell are you talking about? We found Benjie, and we brought him back."

"That," Kenny said sharply, "wasn't the deal. You were supposed to bring me my boots, not the guy wearing them."

Kenny stared at me. He slid a cigar out of his shirt pocket, one of those fat numbers that only moneyed douches smoke. I noticed he was wearing normal clothes, no biker get-up today. Goddamn poseur. He eased the cigar between his lips and carefully lit it, the whole time keeping the gun pointed at me.

"What about those two guys you sent after us? And Eddie?" I said. "Was that part of the deal? Because if it was, I sure missed it."

Kenny held out his cigar and stared at the end of it, the foul smell doing nothing for the ambience of the room. "You really don't get it, do you, Jackson?" he said flatly.

"Sorry, dude, I don't speak asshole."

He chuckled in that unfunny way of his, blowing gently at the burning end of the cigar as he turned it in his fingers.

"You're a funny guy, Jackson. I'll bet you were a real cut-up in school. But the time has passed for humor. The only thing left now is cooperation. So let's just cut the bullshit and lay our cards on the table. You in?"

"It's your show, run it however you choose." I put some extra grit in my voice, determined to give this guy nothing. I wondered what the hell Benjie was doing, and how much more time I had to buy.

"Fair enough," Kenny said. "So here's where we stand. I know Benjie has the contents of my safe deposit box. Those things belong to me. If I get what is rightfully mine back into my possession within, say, the next ten minutes, I'll let you walk out of here with Vince. If not, then I will kill you both."

I nodded at Vince. "Do you mind?"

"Go for it. You have ten minutes."

I moved to the stage. "Wait!" Kenny shouted.

"What now?"

He approached me, the pistol leveled at my heart, and he patted me down. Once satisfied I wasn't armed, he motioned at Vince with his pistol. "You have nine minutes," he said with a smirk.

I kneeled in front of Vince, my back to Kenny. Vince's head was tilted back slightly, his breathing shallow. I noticed his shoulder tweaked at an unnatural angle, surely dislocated, and there was blood trickling from his ear. He was a mess.

"Vince, it's me, Jackson. Can you hear me?"

He moved slightly, one eye opening just a sliver, the other hideously swollen shut.

"Jackson…is…is that you? I can't see too good." Vince's speech was badly slurred, and he blinked his good eye, turning from the spotlights. I moved to shield him and leaned into his face, whispering in his ear.

"Benjie's with me. We're getting you out of here. Just hold on a little longer." Vince's head lolled on a rubbery neck, his mouth forming words. "Easy, don't try to talk. I'm here for you, brother, I'm going—"

"That's it," Kenny said. "Reunion time is over. Step away, Jackson."

"I'm not done yet!" I yelled back. I held Vince's head between my hands, staring into his eyes. "Look at me, Vince. I'm here."

"I feel tired, Jackson. I wanna go to sleep. I wanna see Leslie. Let me go, man. Let me…"

"You can't go. You've got your girls, and they need you. I need you."

"Move away," Kenny said loudly, frustration clear in his tone. I half-cocked my head in his direction, ready to leap over and rip his throat out.

"I'm not moving. Shoot me in the back if that's what you gotta do." I faced Vince. "Listen, buddy, no one goes down alone. Do you hear me? You die, I die. I live, you live. We go down together, Vince. We go—" I felt cold steel on the back of my neck. Kenny jammed the pistol hard.

"Get up, now. I've had enough of your shit for one night." I rose slowly and faced him. "Over there." He waved his pistol toward the bar.

I moved away from Vince, my hand lingering on his shoulder, and stood at the end of the bar. From my position, I could see a round security mirror attached to the ceiling. The mirror reflected the door at the end of the hallway, the one leading to the back parking lot. From where he stood, Kenny couldn't see the mirror or the rear door.

"By the way, I've got some boys covering the back. So whatever Benjie's planning isn't going to work."

"I guess we'll find out soon enough."

"It's a real shame about Eddie," Kenny said smugly. "He was okay, for a weird dude."

Kenny was trying to rattle me now. I stared back blankly, determined to hang tough and deny him to the end. "So tell me something," I said. "Did you ever intend for us to get the boots, or were we simply the bait?"

A casual smirk crossed his face as he took a long drag from his cigar. "I'll let you figure that one out, Jackson." He laughed to himself. "You have two more minutes. If there's a way to reach Benjie, I suggest you do it now."

I saw it then, movement at the back door, reflected in the security mirror. I closed my eyes and thought of Lucinda and our kids, wondering if I'd ever see them again.

"Are you praying?" Kenny said, mocking me.

I opened my eyes. "Fuck you. And the bike you rode in on."

I saw the blur of motion again, and I knew it was time. There was one more question to ask before it all ended.

"Hey, Lopez. Tell me something, before we're done here."

"Sure. Anything for you, pal."

"Are those really James Dean's boots?"

He laughed. Howls of laughter so loud and so hard he had to take the cigar out of his mouth. He laughed for a solid minute, right past the deadline. I started laughing with him, like a scene from a cheap movie. When Kenny finally stopped, he took a drag from that big stinky cigar, and he blew it straight at me.

"Hell no, man. I got those things at Boot Barn, you goddamn fool."

He raised the pistol, and all hell broke loose.

The rear door crashed open and I hit the deck. Shots rang out and I rolled sideways, seeking cover. I looked up, saw Benjie dive across the floor, his black automatic blazing. He stood and charged Kenny, and they both went down. Muffled shots went off, followed by grunts of pain as Benjie rolled away. Kenny got to his knees, his shirtfront bloody, and he pointed his pistol at Benjie, who lay motionless a few feet away. I saw all of this in slow motion, and before my brain knew what my body was doing, I'd leapt from a crouch and speared Kenny, driving him to the floor, his pistol falling at my feet. I twisted and grabbed the gun. On my back, I fired at Kenny as he tried to stand. I didn't stop firing until the slide locked open. And then it was over.

I looked at Vince, afraid he'd been hit in the crossfire. He seemed okay. Then I belly-crawled to Benjie. He was barely breathing. I got up on my knees and cradled his head in my lap.

"That was one helluva signal, partner." He coughed a laugh, blood at the corner of his mouth. "Why'd you do it like that? That was suicide."

He looked into my eyes. "It was the only way, Jackson. It had to be." He grimaced, wheezing hard breaths. "It's been coming for a long time. It was the only way to make it right."

Benjie's breathing rattled in his chest, and he coughed up blood. He closed his eyes, and we sat like that, the sound of sirens faint in the distance. Then Benjie gathered his strength and lifted his head to look at me.

"You did good, Jackson. You did real good. Now finish it. Tell them everything. Give them the box. Kenny has other partners, shut the whole thing down." I looked at him, tears welling as the sirens grew louder. Benjie spoke to me slowly, each word an effort now.

"A man's destiny can only be determined—" he coughed a vicious spasm, struggling to speak, the life slowly slipping from him. "A man's destiny can only be determined…after he has unencumbered himself from the prejudice of his enemies. And the sins of his past."

I stared down into Benjie's eyes, awed by the knowledge that mine were the last he would ever know.

"Somebody told me that once. It was a guy who used to be my friend."

The sirens peaked outside the door, as Benjie's last breath slipped out into the cold and musty air of Weeds Roadhouse. I eased his head back gently, and I cried inconsolably. Great heaving waves of emotion, released into a flowing river of tears shed for the sum total of all that would never be.

Forty-four

I woke to the sound of wind through the trees.

The fragrant smell of pine and sycamore blew through the open window, the curtain dancing lazily as I lingered in a sublime state of mind, calm and peaceful in the bed sheets. After a few minutes I got up and made my way through the living room and into the kitchen. I stood at the window, taking in the morning. The sky was clear and light, the bloom of the trees abundant. Warm winds had been blowing for days, and the temperature hadn't dipped below eighty degrees in a week. I turned from the window and moved to the couch. The living room was clean today, my son's toys neatly tucked away. The kids would arrive in a day or two, and I could hardly wait for the ensuing chaos.

Things were better now, better than they'd been in a long time. Lucinda kicked her boyfriend to the curb three months ago, realizing that he was indeed, an asshole. She was learning the hard way that the grass is rarely greener on the other side. I didn't rub it in, knowing all too well there were no winners in this game.

Once the boyfriend was out of the picture a lot of the acrimony went away too. Lucinda and I agreed to bury the hatchet, and not into each other's head. The attorneys were fired in favor of a paralegal, and any day now an agreement would be signed. I had more custody, which was a good thing, but I was still broke. That was okay too. The thing is, we were talking and working it out. It wouldn't be the fairy tale ending I'd dreamed of, but at least I could live with it.

I never told my kids the truth about my missing week. How could I? Instead, Lou and I concocted a skimpy story about dad leaving town for work, to a place where they had no telephones. Hey, they're kids; we had to keep it simple. I had no qualms about lying to them. Some things the little ones just don't need to know.

Lucinda got the whole story, the truth, with no omissions. Her response was mixed. I think she understood what drove me to take Kenny's deal, but a part of her just couldn't condone it. It was left a stalemate, and thankfully she never held it over my head or judged me in any way. I appreciated her for that.

I stretched out on the couch, feeling lazy. Looking up at my Chinese-Mexican guitar sitting in its case on top of the bookshelf, my eyes settled on the bullet hole. I thought of that morning down in the Mexican desert. It seemed like a lifetime had passed since that awful day. The Mexican authorities eventually found Eddie's body. The other two as well. Johnny didn't make it. I was the one who told them about it.

It's been four months since Benjie came crashing through the door at Weeds and the final act was written. I recounted that night. Waiting there for the cops, spending the night in jail until they had a chance to sort it all out. Vince survived his beating, and after a two-week stay in the hospital and about six weeks of physical therapy, he's as good as new, if not considerably less crazy. Emotionally he's doing fine, and to my great pleasure, my friend has started to open up and deal with a closet full of skeletons.

He took a long overdue trip back home to Lake Charles. His ailing mother gave him Ray Taylor's Medal of Honor, which Vince now proudly displays above his fireplace mantle. He pushed on from Louisiana to Washington D.C., and a visit to the Vietnam Veterans Memorial. Vince told me that seeing Ray's name engraved on the wall was the single most cathartic thing he'd ever done. I'm proud of him for that, and I'm not ashamed to say that I love my friend for all that he is; the good and the bad, and the really annoying shit he still does on a regular basis. But hey, that's Vince.

Once he was back on his feet, Vince broke up his band, focusing instead on solo gigs. He never told the other guys about Eddie, leaving them to wonder about whatever happened to their guitar player. Everyone just assumed the guy moved on to something else. I don't blame Vince for the way he handled that; I probably would have done the same.

As for Kenny and Benjie, they were carted off to wherever it is they take dead people.

I told the cops everything, starting with the night at Weeds when I first met Kenny, all the way to Vince's kidnapping and the subsequent shootout at Weeds. They went to Benjie's house in Santa Ana and retrieved the metal box that held Kenny's stuff, along with a fireproof file box Benjie kept hidden in a closet, the contents detailing every dirty deal and illegal activity Kenny had perpetrated in the last ten years. They had everything they needed to close the book on Kenny Lopez, although I'm not sure how it mattered, seeing how he died and all. Still, I guess they call that a win in the world of law enforcement.

The funny thing is, when the cops inventoried the contents of the box and asked me to review the list, I noticed there was no mention of the computer thumb drive, the one worth twenty million dollars. That one has stuck with me since; where could it have gone?

No charges were ever brought against me, or Vince, and there was no trial for us to testify at. They said that if future investigations ever turned up possible indictments, they might need my help. No problem, I told them, call me anytime.

From the time I first laid eyes on Benjie Cole in the jail at Concepción, to the sad ending at Weeds, I'd spent only a few days with the man. But in truth, it felt like I knew him for a lifetime. I can't really put into words the impact he had on me, and it's taken me a long time to get over his death. I found out later that Benjie Cole was a sick man, a tumor growing in his lung. Would it have killed him? Who knows for sure? I can't help but wonder if that is what drove his final act. One thing I know for certain; Benjie left this world on his own terms, and from what I came to learn of the man, it was never going to be any other way.

And finally there was Lupe, the kid with the dynamite. I check on him once in a while, and I'm happy to say he's doing well. Father Ramon eventually located a relative who lived in Santa Ana, and Lupe was accepted with open arms into a very good life with people who care for him. I never told the cops *that* part of the story.

As I ran through all of these things in my mind, I was struck by the notion that we really don't have control over our lives. Despite exercising our free will, in the end it all comes down to a crapshoot. It's the human factor; you just never know what the other guy is going to do. All it takes is one fool like Kenny Lopez to come along and turn a whole bunch of lives to shit.

Those words Benjie spoke to me that night in Weeds, before he slipped to the other side, have stayed with me ever since. I've tried to take them to heart, and to take a good look at myself. I'm not saying there's been a radical reboot of Jackson Thomas, but progress has been made, and I'm committed to living a different kind of life, a more open and free life. Because each and every breath we take is too precious to waste.

I got up off the couch and pulled down my little guitar, gently fingering the bullet hole. I opened the case and carefully pulled the instrument out. It looked exactly as it did the day I bought it from the jovial fat man. I wondered what he was doing right now. And Milena too, that beautiful young woman who's brief crossing of my path showed a whole new world of possibility. Yeah, a few nice things happened on that trip to Mexico.

Returning to the couch, I lightly strummed the strings, picking up a slight buzzing that I didn't remember from before. I plucked each string individually, and heard it again. I turned the guitar over and shook it, a loose noise coming from the sound hole. Feeling around the inside edge with my fingers, I snagged a piece of tape. I pushed my fingers through the strings and felt something plastic, forced the object out, my heart beating fast when I saw what it was.

Benjie Cole, you devious son of a bitch.

I got up and stumbled to the telephone, dialing numbers as I considered the possibilities. A familiar voice answered on the third ring.

"Vince, it's Jackson," I said.

I took a deep breath.

"Tell me, amigo. What do you know about numbered bank accounts?"

About the Author

John Turner lives in South Orange County, California. He is the father of two beautiful children, an avid reader, and a teller of tales. *Dodging Bullets* is his second published novel.